RAVEN'S HONOUR

Claire Thornton

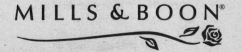
MILLS & BOON®

*MILLS & BOON and MILLS & BOON with the Rose Device
are registered trademarks of the publisher.*

*First published in Great Britain 2002
Harlequin Mills & Boon Limited,
Eton House, 18-24 Paradise Road, Richmond, Surrey TW9 1SR*

© Claire Thornton 2002

ISBN 0 263 83121 3

*Set in Times Roman 10½ on 12 pt.
04-0502-80354*

*Printed and bound in Spain
by Litografía Rosés S.A., Barcelona*

RAVEN'S HONOUR

Claire Thornton

Chapter One

Spain, November 1812

'Come on, Belinda, don't give up on me now!' Honor urged.

The donkey baulked, her ears flicking nervously at the sight of the angry, fast-flowing waters of the River Heubra. Ahead of them, soldiers of the 52nd Regiment of Foot were jumping down the steep banks of the river, then fording through almost shoulder-deep water. Many of the men were holding on to each other to save themselves from being swept away by the current.

Honor couldn't blame Belinda for her reluctance to plunge into the river, but the delay was dangerous. She could hear musket and rifle fire behind her as the rearguard of the Light Division skirmished with the advancing French. Honor gritted her teeth and urged the donkey forward. She'd always kept up with the column, ever since she'd first arrived in the Peninsula over three years ago—she wasn't about to become a French prisoner now.

'*Come on*, Belinda!'

The donkey still wouldn't budge. Honor was just wondering whether to slide off her back and lead her into the water when the decision was taken out of her hands.

She heard a dull thwack behind her—then Belinda bolted forward, half-jumping, half-falling into the rushing water. The shock of icy water knocked the breath from Honor's lungs. The current hammered and sucked at her legs, plastering her shabby skirt against Belinda's struggling body.

The little donkey was already losing the fight against the wild-tempered river. She could barely keep her head above the foaming water. Her eyes rolled with fear and panic.

Honor had no breath to reassure her. The river tossed the donkey like a dead leaf, dragging Honor beneath the surface of the water. Her skirt was caught. For long, desperate moments, she fought to free herself from Belinda's foundering body. Her lungs burned. She could hear nothing but the water roaring in her ears. The current pounded around her head, hard as a clenched fist, battering her bruised body. She forced her head up, sucked in a quick, painful breath, and finally found some leverage against Belinda's side. She tore her skirt free. Relief surged through her that she was no longer anchored to the failing donkey. She made one last effort to get to Belinda's head, to save the donkey and her possessions. It was too late. She was already too tired, and the donkey was too far gone. Just saving herself was going to take all her strength and determination.

She tried to ride the current, to use it to reach the river bank. She'd been swept too far downstream for any of the infantry crossing the river to help her. She was numbed by the heat-sapping cold. Blinded by the stinging water. Choking and drowning…

She slammed up against something hard and unyielding. What little breath she had left in her body was knocked out of her. A strong arm plucked her unceremoniously from the water to lie across the high pommel of a Hussar saddle. She was draped face down, like a sack of corn, her breasts pressed against a muscular leg.

Honor gasped and coughed uncontrollably. She tasted bile in her mouth and was suddenly afraid she might throw up in this undignified position. By an effort of sheer determination, she reasserted some control over her shivering, battered body. Honor blinked water from her eyes and turned her head to one side. She was aware of her hair hanging down towards the ground in sopping rats tails.

She was lying across a tall black horse, her body resting on the hard thighs of its rider. His body heat penetrated her sodden dress, warming her in a shockingly intimate way. The virile, masculine strength of her rescuer stirred a response deep within her—but then she deliberately pushed aside her inappropriate awareness of him.

She focussed her attention on his mount instead. She knew this stallion. Even from her limited viewpoint the horse was unmistakable. But then she'd known from the first moment the identity of her rescuer—and the horse possessed the same fierce courage as his rider. She felt the stallion's hindquarters bunch as it thrust up the river bank. The wild current which had taken her poor Belinda troubled the black no more than a gurgling summer stream might have done.

'Corvinus,' she whispered hoarsely.

'As you say,' said a dry voice, from far above her.

The black stood patiently as strong hands lifted Honor and lowered her to the ground. Her legs were so weak she would have fallen if she hadn't grabbed the front of the saddle and hung on tight.

'Steady.' Her rescuer had released her, but now he caught her upper arm again, supporting her while she collected herself.

Honor shook her dripping hair out of her eyes and lifted her head to peer up at Major Cole Raven.

He was leaning over her, his face only inches from hers. She'd never been so close to him before. She gasped as she met his fiercely probing gaze, almost as shaken by his proximity as she had been by her plunge into the Heubra. Raven's ice-blue eyes were shockingly vivid in his wolfish, stubble-darkened face. Beneath his shako his tawny hair had been bleached by the sun until it resembled the brindled pelt of a wolf. He must have been born with those deep-set eyes, strong cheekbones and square jaw—but years of campaigning had intensified the dangerous edge to his personality.

He was a consummate soldier. His big, rangy body had been hardened by long marches in freezing snow or scorching heat, and tempered by the battles he'd survived. The men joked he had a bayonet for a back-bone and ice water for blood. Even now, after two days of forced retreat, most of it in the pouring rain, without food because the Commissariat had gone by a different route, Honor could see no sign of fatigue or distress in the Major's lean face. Only the thick stubble on his usually clean-shaven face gave any indication of his situation.

Honor normally tried to avoid the man. Whenever she was near him she could sense, beneath his controlled demeanour, currents as deep and wild as the river from which he'd just saved her. Her instincts warned her of danger, so she tried to keep her distance.

Right now her instincts were screaming, but his firm grip on her arm meant retreat was impossible.

She shivered slightly as she met his penetrating gaze. She was numb with cold and shock from her disaster in the river, but this quiver of nervousness was purely in response to Cole Raven's undivided attention.

'Thank you, sir,' she said, as steadily as she could.

He nodded a brief acknowledgement of her thanks. She tried to pull away, but his grip on her arm tightened. A shiver of alarm coursed through her.

'Have your legs stopped shaking yet?' he asked, his neutral tone belying the searing intensity of his gaze.

Her irrational panic receded as she realised he was simply concerned she might fall if he released her. Since she still had a death grip on his saddle with her other hand, it wasn't an unreasonable assumption.

'Yes, thank you, sir,' she said again.

She tried to prove her words by releasing the saddle and stepping away from him. He'd already wasted enough of his time rescuing her. Now she was safe, he had more important duties awaiting his attention.

She was dimly aware of the constant sound of rifle fire as the 95th engaged with the French—but then the shock of what had nearly happened hit her like a wall of freezing flood water. Fear of recently past danger temporarily overwhelmed her awareness of the imminently approaching threat. Instead of letting go, she moved closer and clung tighter for a horrible, desperate, heart-stopping moment.

Corvinus swung his head around to sniff curiously at the bedraggled woman standing by his shoulder. Honor felt his velvet lips mumble against her wet, muddy hair. Then he snorted disapprovingly and straightened his neck, shaking his head vigorously.

Honor's mood broke. She laughed and stroked the stallion's smooth, glossy neck.

'Show off,' she said, unaware of the note of affection in her voice as she spoke to the horse. 'Just because *your* mane's in such fine, untangled condition…*I* haven't got a lady's maid to pick the twigs out of *my* hair every—' She broke off, embarrassed to be caught talking like that to Corvinus in the presence of the stallion's master—particularly in the current, precarious circumstances. The shock of nearly drowning must have unhinged her mind.

She forced herself to look up at the Major, but to her relief he was looking beyond her.

'Your wife, Corporal,' he said curtly.

'Thank you, sir.' The relief in Patrick O'Donnell's voice was heartfelt and unmistakable.

Cole Raven released Honor into her husband's arms and rode away, rapping out quick orders as he did so.

'I thought I'd lost you, girl.' Patrick hugged her.

'Not me, just poor Belinda—and all our belongings.' Honor replied, hugging him back, grateful for the safe, unalarming warmth of his embrace.

She was missing one shoe. Her shabby skirt was ripped almost to her knees. She'd taken off her coat to make it easier to cross the river, and now it was lost with all their other possessions. She was covered in mud, her sodden hair dripped cold water down her back, and she couldn't control her bone-aching shivering—but at least she was still alive.

Patrick shrugged out of his greatcoat and insisted she put it on.

'But you're just as cold and wet as I am,' she protested, reluctant to take it from him. Shabby though the coat was, it was both warm and dry because Patrick had folded it and carried it across the river tied to the top of his knapsack.

'I'm dry from the shoulders down, girl,' he pointed out cheerfully, 'you look like a drowned rat.' He thrust the coat into her arms before hurrying to do his duty.

Honor wrapped herself gratefully in the coat and squeezed as much river water from her hair as she could. She smiled ruefully as she fell into step beside the marching men. She and Patrick had been through some difficult times in the past, but they'd never before been reduced to only one coat between the two of them. When she was warmer, she would insist Patrick took his turn wearing it.

The battalion had been ordered downstream to defend the ford at San Muñoz. Cole rode beside the column, his outward demeanour as calm as ever, and tried not to remember his horror when he'd seen Honor disappear under the dark surface of the Heubra.

She had been a married woman—not only that, but a loyal, devoted wife—for as long as he'd known her. She'd done nothing to attract his interest, yet he desired her more than any other woman he'd ever known. When Honor was nearby Cole always knew where she was and what she was doing. He could sense her presence with every fibre of his being. He knew all the expressions on her fine-boned face. He'd been intensely aware of her even before he'd joined her husband's regiment—though he was damn sure that hadn't influenced his decision to seek promotion into the 52nd.

He'd watched from a distance as the sun bleached her golden blonde hair until it was nearly white. He'd watched her naturally slim body become almost painfully thin as she'd adapted to the rigours of army life. He'd seen her smooth skin darken to a rich golden brown under the Iberian sun. In her own way, she was as seasoned and battle-hardened as any of the troops around him. Yet her large hazel eyes were bright and expressive. And she possessed an inherent grace which was never eclipsed by the shabby clothes and clumsy shoes she wore.

Cole told himself he didn't approve of women submitting themselves to the brutality of war. He told himself that Honor had unsexed herself when she'd followed her man to the battlefield, marching beside him with no shoes on her feet and her skirt ripped in tatters almost to her knees. He told himself fiercely that Honor O'Donnell was a married woman—and he reminded himself almost daily that he had a fiancée waiting for him in England. But nothing he told himself altered the fact that, every time he looked at her, he wanted her.

The most important consequence of his inner battle was that, until today, he had taken great care to keep a physical distance between them. The moment when he'd hauled her out of the swirling water was the first time he'd ever touched her in the two years or more she'd been destroying his inner peace. He could still feel her slim, shivering body laid across his thighs, her slight breasts pressed against his leg. Despite the cold

discomfort of his present situation, fierce heat flooded
him at the memory of holding her so intimately against
him. She was too thin, he thought, and there would be
nothing for her to eat tonight. She didn't even have a
blanket—it had been lost with the donkey in the
Heubra.

He savagely damned the Quartermaster-General for
sending the supply train by a different route from the
troops, and himself even more savagely for acting like
a lovesick fool over a woman he could never have.
She had a husband to take care of her. Cole had seen
the expression in Patrick O'Donnell's eyes when he
looked at his wife. No doubt he was more than willing
to keep her warm on a cold night.

'Damn!' Honor slipped in the mud and nearly fell
over, cursing the quagmire even though she had reason
to be grateful to it. A shell hit the ground near her,
burying itself in the mud and throwing up a shower of
clay that half-blinded her, but didn't otherwise hurt
her.

They'd reached San Muñoz just in time to be caught
up in a skirmish with the French artillery.

She saw a soldier in Patrick's company hit and
crawled over to him. There was blood mixing with the
mud on his arm, but he was bright-eyed when he
looked up at her.

'Shouldn'a' spooked the donkey,' he said jerkily,
slurring his words. 'Di'n' mean to drown you, Miz
O'Donnell.'

'I know, Danny,' she said, smiling at him through
a mask of mud. She ripped a strip off her wretched
skirt, tying it round his arm to slow the bleeding. 'It's
not your fault Belinda wasn't much of a swimmer.'

Another shell landed close by. She leant over Danny, protecting him with her body from the shower of sticky clay. The sound and smell of battle were overwhelming.

A hand grabbed her shoulder and dragged her backwards.

'For the love of God, get to the rear!' a voice grated in her ear.

Before she could respond, Major Raven had gone.

'Best follow orders, ma'am,' Danny Thompson croaked.

Honor lifted her head, pushing her filthy hair out of her eyes as she sought out Patrick. It was very unusual for her to be this close to him when he was fighting. It was a complete accident she'd been caught up in the skirmish.

Just as she found him, she saw him stagger and fall into the soft ground, his musket still clutched in his hand.

'Patrick!'

She stumbled to her feet, slipping and sliding through the mud to reach him. She tripped over a wounded man and sprawled headlong in the glutinous mud. Gritty clay oozed through her fingers and covered her from head to toe. She pulled herself up, staggered a few more yards and fell down beside her husband, ignoring the other men around them.

'Patrick?' She tugged desperately at him, barely noticing the cold rain which had begun to fall.

He drew in a deep, unsteady breath, coughed, and pushed himself shakily onto his hands and knees, his head falling forward as if it was too heavy to lift.

Honor threw her arms around him, supporting his

weight against her slender body as he recovered his senses.

'It's a scratch, sweet lamb, just a scratch,' he said hoarsely, his soft brogue more noticeable than usual, as he finally sat up unsupported.

'Oh, God!' Honor was so relieved he could talk coherently that tears burned her eyes.

She blinked them back because tears were certainly not what Patrick, or any one else, would expect from her. As she did so, she realised that the French firing had stopped. They were no longer under attack, but now it was pouring with icy rain.

'Damn the weather, damn the French, damn the Commissariat!' she muttered like a chant.

Patrick was trembling from shock and cold. They'd all been cold, wet and hungry since they'd left Salamanca two days ago. First the torrential rain, then the river, now the rain again.

'Let me see,' she said, gently opening Patrick's jacket. He'd been wounded in the side by a piece of case-shot. It was a long, shallow gash. She'd seen men recover from much worse injuries—and die from apparently less serious wounds. She knew of a woman who'd died simply because she'd pricked her finger on a pin which had fastened a bandage around an infected wound.

It was the first time Patrick had ever been hurt and Honor was afraid for him, but she couldn't let her fear show.

'Just bind it up with a strip of your petticoat and I'll be fit for another day's march,' Patrick said bracingly.

'Yes, sir!' Honor snapped, anxiety putting an edge on her voice. 'Clean? clean?' she muttered, glancing around. 'There's nothing clean in this whole damn world.'

The relentless rain plastered her hair to her face, her clothes to her back. Dirty water ran down Patrick's body and mingled with the blood seeping from his wound.

'Honor, girl, I don't like to hear my wife curse so freely,' Patrick chided her gently.

'I'm sorry.' Honor bit her lip. She'd never felt so helpless, or so worried. She would have given everything she possessed for clean water, clean linen and a dry place to tend her husband's wound. Unfortunately, everything she possessed except the clothes on her back were lost in the river.

Before she had time to do anything further a clean, dry handkerchief was thrust into her hand. She instantly pressed it against Patrick's side, leaving it up to him to thank the donor, who'd already moved on.

'Hold this,' she commanded, putting Patrick's hand against the handkerchief, hiding her fear beneath her brisk manner.

Her petticoat was in no better shape than her skirt. She had to tie three strips together before she had a makeshift bandage long enough to go round Patrick's body. When she was finished she helped him to his feet. There was no provision for the wounded on this march. If he couldn't keep up, he would be left for the enemy. Of course, everyone believed the French treated wounded enemies with humanity, but neither Patrick nor Honor wanted to put that belief to the test. She was relieved to see that he seemed quite steady on his feet, though still somewhat dazed.

'Give me your musket,' she said. It weighed more

than ten pounds, a heavy burden for anyone to carry, much less an injured man.

'I can carry my own weapon,' Patrick protested.

'Then give me the rest,' Honor countered. 'I've carried more, and now I have nothing to carry.'

Patrick hesitated, then let her take his knapsack, haversack and even his water canteen. He started to protest when Honor made him take back his greatcoat, but his objections faded when he saw her strip the coat from one of their fallen comrades.

'He doesn't need it any more,' she said quietly. She touched the dead man's face gently. 'Poor Samuel,' she said sadly. She checked to see if he had any personal belongings she could save for his family.

Then she stood up and put on the coat. It was tattered, muddy and stained with blood, but it still provided some protection from the weather. She distributed Patrick's equipment about her person and then she was ready to march beside him in the column. Normally she followed at the rear of the battalion, with the other womenfolk and camp-followers—or even went ahead to prepare the camp for the men's arrival— but today Patrick needed her. She wasn't the first woman to help her man on the march.

Danny Thompson was near them in the column, his arm held in a crude sling. They'd lost several good men in the brief skirmish, including the two senior officers of Patrick's company. Honor was inclined to think the whole retreat had been mismanaged, but grumbling wouldn't help. All she really wanted was a dry billet and a chance for Patrick to rest.

A dry handkerchief. In this whole, Godforsaken world, all he could give Honor was a dry handkerchief to ease her misery. Cole turned up his collar against the sleeting rain and cursed his helplessness, while mud sucked at Corvinus's hooves with every step the stallion took.

This retreat was a grim business. The Light Division hadn't lost a battle. They'd marched into Madrid in triumph in August and, along with the Third Division, had been comfortably quartered in the vicinity until October. Wellington had left the Fourth Division at Escurial and marched north with the First, Fifth and Seventh Divisions. He'd laid siege to Burgos in September, but a month later the fortress was still in enemy hands, and the French and their allies had had time to gather their forces. Wellington had been forced to retreat from Burgos, while the Divisions he'd left behind had retreated from Madrid under the command of General Hill. The Allied army had reunited at Salamanca, the scene of its victory in July, but this time there'd been a stand-off between the French forces and the Allies, and now Wellington's army was in retreat.

As a member of the Light Division, Cole hadn't taken part in the siege of Burgos. Privately, he thought it had been a badly mismanaged affair—both the siege train and the provision of trained engineers had, by all accounts, been laughably inadequate—but he preferred to voice his opinions only when they might make a difference. Right now his first priority was to ensure the safety of his own men.

The country between Salamanca and Ciudad Rodrigo was a flat, wooded plain. The road was criss-crossed with rivulets of water which in wet weather turned the route into a muddy quagmire. The road was littered with the carcasses of dead horses and oxen. Cole had seen an exhausted Portuguese soldier buried so deep in the mud he couldn't pull himself out. There had been no help for it but to leave him behind. There were many sick, weary men on the march. O'Donnell could still stand, he could still walk—he was not the worst of them.

With curt words of encouragement, and the occasional black joke, Cole put heart into the wet and disheartened men of his regiment. But even under these conditions he would not tolerate even a hint of insubordination from the hard-used men.

There was no warm billet that night, and nothing to eat but acorns. Honor tried not to think of poor Belinda, who'd carried their remaining rations away with her on the bitter waters of the Heubra.

Most of the ground was ankle-deep in slushy mud, so the men congregated in groups on the higher ground around the roots of trees. There was only green, wet wood to burn, but they managed to light a smoking fire. When Major Raven's servant, Joe Newton, brought her a blanket, Honor accepted it with gratitude. Joe and Patrick had become friends soon after Raven had joined the 52nd. They were united by their love of good horseflesh—a love Honor shared. She knew the Major's black stallion well, although she'd always avoided Cole Raven when she and Patrick visited with Joe. She wasn't surprised by Joe's kindness to them, and it didn't occur to her to wonder whether Cole Raven had had any hand in the matter.

Beyond the small circles of light cast by the struggling campfires the night was cold and unfriendly. In the distance, hidden by the black, dripping tree trunks, wolves howled. Honor shivered at the eerie music. So many fallen horses and men meant easy pickings for the beasts.

'Sing for me,' Patrick urged.

He was lying on the ground, his head on her lap, wrapped in the blanket Joe had given them.

Honor hesitated. In all the time she'd been in the Peninsula, she'd done nothing to remind others of her life before her marriage. She was Mrs Patrick O'Donnell, the respectable wife of a steady, dutiful man. She'd left Honor Meredith, toast of the fashionable London stage, far behind her. Patrick had never questioned her behaviour, and never before asked her to do anything which might compromise her relationship with the other men or wives. She was surprised by his request, but she had no thought of refusing him.

She began to sing softly, choosing one of Thomas Moore's Irish melodies which she knew Patrick particularly liked. If she closed her eyes and concentrated, she could almost imagine they were back in London. She was onstage in a crowded theatre, trying to hold the attention of an audience which was more interested in gossiping than in watching the performance. It had required courage as well as talent and persistence for Honor to establish a career under such circumstances.

Now, singing for Patrick in a dark, alien landscape, Honor imagined she was back in the gaudy, fantastical world of the theatre, where the forbidding black trees were only painted on to a flimsy backcloth, and when the performance was over they'd wash off the blood and eat a comforting meal in a firelit room.

She tried to put the cosy warmth she imagined into her voice, but tears seeped beneath her closed eyelids. It was so hard to drive the cold away.

* * *

Cole returned from checking the picket and paused in the shadows of the dank trees, listening to Honor sing. He'd never heard her do so before, though some of his fellow officers claimed to have seen her perform in London. She'd been a fêted actress before her marriage. He could only assume she loved Patrick O'Donnell very much to give up a pampered life to follow the drum.

Her clear, musical voice was husky with weariness, but it conjured happier, warmer times. When she stopped, someone asked her to sing again. Her voice pierced the cold and darkness which isolated them all in this miserable corner of existence.

Cole's heart twisted with foreboding. Honor had never sung before. He wasn't given to fanciful ideas, but her song seemed prophetic. Even the wolves had ceased their own song to listen. *Not a swan song. Please God, don't let it be a swan song,* he thought. *Not for Honor.*

The next morning, as usual, the men stood to their arms an hour before dawn. Honor watched Patrick anxiously in the uncertain light, but he seemed fit enough. She danced from foot to foot and hugged herself in a vain attempt to get warm as they waited for the orders to move off. The French were not far behind and the delay seemed inexplicable to her.

She snooped around a little and overheard a conversation between some officers which indicated that the Light Division couldn't move until the First Division had done so—and the First Division couldn't move because its officers didn't have a guide and they were lost.

Honor bit her lip and hid discreetly behind a tree

trunk as Cole Raven stalked past, a scowl on his face. The Major had transferred to the 52nd Foot a year ago from the 16th Light Dragoons. According to stories she'd heard, while he was in the cavalry, he'd often acted as an intelligence officer for Wellington. It occurred to her that a man whose previous duties had not only included leading patrols deep into enemy territory, but also sketching accurate maps of Spain and Portugal during his first months in the Peninsula, was unlikely to be impressed by the excuse that an entire Division was lost!

Unfortunately, Honor's own sense of direction was so poor she didn't feel able to criticise the officers of the First Division as freely as she might have liked. If she'd known where Luis was, the goatboy who often acted as her own guide, she could have offered his services—but Luis, like the Commissariat, had disappeared along another route.

One of the Light Division officers provided the First Division with a guide, and finally the Light Division itself was able to move off. Honor listened anxiously for any sign of pursuit by the French. She knew her companions were equally eager to avoid a confrontation. In the present situation there could be no victory, only unnecessary losses.

The sun shone, which was a relief after the endless rain of the previous day, but the roads were still swamped with mud, which hid potential hazards from the unwary. Honor bit back an exclamation of pain as she stubbed her bare foot against a buried tree stump. Her feet were already so numb from cold that it didn't hurt as much as it might have done, but she was afraid of doing real damage to herself. She wouldn't be able to keep up with the column if she couldn't walk, and then she wouldn't be able to help Patrick.

She was keenly aware of every movement he made. He seemed well enough in the morning, but when they set off again after the midday break he was obviously having more difficulty. He stumbled several times, before he finally allowed her to take his musket, concentrating all his strength on putting one foot in front of another.

When they eventually halted for the evening she looked at Patrick's wound. At the sight of it, she swallowed tears of fear and anxiety. It was far worse than it had been when he'd first been hit. She did her best to tend it, then huddled against Patrick, wrapping them both in the damp blanket, trying to keep them warm and alive through the cold night. She was too exhausted to stay fully awake, but too anxious and uncomfortable to rest properly. She dozed fitfully, nightmarish images chasing each other through her mind.

The next morning they tried to set off with the others, but it was soon clear that Patrick could barely stay on his feet, much less keep up with the column. The rest of the men in the company were too weakened and weary to offer more than verbal encouragement. Honor struggled to keep Patrick moving for a while, her arm around his waist. In the end it was too much for both of them.

'If you wait here, you may be able to get a ride on one of the wagons that are following us,' said Lieutenant Gregory, harried and anxious.

The death of the Captain and the other Lieutenant had given him added responsibilities under particularly difficult conditions. He wanted to get all his men to safety, but there was not much he could do for one who couldn't walk. Especially since his own mare had foundered the previous day and he was compelled to march beside his men.

'I'll wait,' Patrick wheezed. 'Take Honor with you, sir,' he begged.

'No,' said Honor flatly. 'I'm staying with my husband.'

The Lieutenant hesitated, meeting Honor's unwavering gaze. He was barely twenty years old, and not long in Spain, but he knew a lost cause when he saw one.

'Mrs O'Donnell will do her duty as she sees fit,' he said stiffly. Honor knew he didn't want to leave them behind, but he had no choice.

'I'll be looking out for you tonight,' Maggie Foster told Honor sharply. She was the wife of one of the other soldiers, a raw-boned, harsh-voiced woman who often fell foul of the military authorities. 'The Corporal could have ridden on my donkey if the Provost Marshall hadn't shot it!' she continued belligerently, flashing a hostile glance at Lieutenant Gregory.

It was the Provost Marshall's business to prevent women and other camp followers from impeding the progress of the troops—or plundering the surrounding countryside. In extreme circumstances he might even shoot a woman's donkey—and Maggie's had been shot the previous day.

The Lieutenant flushed, but refused to be drawn into an argument with the formidable woman.

'Thank you,' said Honor, genuinely grateful to Maggie, who'd often looked out for her since Patrick had joined the Regiment. 'We'll manage.'

'I'm counting on it,' said the older woman. Her eyes

were hard, but her brief grip on Honor's hands was painfully tight.

She nodded grimly to Honor, then stepped back and ordered her children to get up from the muddy ground. When she walked away two little girls were clinging to her skirts, while an older boy kept pace beside her, carrying some of their belongings.

'God be with you both,' Lieutenant Gregory said, his voice cracking. He spun on his heel, and Honor and Patrick watched in silence as the company marched away.

They sat beneath a tree on some relatively dry ground. Honor huddled against Patrick. She'd wrapped him in the blanket and loosened the uncomfortable leather stock from around his neck. Occasionally cold drops of water splashed down on them from the branches above. Their surroundings seemed to be composed only of stark, monochrome shades. Patrick drifted between delirium and brief moments of consciousness. He was far too ill to talk to her or to share any of the responsibility for their predicament. Honor had never felt so alone in her life.

She was cold and scared and hungry. The cold numbed both her body and her mind. Despite the extreme danger of their situation, her thoughts became lethargic and detached, with the surreal quality of dreams. Her mind ranged over many unrelated people and subjects. She thought of her mother, who'd never been daunted by any of the enormous obstacles she'd had to overcome in her life.

But thinking about her mother made Honor feel inadequate and unhappy. Annie Howarth would never have allowed herself to fall into such desperate straits. Honor knew her mother wouldn't be at all impressed by the mess her daughter had made of everything—so she thought about Major Raven instead. Thinking about Cole Raven warmed her. When she summoned his image into her mind her body inexplicably responded. When she remembered how the furnace-like heat of his body had burnt through her clothes after he'd rescued her from the river, her cold, turgid blood once more flowed hotly through her veins. She knew she shouldn't think of him like that but, just briefly, she allowed herself to indulge in the strangely comforting memory.

She hadn't seen either the Major or Joe Newton since the previous evening. She wondered where they were. Joe Newton was a good friend to Patrick. She would have asked for his help if she'd had the chance. Now there was no one to help them.

Honor and Patrick waited for hours on the dreary, inhospitable road. No wagons came.

'Leave me,' said Patrick, during one of his brief moments of coherence.

'No,' Honor replied. She bit her lip, shaking herself out of her cold-induced apathy. She looked up and down the road, searching for a solution to their problem. If only she still had her donkey. She cut off that line of thought before bitter frustration overwhelmed her.

'You have to,' Patrick insisted, more strongly. 'If you stay here, I will die and you will be at the mercy of any man who comes—French, Spanish, deserter.' He broke off, breathing quickly. 'I didn't marry you in London to let you suffer a worse fate in Spain,' he gasped. 'Honor, girl, you have to leave me.'

'Would you leave me?' she demanded.

''Tis different,' he protested.

'Hah!' Honor forced her cold, numb body into activity. She divested herself of everything she'd been carrying except the musket, ammunition pouch and canteen. Then she twisted the musket until it was hanging diagonally across the front of her body. It wasn't comfortable, but if she adjusted it carefully it didn't impede her legs.

'Now get up,' she ordered Patrick.

His eyes widened at the steel in her voice.

'You sound like your mother,' he said, astonished, and not quite approving.

'Get up, damn you!' She hauled him to his feet, using her anger at being compared to her mother to give her the strength she needed for the task ahead. She didn't want to be unkind to Patrick, but somehow she had to find the strength of will and courage to save them both. If the only way she could do that was to call upon the spirit of her sharp-tongued, fierce-tempered mother, then so be it.

As soon as Patrick was upright she turned her back on him and dragged his arms over her shoulders, holding on tight as she bent forward and lifted his feet clear off the ground.

'Help me!' she gasped.

He locked his arms around her neck and she managed to jerk him a little higher up her body, until she could get her arms beneath his legs. He grunted with pain when she jolted his wound, but it was impossible to be gentle. They had to make some adjustments before Honor started walking. At first, Patrick's arms pressed the musket into her body so hard she could barely breath; but soon she was ready to plod after the long-gone column of men.

* * *

Cole snapped his telescope shut with an impatient gesture. He'd spent the past twenty-four hours checking on the position and movements of the French. Normally he enjoyed the opportunity for independent action. He was an experienced outpost officer. At different times he'd worked with both the regular Spanish army and the guerilla bands. But since joining the 52nd Foot his activities had been more circumscribed. He should have relished this chance for a little more freedom of action. Instead he'd been irritated rather than pleased when he'd received his current orders. He hadn't wanted to leave the battalion as it struggled towards safety. He was concerned for the well-being of all the men who served under him, but he couldn't deny that the gnawing anxiety he felt for the O'Donnells—for Honor—was particularly intense.

But now that Cole was satisfied that the French had no intention of pursuing them any further, his task was completed. He was free to rejoin his men as soon as possible.

He glanced at Joe Newton. His servant had been ill at ease from the moment they'd left the column; now he was positively fidgeting with impatience.

'We're going back, sir?' he burst out.

'Yes, we are.'

'Thank God for that.' Joe didn't waste a moment in turning his horse towards Ciudad Rodrigo.

Cole frowned, briefly puzzled by Joe's uncharacteristic vehemence. But since Cole was equally keen both to rejoin their comrades and to reach a comfortable billet, he didn't question him.

Honor walked steadily, keeping to the least rutted part of the road, taking every step with care, fearful of stumbling over a mud-covered obstacle. She was a tall woman; at five foot four, Patrick was actually an inch or two shorter than his wife. That made it easier. So did the fact that he was a skinny, wiry man, without a spare ounce of extra flesh. But he was still a heavy burden, and she was already tired and undernourished.

The light was fading and she knew they wouldn't reach safety by nightfall. Her awareness shrank to the next few feet of muddy road. To look ahead and see how far she had to go would have invited despair. Perhaps that was why it took her so long to realise she wasn't alone on the road. She couldn't hear anything, she certainly hadn't seen anything—but she slowly turned around and looked straight into the amber eyes of a wolf.

The wolf was so close she could see its breath misting on the cold air. There were two others, circling behind it.

'My God!' She exhaled in shock. 'Patrick, let go.'

All she could think was that she couldn't fire the musket with him hanging around her neck. But Patrick was barely conscious. He was clinging on by instinct, unable to respond to her desperate request.

The wolf padded closer, head outstretched towards her, golden eyes focussed on Honor.

'Patrick, let go!' she screamed. He tumbled off her back. The wolf shied away, snarling at her sudden screech.

Honor fumbled with cold, unresponsive fingers in the ammunition pouch. A moment ago she'd thought she was too tired to care what happened to them, but now anger stirred her numb limbs. She was damned if they were going to survive so much, just to become some damned dog's dinner! She tore off the end of the paper cartridge with her teeth, primed and closed the pan, then rammed the powder, torn cartridge and ball into the muzzle of the musket.

Don't fire away the ramrod, she reminded herself a little hysterically. She thrust it into the ground by her feet and lifted the musket to her shoulder. At least the wolf couldn't shoot back. Patrick had to do this under enemy fire.

She aimed at the nearest wolf. The musket kicked so hard her shoulder went numb, but she was too frightened and excited to notice. She was more concerned about the brief interval of blindness when the sudden flash and cloud of smoke obscured her vision.

Had she hit the wolf? Would she feel its teeth in her throat at any second?

The smoke cleared and she saw the wolf was either dead or so severely wounded it would never hunt again.

Excitement surged through her and she gave a hoarse, wordless shout of victory. One of the remaining wolves turned tail at her loud cry. The other sniffed cautiously at its fallen companion and bared its teeth at her, its head low to the ground.

Honor reloaded the musket with shaking hands.

'Mangy cur!' she raged at the wolf. 'Eat the dead meat! That's all you're fit for!'

She fired again. This time she missed, but the solitary wolf had had enough. It disappeared into the trees and Honor was suddenly alone with Patrick. It was only then that she realised two horsemen were approaching. She lifted the unloaded musket instinctively, afraid she was going to be ridden down by French cavalry, then she recognised the leading horse—and his rider.

'Corvinus,' she whispered. The musket was suddenly too heavy to hold and she dropped it, falling on her knees beside Patrick.

Cole heard the first shot before he saw Honor in the failing daylight. When he saw the wolf she'd shot, his heart lurched with admiration for her courage and resolution.

By God, she was a woman among women! he thought exultantly.

Then Honor collapsed beside her husband's hunched body, and the sight chilled his triumphant mood.

He leapt to the ground and seized Honor's arms in an urgent grip.

'Are you hurt?' he demanded fiercely, all his cool composure forgotten.

Beside them, Joe Newton crouched over Patrick.

Honor stared at Cole blankly, as if she didn't recognise him. Her hazel eyes were red-rimmed and sunk in deep, dark circles. Her face was so thin it twisted his gut to see it. Her cheeks were streaked with mud, her hair so matted it was impossible to tell its true colour.

'Honor!' Her name ripped from his lips.

'Patrick,' she whispered, staring past him towards her husband supported in Joe's arms. It was as if Cole's presence had barely registered with her.

Cole released her, feeling a kick of jealousy, because her only thought was for her husband. That emotion was quickly followed by self-disgust and shame at his wildly emotional response to the situation.

'O'Donnell?' Cole bent over the sick man, his voice

expressionless, but his touch gentle as he pressed the back of his hand against Patrick's forehead.

'Take care of Honor, sir,' Patrick croaked. His eyes were clouded by sickness, but no sign of confusion when he met Cole's guarded gaze.

Cole's conscience pinched. Did the man have any idea how he felt about his wife? He glanced at Honor, but she was kneeling in the slush like a statue, her face devoid of expression or response, as if the last of her reserves had finally been exhausted. Joe Newton waited woodenly for orders from his master.

The stallion nuzzled Honor's shoulder gently, then nudged her back with his head a few times, in an almost human gesture of affectionate impatience.

'Corvinus.' Honor turned her head and focussed on the black. 'Come here, boy.' Her voice was utterly flat but, to Cole's amazement, the stallion obediently took a few steps forward.

Honor took hold of the stirrup and hauled herself to her feet. Her stoic determination was so mesmerising that, by the time Cole recollected himself enough to help her, she was already on her feet.

She looked at him directly for the first time.

'We can put Patrick on Corvinus,' she said. It was a statement of fact, not a supplication to an officer.

'Yes, ma'am.' Cole was startled to realise that he'd just given her the same response she often elicited from the privates in her husband's company. Honor didn't seem to notice. Unseen by either of them, a brief smile lightened Joe's sombre expression.

'I intend to put you both up,' Cole said drily, reasserting his authority. 'You first. I will lift...your husband up to you.'

Honor barely acknowledged his words, but she allowed him to help her on to the stallion's back. Cole cursed himself for his momentary hesitation. Why was it so hard to call the man her husband? Cole had always known they were married.

Perhaps his emotional turmoil now was the result of being forced to see, at first hand, the depth of devotion Honor felt for Patrick O'Donnell. She would do anything to keep her husband alive.

He took Patrick from Joe's supporting arms, steadying the man's feverish body briefly before he hoisted him on to Corvinus.

'She carried me.' Patrick's voice was little more than a hoarse whisper against Cole's shoulder. 'No wagons—so she carried me. I was meant…to take care…of her…' His words faded to nothing on the frosty evening air.

The man's words only intensified Cole's self-disgust, but he kept his face expressionless as he lifted Patrick into Honor's arms. Then he turned to Joe.

'Ride ahead, find us a billet, and inform the surgeon he will be needed,' he ordered harshly.

'Not the hospital.' Honor said flatly. 'I'll take care of Patrick.' Her voice sounded rusty and unfamiliar in her ears. 'Don't take him to the hospital.'

She'd seen the conditions in the hospitals. Two or more men crowded in one bed, in airless, filthy wards. A man could go into hospital with a broken leg and die of the fever he'd caught from his unfortunate bedmate. Some of the medical staff were conscientious, but too often the men were left in the care of hospital mates who were ignorant and inattentive to their patients. While Honor still had breath in her body, she would not permit Patrick to be submitted to such an ordeal.

'No, not the hospital,' said Cole, his steady voice inviting her trust.

'Good.' Honor nodded, accepting his assurance. She wrapped her arms around Patrick, holding him in place on the stallion's back as Cole began to lead his little party towards Ciudad Rodrigo.

Patrick was barely conscious, but he'd been around horses all his life. Deep-rooted instincts kept him in the saddle—and Honor did the rest. She'd thought many times that, if Patrick had to be a soldier, he might have been happier in the cavalry—but it had been an infantry recruitment party which had finagled him into the army.

She was hardly more alert than Patrick. From the moment she'd seen Corvinus—and the unmistakable broad shoulders of his master—her relentless determination had begun to unravel. Raven would save them. She had no doubt of it. She closed her eyes, letting him lead them where he chose. Just before her weary, overburdened mind lost all coherence, a stray thought drifted to the surface. What luxury, for once in her life, to be able to rely on someone else's strength and determination.

Chapter Two

The regiment was bivouacked outside Ciudad Rodrigo, but Joe Newton and Maggie Foster met Raven's bedraggled little group as they approached the fortress. Joe led them into the suburbs. Honor was too tired to wonder what he had arranged, she was simply grateful that they had somewhere to go.

The next few days passed in a blur. Later she was able to remember only a few random incidents from that time. She had been billeted with Patrick in the house of an elderly Spanish gentleman and his two sisters. Their hosts were discreet and remarkably tolerant of being burdened with a very sick man. Honor expressed her gratitude to them, but she was too distracted to pay much attention to her surroundings, and too worried about Patrick to question the unexpected comfort of the billet Raven had arranged for them.

Joe was frequently in attendance. Honor never wondered what his master thought of his long absences from his duties. Maggie Foster left her children in her husband's care and helped nurse Patrick. It turned out that Joe had met her trudging back along the road to look for Honor and Patrick, and had told her they'd been found.

The O'Donnells' Spanish hosts brought a priest who made little impression on Honor, though she thought his presence comforted Patrick. Lieutenant Gregory came to see them, grateful that they had not died on the road, sorry that Patrick was so ill.

Major Raven visited, bringing with him the battalion surgeon, but otherwise saying little.

Patrick received the best care available—but it wasn't enough.

He rallied briefly, then his condition deteriorated. Most of the time he was too weak or confused to speak to Honor. She remembered only two things he said to her.

'You're a good wife,' he whispered once, when she lifted his head to help him drink.

For a while his memory drifted back to his childhood in Ireland, and Honor could do little more than guess the correct response to his ramblings.

'You must make peace with your mother,' he said suddenly, his voice surprisingly strong. It was the last thing he said to her.

He died the next day. Honor prepared his body almost mechanically. She was too weary to cry, or even to grieve. Then she lay down beside him, knowing only that her long struggle to take care of him was over and she could finally rest.

Cole found them like that half an hour later. His first, appalled thought was that they were both dead.

'Honor! My God!' He pulled her into his arms. Her head lolled on to his shoulder. Then she sighed, an effortful breath, and relief thudded through him.

He tightened his hold on her. She was too thin. She weighed nothing in his arms. Her hair and her clothes were clean, but she looked more waif-like than ever. He hadn't realised quite how much the fierce determination of her will counterbalanced her fragile appearance. With her eyes closed it was hard to associate her with the woman who'd moved Heaven and earth to bring her husband to safety.

Then he saw that Patrick was dead, his body laid out for burial, and a chill invaded Cole's soul. Was Honor's life so bound up with her husband's that she no longer believed she had a reason to live?

'Honor!' he cried, fear edging his voice.

'Mmm.' She moved slightly in his arms, pillowing her cheek against his scarlet uniform. She drew in another deep breath. 'Tired,' she mumbled on an exhaled sigh. The rhythm of her breathing changed. To Cole's amazement, he realised she'd fallen into a peaceful sleep in his arms.

'Honor?' he murmured, an unfamiliar calm soothing his anxiety as he cradled her against his heart.

He didn't move—he couldn't. He could not bear to lay her down. She felt so warm and trusting in his arms. If he lowered his head, he could brush his lips against her sun-streaked hair. The temptation was overwhelming. He stroked a stray tendril back from her face. Her skin was soft and smooth, her fine bones as delicate as a bird's.

That brief, gentle touch was the only liberty he allowed himself to take with her. She was so vulnerable in her sleep that it stirred an ache deep within him. He could not protect her from the pain and grief she would feel when she woke and realised that Patrick was dead. She needed this interlude of unburdened rest.

She was still asleep when Joe Newton arrived.
Shrewd eyes observed the care with which Raven held
Honor, but the servant didn't comment. Cole didn't say
anything either. His angular face was typically expressionless as he watched Joe briefly examine Patrick.

'She laid him out?' said Joe, a question in his low
voice.

Cole nodded. Honor had been alone when he'd
found her. He doubted anyone else had performed that
chore for her.

'Her last duty,' said Joe. 'She ploughed her furrow
to the end.' His eyes softened as they rested on
Honor's sleeping face. 'No one could have asked more
of her than that—not Patrick O'Donnell, at any rate.'

Honor slept for hours. Cole carried her out of sight
of curious eyes while Patrick's body was removed,
held her in his arms while Newton set the small room
to rights, and then—reluctantly—put her gently down
on the crude bed. He sent Newton away, knowing his
own actions had betrayed him, but trusting the man's
loyalty and goodwill would keep him silent.

Cole didn't leave. Honor was alone and unprotected
in a strange place. She needed him.

Honor woke slowly and reluctantly. She ached in
every bone and muscle of her body, which had become
normal. She was also warm—which was a miracle.
And she had a nagging, aching awareness that something was dreadfully wrong.

Patrick!

She turned her head, but he wasn't beside her. She
thrust upward, staring wildly around. Patrick was
gone—but she wasn't alone.

There was a candle burning on the table, and she saw Cole Raven sitting in the dim light. His presence shocked her, but somehow it didn't surprise her. He'd been a constant—though distant—presence in her life for a long time. Her first, instinctive response was to feel comforted by the familiar sight of his broad shoulders.

At her sudden movement he turned his head towards her. The hard planes of his face could have been carved from teak, they showed so little expression. His deep-set eyes were hidden in shadows and unreadable. He didn't speak. Suddenly his presence didn't seem quite so reassuring. He was too powerful, too inscrutable, too much at ease in the darkness which surrounded them. Terrifying images crowded into her mind as she recalled the traditional association between ravens and the battlefield—ravens and the dead. Was Raven here because Patrick had died? A human emissary of death?

Honor shuddered and put her face in her hands. Her imagination had always been as much a curse as a blessing. Normally she tried to conjure only warm, positive musings, but tonight all her defences were down. She took a deep breath and tried to clear her thoughts. She had no idea what time it was or how long she'd been sleeping. Why had Raven watched her sleep?

'Do you remember what happened?' he asked after a few moments.

'I know Patrick is dead.' Her voice was muffled by her hands.

Grief welled up inside her for her husband, but she choked it back. She was acutely aware of Raven's scrutiny. She didn't understand what he was doing beside her, but she was determined not to give in to her emotions while he was watching her. Her mother's teaching had been unequivocal in that respect. Annie Howarth firmly believed that one should be rational, practical and, above all, *businesslike* on all occasions.

'There is food if you are hungry,' Raven said. 'You must be hungry. You've been asleep for hours. God knows how long it is since you ate.'

Honor swallowed her tears and lifted her head. She wouldn't allow herself to grieve for Patrick until she was alone. In the meantime, although she didn't feel hungry, she knew Raven was right, she needed food. She pushed back the covers and discovered she was still dressed, although her shoes were on the floor beside the bed. She put them on and drew in a deep breath, light-headed from the mild exertion.

'Here.' Cole put a plate of food into her hands.

There was only one chair in the room and Raven had it, so Honor sat on the side of the bed to eat.

Garlic sausage, cold pork and bread. Real bread, not the weevil-infested biscuit which was the staple of army rations. Despite her wariness over Raven's intentions, she was touched that he'd given her food. She couldn't remember the last time she'd eaten food she hadn't been responsible for providing.

She ate slowly, doing her best to ignore Raven's watchful presence, focussing instead on her meal. She seldom had the opportunity to enjoy the sheer pleasure of eating good food. If there turned out to be a price for this meal, she would conduct the negotiations with the food safely in her stomach.

'Brandy?' Cole poured her a glass from the bottle on the table.

She accepted it wordlessly and took a cautious sip.

The strong liquor burned her throat and she handed it
back to him immediately. Gin had been the undoing
of the normally abstemious Patrick. She had no intention of letting her own wits be clouded by drink.

'Or tea?' Cole smiled faintly, and she saw a tin ket-
tle sitting on the hearth.

She waited while he made the tea, not surprised at
his competence. The food had strengthened her, and
now she had the energy to notice things that had previously eluded her.

She was wearing a warm brown skirt and jacket,
just like so many of the local women. There were
good, square-toed shoes on her feet. There was a black
shawl lying across the foot of the bed. She barely remembered the moment when Joe Newton had given
her the new clothes; she'd been too tired and too preoccupied with the task of nursing Patrick. Now she
had time to consider the implications of those gifts.
Joe had presented them to her, but he hadn't paid for
them.

She accepted a cup of tea from Major Raven, and
saw that he'd poured one for himself as well. She studied him carefully, refusing to be daunted by his cold
reserve, as she tried to remember everything she knew
about him.

He was a big man with enormous physical stamina.
She'd heard he had been wounded while he was still
in the dragoons, but he'd survived both injury and the
tortuous medical treatment he'd received. He was a
head taller than Patrick, and Honor had noticed that
tall men often suffered most on the march, but Raven
seemed immune to the discomforts of campaigning.

He also possessed a forceful personality. After the
bitterly costly siege of Badajoz earlier that year, all

discipline had been lost among the British soldiers. They had rioted drunkenly in the streets of the town. Raven had been among the few officers who could still exert any control over his men. Patrick had told Honor how the Major had saved a Spanish girl from rape, relying simply on the strength of his personality. No sane man, looking into those crystal blue eyes, would willingly cross him.

Honor was grateful for Raven's help, but she was wary. Experience had taught her that most interactions with other people involved negotiations of some kind. She preferred those negotiations to be as unambiguous as possible.

'What do you want from me?' she asked quietly.

Cole's eyes narrowed as he studied her intently.

Honor met his gaze steadily, refusing to be cowed by his keen-eyed inspection.

'Nothing,' he said at last. He finished his tea and set the cup down on the table.

His denial puzzled Honor, but she didn't let her confusion show.

'I will pay for the clothes as soon as I can,' she assured him. 'There will be work I can do.' There was always work—mending, washing or cooking for different officers.

'That's not necessary,' said Cole brusquely.

'It is for me.' Honor lifted her chin stubbornly. 'I don't accept charity.'

He held her gaze with his hawk-like blue eyes for a long, tension-filled minute. Her heart rate increased as she realised more fully the hazards of crossing his fierce will. The Major did not tolerate any form of insubordination.

To her relief he broke eye contact first, glancing sideways at the shadow-filled room.

Honor drew in a deep, steadying breath. 'Thank you for all you did for Patrick,' she said.

'He was a good man.' Raven moved his long legs restlessly.

Was. Honor swallowed back her flash of anger at Raven's use of the past tense. She did not like the idea that Patrick's life could be dismissed in a few brief words.

'Yes,' she agreed raspily.

There was a heavy silence between them for several minutes, then she roused herself to speak once more.

'Patrick told me you saved his life at Badajoz,' she said.

Raven shrugged impatiently. 'In the heat of battle, who can be sure of such things?' he said, disclaiming responsibility for being considered any kind of saviour.

'God! You're a stubborn, contrary man!' Honor exclaimed, surprising herself as much as Raven with her unexpected outburst.

Raven's eyebrows quirked ironically. '*I'm* stubborn?' he said, a gleam in his eyes. 'I'm sure you could give me lessons, Mrs O'Donnell.'

'At least I say what I'm thinking!' she said forcefully. 'Talking to you is like debating with a baggage mule. You don't say what you want, but you're bound and determined to do things your own way! Hah!'

She grabbed the plate and chomped down on another piece of bread, suddenly ravenously hungry.

Raven blinked at the force of her attack then, to her amazement, grinned. The expression completely transformed his angular face, making him seem both younger and far less threatening.

'What do you think I want?' he enquired blandly.

Honor was momentarily startled to see a rakish smile hovering on his lips, but the unexpectedly suggestive gleam in his eyes fuelled both her suspicions and her growing annoyance.

'That's what I'm talking about!' she snapped, hastily swallowing the mouthful of bread, and waving her hand at him crossly. 'Answering a question with another question. If you can't say anything to the purpose, go away.'

Raven chuckled softly, apparently not offended by her bluntness. 'You don't mince your words, do you?'

Honor ate some more sausage, glowering at him, trying not to acknowledge the small thrill of pleasure she got from sparring with him. She might be playing with fire—but at least the flames warmed her, driving away her memories of the recent endless cold.

'What will you do now?' Raven asked, his expression sobering.

Honor wasn't ready to face that question. Instead of answering directly, she instinctively went on to the offensive.

'Me, me, me!' she exclaimed. 'Why is this whole conversation about *me*? I want to know what *your* part in this is. Why were you sitting beside my bed when I woke up, with a plate of food and a bottle of brandy at hand? Exactly what kind of bamboozling game are you trying to play with me?' she demanded recklessly.

Raven's expression darkened.

'In case you've forgotten, I saved your life,' he said icily, all humour wiped from his dark face.

'I *know*!' Honor leapt to her feet in agitation. The candle flame danced in response to her hasty action, sending long shadows plunging around the room. 'The question is, *why*? This is the third time you've come to my rescue. Why did you fish me out of the Heubra? Why did you give me these clothes? What do you want in return?'

She stood over him, her hands on her hips as she fiercely confronted him with his own actions.

Raven flushed, tilting his head back to look at her. 'Don't you know better than to look a gift horse in the mouth?' he growled furiously.

'Why? Have you got plaster teeth?' she threw at him.

'Try me.' He bared his teeth at her in a silent snarl.

Honor froze. She was pitched back to the moment on the road when she'd stared into the amber eyes of the wolf. Raven's eyes were blue, but the expression in them was as dangerous and unfathomable as the wolf's. Despite the fact that Raven was still sitting, while she stood over him, the feral, masculine power in his lean body threatened to overwhelm her. Tension crackled in the air between them.

She stepped back slowly, never taking her eyes from Raven's face. She had an irrational fear that, like the wolf, he might spring at her if she dropped her guard for an instant. But she knew she must never let him see she was afraid. She clenched her hands to hide the fact she was trembling.

'I…I am grateful for all you have done for us,' she said, unsteadily. 'I have no wish to insult you by questioning your motives. But I prefer to know exactly what I'm dealing with. I am sure you understand that…sir.'

The last word was not said in a disrespectful tone, but to emphasise the difference between them. Raven's generosity to Patrick was not unprecedented. His personal attentions to her were...unusual...to say the least—unless he had a very specific role in mind for her.

He scowled at her. Her throat was so dry she couldn't swallow. Her ribs ached with tension when she tried to draw a breath—but she didn't dare take her eyes off his face.

'I will arrange for your return to England,' he said abruptly.

'What?' Honor's jaw dropped in amazement. She was so surprised she forgot her nervousness. 'In what capacity?' she exclaimed, finally recovering her wits.

'Dammit, woman! I'm not trying to make you my mistress. I'm simply trying to ensure your safety,' he snarled at her impatiently. 'That *is* what your husband wanted, isn't it?'

'Patrick?' She was bewildered by his reference to her husband.

'"Take care of Honor", that's what he said to me on the road,' Raven reminded her savagely. 'I wonder if he knew just how difficult you'd make it?'

'You're here because you feel some sort of obligation to *Patrick*?'

Honor's legs were suddenly too weak to support her. She flopped down on the bed, staring at Raven in bewilderment. Somehow his attentions to her had seemed a lot more personal than that. Had she completely misread the situation?

'What else?' He glared at her. 'Let me tell you, Mrs O'Donnell, your opinion of my morals is insulting, to say the least. I do not customarily take advantage of grieving widows.'

The lash in his voice stung. It was an indirect criticism of her own conduct since waking.

'Would you have preferred me to collapse in tears at your feet?' Honor demanded, in a low, shaking voice. 'You are *not* the arbiter of my conduct. You did *not* need to watch me sleeping—like a vulture gaping for the feast. Your intentions could just as well have been conveyed to me by Joe later, when I was in a state to consider them. Not now, in the middle of the night, when I'm alone, tired and confused.'

Raven's hands clenched into fists. He was pale beneath his tan. His face might have been chiselled from granite as he stared at her in the flickering candlelight.

'I have seldom witnessed anyone less confused—or more calculating and suspicious in their response to disinterested kindness,' he grated. 'No doubt O'Donnell is giving thanks for his merciful release.'

Honor's lips parted wordlessly. All colour drained from her face. She was stunned and bitterly hurt by his cruel accusation.

'Patrick,' she whispered. Tears blinded her.

'Honor? My God!' Raven was suddenly on his knee before her. 'That was unforgivable.' He seized her hands in his. He sounded as shaken as she felt, but she was almost too distraught to notice.

'Go away,' she whispered. 'Please. Go away.'

'Honor.' His hands tightened over hers.

She turned her head away.

'I did not mean what I said.' His voice was strained and ragged. 'Forgive me. No man could have wished for more from his wife.'

She didn't reply. She couldn't trust herself to speak.

Raven stood up.

'We will discuss your return to England at a more suitable time,' he said grittily. 'Goodnight, Mrs O'Donnell.'

Honor sat like a statue for several minutes after he'd gone, fighting for self-control. At last she reached a shaking hand for the glass of brandy and swallowed it down. It seared her throat and she coughed, fresh tears stinging her eyes. But these tears had a physical cause and she was not afraid of them. She was afraid of the grief which threatened to consume her. She clutched the glass against her chest, realising suddenly that she had nothing left from the last few years—not even her wedding ring. She'd traded it for necessities when Patrick's pay had been late and their funds were low. She was penniless, possessionless, and alone. This bleak room in an alien country was certainly not the place to surrender her self-control. If she gave up now, she would betray Patrick, as well as herself.

Cole stood in the street, leaning against a wall as he struggled to discipline his raging emotions. He'd known Honor was a determined woman, but he'd never expected to be on the receiving end of her temper. Always before she'd treated him with the courtesy and deference his rank required. Now she treated him as an equal. It was a novel sensation for Cole. Very few people were prepared to challenge him head on.

He was furious with her suspicions. He'd only been concerned for her safety, yet she'd accused him of being some kind of foul scavenger, preying on her misfortune. He clenched his fists angrily.

Damn Honor. Damn his own soft-minded weakness where she was concerned. He hadn't considered how she would interpret his presence by her side when she woke, he'd only known he couldn't leave her alone when she was so vulnerable.

If he'd expected anything from her awakening in

such circumstances it had been grief, confusion—or even gratitude that he'd considered her plight and would protect her. But she'd gone from sleep to wakefulness with a campaign-hardened efficiency that would have done any soldier proud. That was not how Cole wanted to perceive her. He ran a hand through his dishevelled hair. If he had any sense, he'd leave her to fend for herself. She was clearly more than capable of holding her own against anyone.

Within a day of Patrick's death, Honor received marriage proposals from four of the men in his company. It was usual for widows to remarry quickly. Without a man, and with no easy means of getting home again, a woman was very vulnerable. Sometimes a woman could be married and widowed more than once within a few months. Honor turned all the proposals down, careful not to offend any of the men.

She also received considerably less respectable proposals from a couple of officers. She turned them down as well. She had no desire to become any man's mistress. She knew Raven's offer to send her safely back to England was intended to save her from such indignities, but she wasn't ready to leave Spain—and when she did leave, she would make her own arrangements. In the meantime, with Maggie Foster's help, she found employment as the maid of the Spanish mistress of an officer in the 43rd Foot.

The Light Division was to spend the winter in various villages around Ciudad Rodrigo. Honor was relieved to discover that her new employer, Captain Arthur Williams, was quartered in a different village from Major Raven. The empty cottage assigned to Captain Williams and Dolores, his mistress, consisted

of two mud-floored rooms. The outer chamber was intended for the use of both pigs and people, while the
inner was divided into sleeping chambers around a
central sitting room. The bedrooms were dark or light
depending on whether the small windows were shut-
tered or left open. The fire was in the middle of the
floor, the smoke was supposed to escape through a
hole in the roof.

Honor threw herself into the task of making the
place habitable for herself and her new employers.
Within a short space of time she'd had a hole knocked
in a wall and an outside chimney built, cleaned the
rooms, and even found crockery and wall-hangings to
make the place more comfortable.

She welcomed the hard work. Sooner or later she
would have to think about the future, but for now she
preferred simply to live from day to day.

'A woman of many parts,' said Captain Williams
appreciatively, a week after she'd started working for
him. 'With a gift for making a hovel into a gracious
home.'

'Thank you, sir,' said Honor.

'Most remarkable,' he said. 'I saw you perform as
Rosalind at Drury Lane a few years ago. Captivating
performance. Tried to offer my compliments later—
but couldn't get near you for all your other admirers.
Now, here you are cooking my dinner in Spain. Quite
a turn-up, hey?'

'Yes, sir,' said Honor calmly, her heart sinking as
she heard the satisfaction in his voice.

'Well, well,' said Williams jovially. 'They must
have been heady days. I don't suppose you ever
thought you'd end up here, did you?'

'I don't think any of us can predict with certainty where we will be in a few years' time,' Honor replied. 'Even during peacetime.'

'Why did you marry O'Donnell?' Williams burst out. 'You could have had every luxury. Pampered, privileged… Selhurst would have given you anything you asked for! Instead you threw yourself away on—'

'Unfortunately the Duke of Selhurst didn't have anything I wanted,' Honor interrupted crisply. 'I'm glad you find my work here satisfactory, Captain. But I must inform you, I'm not willing to discuss my personal life. If that is not acceptable to you, then let us terminate this arrangement forthwith.'

'B-but what will you do if…?' Captain Williams's startled response faded into silence in the face of Honor's unwavering gaze.

Her heart hammered in her chest, but she didn't reveal her agitation by the merest flicker of an eyelid. She was angry at the Captain's disparaging reference to Patrick, and she wasn't willing to discuss her personal history with anyone. On the other hand, she needed both the money and the relative security that this job gave her. She didn't want to alienate her employer unnecessarily.

'Come, sir,' she said, offering Williams a friendly smile. 'Surely we can agree that the past is done with, and hardly worth the effort of discussing?'

Williams frowned at her attempt at conciliation. Honor held her breath and tried to project an aura which was both respectful and respectable.

'Dolores likes the way you do her hair,' said the Captain at last.

'She has beautiful hair,' said Honor, grateful the Spanish girl wasn't present. She thought Williams might have been less willing to tolerate the minor challenge to his authority if his mistress had witnessed it.

'Very well.' Williams came to a decision. 'You may continue as Dolores's maid. But if I detect the slightest impertinence in your behaviour you will be dismissed immediately.'

'Yes, sir. Thank you,' said Honor, bowing her head slightly to show her acceptance of his terms. 'I must fetch some water.' She wrapped her black shawl around her head and shoulders and hurried out of the cottage before he could say anything further.

Once outside she picked her way carefully over the uneven, rocky road. The wet, slippery stones beneath her feet were uncomfortable to walk on, and for a few minutes she focussed all her attention on taking each step.

At last she took a deep breath and tried to relax the tension in her muscles. Everywhere she turned she seemed to face obstacles. She wasn't comfortable with Captain Williams. She didn't like his casual dismissal of Patrick, and she didn't care for the way he seemed to derive pleasure from the reversal in her fortunes. Had he employed her simply so he could boast about how the one-time darling of Drury Lane had been reduced to working as his mistress's maid?

She'd wanted a few months' peace while she considered her future. She still hoped that might be possible, but she would have to be careful of the Captain. She didn't want any more trouble.

She looked up and saw Cole Raven riding through the village towards her. His unexpected arrival startled her. Her heart thudded with apprehension. She hadn't seen or spoken to him since the night she'd woken to find him sitting beside her bed. Her first impulse was to run and hide. She even glanced about, looking for an escape route—then she realised such an attempt would be futile.

Instead she braced her shoulders against the wind and stood still, waiting. It was possible he wasn't coming to see her—more than possible. It was highly likely he had other business in the village. Strangely, she didn't find that idea as consoling as she should have done.

She watched as he came nearer. He was riding Corvinus. The big black tossed his head proudly and she heard the jingle of the bridle carried to her on the cold wind. Despite herself, she had to admit that man and horse made an impressive sight. Corvinus was sure-footed on the rocky ground: powerful muscles moved easily beneath his shining black hide. Raven was completely at home in the Hussar saddle he still favoured. A consummate horseman. He and the stallion were so closely attuned to each other they almost seemed to be two parts of a single entity.

Raven looked straight at Honor and inclined his head in a brief acknowledgement. He continued to look at her as he rode straight towards her. Even over a distance of several yards she was aware of the intensity of his scrutiny.

She clutched her shawl tighter, hating how easily Raven could reduce her to nervous uncertainty. She'd wondered if Raven would seek her out again. She wasn't sure if she'd hoped for or feared their next encounter, but with her heart beating up into her mouth she would be lucky if she could talk at all when he greeted her.

At last Corvinus closed the distance between them. Honor tipped her head back to look at the man high

above her. Last time they'd been in a similar situation—when Raven had fished her out of the Heubra—
he had bent over her, reducing the difference in their
heights. Now he towered more than four feet above
her head. For a few long moments they stared at each
other, the tension thick between them—then Corvinus
nudged Honor's shoulder impatiently.

She gasped and immediately turned her attention to
the horse, grateful for the distraction. She petted him,
murmuring soft words of praise as he tossed his head,
his black mane flying.

'You speak as old friends,' said Raven. His voice
sounded gravelly. 'I noticed it before.' He dropped
lightly to the ground and stood beside Corvinus's
shoulder.

'Ah, yes.' Honor looked up at him warily, unable to
read anything from his tone or his expression. 'Patrick
was Joe's friend. And we both—Patrick and I—we
both love good horses.'

'I see,' said Raven. He removed his shako and
tucked it under his arm. Honor noticed how the black
feather plume brushed against his sleeve. All her
senses were fully alert, trying to interpret Raven's intentions towards her. She'd never been so close to him
when they were both standing. He was taller even than
she had imagined. The scarlet of his uniform jacket
contrasted dramatically with his sun-browned, angular
good looks. His silver epaulettes drew attention to the
breadth and power of his shoulders.

At five foot six inches, Honor was used to looking
most of the men in Patrick's old regiment in the eye.
Raven was over six feet tall. She felt dwarfed in his
presence—almost intimidated by his size and the controlled masculine energy which radiated from his per-

son. Apparently the cold wind didn't bother him as much as it bothered her.

She took a deep breath, determined not to let herself be overawed by the formidable major.

'Joe always puts the interests of the horses first,' she said, belatedly afraid she might have caused trouble for the servant.

'Not always,' Raven replied coolly.

'He does!' Honor fired up immediately on behalf of the absent Joe. 'I assure you—' She broke off as Raven raised a hand to silence her, a slight, enigmatic smile on his lips.

'I have no quarrel with his priorities,' he said calmly, taking the wind out of Honor's sails. 'Is there somewhere we can talk?'

'I really don't—'

'I fully intend to talk to you—in the wind or out of it,' Raven interrupted her again without apology. 'But I'm sure Corvinus would appreciate a more sheltered location.'

Honor pressed her lips together, annoyed at the way Raven had manipulated her.

'This way,' she said shortly. 'There are two empty barns further up. Captain Williams keeps his horses in one of them. I'm sure Corvinus will be comfortable in the other.'

'Good. Lead on.'

Honor disliked the peremptory note in Raven's voice. It clearly hadn't occurred to him that she might not obey his command. She told herself that the only reason she was doing so was from simple courtesy— she still owed him a debt of gratitude for his help with Patrick—but she was also uncomfortably aware she preferred to avoid arousing his displeasure.

She'd woken in the night from disturbed dreams about Patrick, Raven and the wolf she'd shot, only to realise that she really was listening to the eerie, terrifying howls of a wolf pack as it circled the village. For a few seconds, images of Raven had been indistinguishable from the savage eyes of the wolf. She had no doubt that, in some ways, the man was more dangerous than the wild beast.

But she'd had other dreams associated with Raven that made less sense to her—of warmth, comfort and peaceful rest. Could a dangerous predator also be a protector?

She listened as Corvinus's hooves struck the hard ground behind her. Raven walked without making a sound. How could such a large man move so silently? She turned abruptly to check he was still following her. He was less than two feet behind her.

He raised his eyebrows in a wordless query.

'Here we are,' she exclaimed, hating the breathless quality of her voice. Hating the way Raven seemed to tower over her.

'Good.'

The stone-walled barn had been damaged in one of the many skirmishes that had taken place in the area. There was a hole in the roof and in one of the walls. Rubble lay in one corner of the floor, but the building still offered reasonable shelter from the cold wind.

Raven efficiently tended to Corvinus, then turned his attention to Honor.

She wrapped her black shawl firmly around her head and shoulders, her hands tucked safely inside. She didn't want to risk the possibility that he might see them tremble and think he had gained an advantage over her.

'I've come to arrange your return to England,' he said bluntly.

'Thank you,' she said tautly. 'I appreciate your concern—but I will make my own arrangements, Major.'

'Don't be ridiculous,' Raven said curtly. 'If you had the means to arrange your return home, you wouldn't be skivvying for Williams and his doxy. Pay attention. I will shortly be making a brief visit to Lisbon. You will accompany me. In Lisbon I will select someone suitable to travel with you on the packet boat to Falmouth and thence to London. I'm assuming you wish to return to London?' He cocked a questioning eyebrow at her. 'All I require from you at this moment is the name and direction of the individual in England into whose care I will be delivering you.'

'Why? So you can check their references?' Honor demanded, too stunned by his announcement to consider her words—or even to feel indignation at his high-handedness.

Raven flushed. 'This is not a subject for levity,' he growled. 'The name and direction, if you please.'

Honor walked around him to stand beside Corvinus. She patted the stallion's shoulder affectionately. He swung his head round to mumble his lips at her shawl. He snorted disapprovingly and, despite herself, Honor laughed. She pushed the shawl back to reveal her sun-bleached hair and moved to stand at Corvinus's head. She knew that stallions could be dangerous and unpredictable creatures—but Corvinus had always been exceptionally good-mannered with her.

She always enjoyed her encounters with the fine black horse, but on this occasion she was simply giving herself a little time to think. Raven's plans for her, not to mention the autocratic way in which he'd conveyed them to her, dumbfounded her.

'Aren't you handsome?' she murmured, threading Corvinus's forelock gently between her fingers, then gently drawing her hand along his silky black ear.

Corvinus nodded and nudged his head against her chest, pushing her back a couple of steps.

'Be careful!' In a couple of strides Raven was beside her, seizing the bridle in his strong hand. 'He's not a child's pony.' With his other hand on Honor's shoulder, he moved her firmly away from the stallion.

Corvinus snorted in annoyance and pulled against his master's controlling hand on the bridle.

'I know he's not a pony,' Honor said in exasperation. 'He's a great big dangerous beast who could stomp me into the ground if he wanted to—but he's not going to. He's always been a complete gentleman whenever we've met.'

She sensed the swift glance Raven threw in her direction, but she kept her attention on Corvinus. She could still feel Raven's touch on her shoulder, even though he'd released her immediately. She had no doubt that he'd moved to protect her—just as it seemed he wanted to send her back to England for her own safety.

She had very mixed feelings about that. She didn't want Raven interfering in her life—but it was a long time since anyone had tried to take care of her so competently.

'Mrs O'Donnell, kindly tell me the names of your friends in England,' Raven said impatiently.

'I really don't see why you need that information,' Honor demurred, looking sideways at Raven. 'Even supposing I might be willing to accept your help getting back to Falmouth, I certainly don't need anyone else's help to take the stagecoach back to London.'

'Your husband asked me to take care of you,' he replied grittily. 'To my mind that includes making sure you do *have* somewhere to go once you arrive back in England.'

'Somewhere suitable, you mean?' Honor couldn't help teasing him, despite his glowering expression. 'You *do* want to check the references of my friends. If they aren't up to your exacting standards, what will you do?'

'Dammit, woman! I don't have time for this!' Raven threw up a hand, jerking it impatiently through his dishevelled hair. 'The name, if you please!'

For some reason his frustrated gesture both amused and reassured Honor. She thought perhaps Raven wasn't quite as sure of himself, or the situation, as he wanted her to believe.

'What if I don't have anyone to return to· in England?' she asked curiously.

'I know you have,' he replied curtly. 'You send and receive letters regularly.'

'Have you been spying on my correspondence?' Honor demanded, disturbed that he should know so much about her.

'Of course not! But not many of the men—let alone their women—have regular communication with England,' he pointed out.

'I see. So now you want the name of my correspondent. Since you obviously believe that I *do* have somewhere to go once I reach England, why are you so determined to find out where? Surely you don't think you have a right to know my personal business—

simply because Patrick asked you to take care of me?'
Honor challenged him.

Even in the dim light of the barn she saw Raven
flush.

'I have no wish to intrude in your personal affairs,'
he denied grittily. 'I will be more than happy when I
can transfer responsibility for your care to someone—'

'Responsibility for my care!' Honor interrupted
hotly. Her initial shock and mild amusement at
Raven's overbearing attitude had now given way to
annoyance. 'I've been responsible for my own care
since I was seventeen years old. I do not need or want
your help, Major. I will make my own arrangements
when I am ready.'

'You are impertinent and ill disciplined,' Raven said
icily. 'I will inform you when it's time to leave.'

'The only way I'll leave here with you is against
my will!' Honor declared fiercely. 'Abduction, sir!
What will that do for your reputation—if it becomes
known you forced a dead soldier's wife to go with you
against her will? Bathsheba to King David…'

Raven reared away from her as if she'd struck him;
his expression dark with anger. His hands, held rigidly
at his sides, were clenched in fury at her insult. Every
muscle in his powerful body was taut with barely contained rage. Honor's breath stuck in her throat as the
terrifying currents of Raven's wrath swirled around
them. Corvinus danced backwards, edgily responding
to the highly charged emotional atmosphere in the
barn.

'For God's sake!' she gasped, stunned by the violence of Raven's reaction to her biblical allusion.

Bathsheba had been the wife of one of the officers
in King David's army. The King had made Bathsheba

pregnant, then given the orders which had led to the death of her husband in battle. After that the King had taken Bathsheba into his harem.

Honor didn't think the story of Bathsheba and King David bore any resemblance to her relationship with Raven. She'd only mentioned it because, in her exasperation with Raven's dictatorial manner, she hadn't been able to think of a more appropriate retort. But it seemed as if Raven had taken her words as a mortal insult.

'Surely…?' Her voice faded away as she stared at him, trying to decipher the cause of his fury.

His blue eyes seared her with the ferocity of his emotions. She thought she saw hatred and disgust as well as anger in their stormy depths.

She started to tremble uncontrollably, appalled at the hostility she had unwittingly aroused.

'You think I'm the kind of man who could order another man to his certain death—just so I could take his woman?' Raven demanded, his voice low and throbbing with outrage.

'*No!*' Honor stared at him, struggling to regain her own composure. 'No, of course not.'

'You as good as said so when you first woke after O'Donnell died,' Raven said, with harsh contempt. 'Now you've repeated the accusation. You overrate yourself. The sooner you're safely away from here, the better. You'll be informed when it's time to leave for Lisbon.'

He lead Corvinus out of the barn into the cold dusk and mounted in one easy movement. He didn't look back at Honor as he rode away through of the village, his back ramrod straight.

'Oh my God,' Honor murmured, shaken to her core.

She staggered back and leant against the rough stone wall of the barn. Her trembling legs were too weak to support her unaided.

Raven had indeed taken her hasty words as a mortal insult, though she'd never intended them as such. She remembered the fleeting impression she'd received of disgust—even hatred—in his eyes, and shuddered. Did he really have such a low opinion of her?

She found the idea deeply distressing—so hurtful that a physical pain clutched at her midriff. She bent forward, wrapping her arms protectively around her body as she waited for the first intensity of her distress to subside. At last she straightened up and resolutely squared her shoulders. She had no intention of letting Raven dictate her actions—but nor could she allow him to believe she thought so badly of him. She took a deep breath, trying to calm her apprehension at the thought of facing Raven again.

Chapter Three

'Mrs O'Donnell wishes to see you,' Joe Newton said expressionlessly.

Cole looked up, startled by his manservant's announcement. It was two days since his confrontation with Honor in the barn and he still couldn't think calmly of the incident. She'd accused him of lusting after her, of manipulating events—perhaps even hastening Patrick's death—so that he could have her. Her reference to Bathsheba and King David had been far too apposite. The Old Testament story of the King's sinful action had never been far from Cole's mind over the past few weeks. So Honor's accusation had cut like a whiplash across his already tormented conscience, laying bare his guilt and precipitating his wild fury.

'She's here?' he said sharply.

In future he intended to discuss nothing with Honor except for the essential, practical details of her journey home. Under no circumstances did he want another, gut-wrenching, emotionally devastating argument with her.

He was just about to send her away when it occurred to him that perhaps Honor wanted to see him for the same reason. She'd obviously realised the wisdom of leaving Spain and wanted to talk about the arrangements. Bolstered by that possibility, Cole stood to greet his uninvited guest.

'Show her in,' he said brusquely.

'Major Raven.' Honor stopped just inside the door, briefly meeting his eyes before glancing nervously around at the sparsely furnished room.

As always when he saw her, Cole's heart leapt with a combination of fierce, conflicting emotions. She was always beautiful to him, whatever she was wearing, but it pleased him that she was dressed in the warm new clothes he'd given her.

He instinctively checked her countenance for signs of fatigue or illness. She was still too thin, and far too fragile for the brutal life she'd been forced to lead— but she no longer looked as if she was on the brink of exhaustion.

Her slender fingers clutched her shawl tightly. He saw that her expression was both wary and resolute. He'd always admired her courage, but he was filled with self-disgust when he realised that today she was afraid of him. No doubt she saw him as some kind of ogre who lusted after another man's wife without a thought for the feelings of others.

'Mrs O'Donnell.' He stopped, uncertain what to say next. He cleared his throat and started again. 'I have not yet made all the arrangements for the journey to Lisbon—'

'No, no,' she interrupted him quickly, 'that's not why I came.'

'You wish to tell me the name of your friend in England?' he asked hopefully, though he tried to keep his voice businesslike.

'No. I didn't come to talk about my return home at all,' she said firmly.

'We have nothing else to discuss,' Cole said roughly, his stomach clenching at the prospect of a more personal conversation.

'Perhaps not to discuss,' Honor agreed, looking at him warily. 'I mean, I came to tell you something…'

'I have no interest in your self-willed opinions,' Raven said, his harshness prompted simply by his need for self-preservation. 'I promised your husband I would take care of you. I fully intend to do so—with or without your co-operation.'

He saw Honor take a deep breath and press her lips together before she replied. He realised he'd angered her—as he so often seemed to—though that hadn't been his intention. All he wanted was to bring this interview to an end as quickly as possible.

'I came to apologise,' Honor said grittily.

Cole stared at her in silence.

'I should not have accused you of such a dishonourable thing—even in jest,' she said tightly.

'You were not jesting.' He wasn't mollified by her attempted apology. He found even the most oblique reference to his feelings for her extremely painful.

'No, but I spoke in haste.' She clutched her shawl tightly as she watched him across the width of the room. 'I was angry…' He saw her take another deep, unsteady breath. 'You can be very free with your orders, Major.'

Cole gritted his teeth together as he stared at her through narrowed eyes.

'I'm very conscious of your kindness to Patrick before he died,' Honor continued. 'And your kindness to me—'

'I don't want your gratitude,' Cole growled.

She blinked at him in confusion and he wished he could recall his hasty words. He could almost see the question forming in her mind—if he didn't want her gratitude, what did he want?

'Patrick O'Donnell was a good man. It is not a hardship to carry out his dying wish,' Raven said quickly. That much was true, and he could say it with a clear conscience.

'Or it wouldn't be if I weren't so damned contrary,' Honor replied wryly.

Her smile took Cole by surprise. It transformed her face, hinting at the sense of humour he'd almost forgotten she possessed. He'd first been drawn to her, even from a distance, by her laughter and the good humour with which she faced the discomforts of army life.

His own mood lifted in spite of himself. He liked seeing Honor smile. He wanted her to be happy.

'If you know that, why are you so determined not to co-operate?' he asked, his tone warmer than before. 'There would be no need for any of this if you would simply—'

'Do as I'm bid?' Honor finished for him. 'I am not biddable, Major.'

Cole couldn't help uttering a wordless, but emphatic, grunt of agreement with her statement.

She raised her eyebrows slightly in response, then smiled and pushed her shawl back from her pale hair.

'I respect your determination to keep your word to Patrick,' she said, 'but I really think you should also take my preferences into account.'

'You prefer to work your fingers to the bone for Williams and his—'

'She's a very nice, kind girl,' said Honor quickly, before Raven could make a disparaging reference to Captain Williams's mistress. 'Dolores. Her family were killed by the French. She really doesn't have many options available to her—and Captain Williams is kind to her.'

'I see,' said Cole. He ran a hand through his hair, wondering how the devil he was going to deal with Honor. Even when she wasn't flatly contradicting him she was as difficult to get to grips with as a greased eel. 'Nevertheless, however considerate your employers, your life here is hardly a sinecure,' he pointed out.

'Life is never a sinecure in my experience,' Honor retorted. 'May I sit down—or would that be an affront to your views on military discipline?'

'I'm surprised no one has strangled you yet!' Cole exclaimed, thoroughly exasperated, as he gestured towards a chair.

'No doubt they've considered it,' she said, seating herself with annoying composure.

'May I offer you some refreshment?' Cole offered, doing his best to impersonate a genial host, since that was the role she'd apparently chosen for him.

'No, thank you.' Honor folded her hands primly in her lap. 'I simply wanted to clear up a few points of confusion between us.'

'I am not confused,' Cole stated baldly.

'Then the confusion must be all mine,' she replied equably. 'I'm sure you'll be generous enough to clarify things for me.'

'Are you, indeed?' Cole said drily.

'Oh, yes,' said Honor. 'You're a very generous, honourable man, Major. There is no doubt about that.'

Cole's sharp riposte died on his lips as he saw the

sincerity in her hazel eyes as she looked at him. He glanced away, shaken by the possibility that maybe she did believe him to be an honourable man. If so, her judgement was sadly lacking. An honourable man didn't desire another man's wife.

'We were discussing your confusion,' he said rustily.

'We were discussing your determination to eject me from Spain before I'm ready to leave,' she corrected him.

Cole's familiar temper rose at her persistent stubbornness—but then it occurred to him to wonder why she was so resistant to leaving.

'Why don't you want to leave?' he asked.

Honor hesitated, her eyes narrowing as she gazed into space, and he realised she was choosing her words carefully.

'I'm not ready to go,' she said at last.

'That's hardly an answer,' he said impatiently. 'Why not?'

'Patrick has not yet been dead two weeks,' she said. 'I haven't become accustomed to…to…'

'You can become accustomed just as easily in England as you can here,' said Cole roughly.

Honor lifted her eyes to meet his. 'Why are you so eager to get rid of me?' she asked curiously.

'I'm not!' he replied angrily, guilt sharpening his response. Despite his determination to send her away, he didn't want her to leave.

'Perhaps we can find a compromise,' she said after a few moments. 'When I'm ready to leave, I will allow you to help me with the arrangements.'

Cole raised his eyebrows at her terminology. 'You will *allow* me to help you?' he repeated sardonically.

'I am not one of your men,' she reminded him.

He resisted the urge to tell her how he would have dealt with her if she had been.

'And when do you suppose you'll be ready to leave?' he asked drily.

'I don't know,' she replied. 'I will tell you when I am.' She stood up and he did likewise.

'You haven't told me the name of your friend in England,' he reminded her.

'No, I haven't,' she agreed. She looked up into his eyes and surprised him by smiling. 'Were you planning to write to them in the hope they might use their powers of persuasion on me?' she asked.

He gritted his teeth, unwilling to admit that what he'd really been seeking was the assurance she did have somewhere safe to return to in England.

'Will you go back to the stage?' he asked instead.

He didn't like the idea of her putting herself on public display once more. He'd never enjoyed the theatre himself, but he'd heard enough comments by his fellow officers to know how they viewed actresses. Even Honor's status as a devoted wife had not saved her from being the subject of several lewd remarks during her time in the Peninsula.

'You don't approve of actresses, Major?' Honor asked him.

'I don't approve of the life they must live,' he said stiffly.

'Ah.' She went very still, studying his expression intently. 'I see. No wonder you are so impatient to fulfil Patrick's wishes. Your approval of him does not extend to me.'

Cole's ribs expanded as he dragged in a deep breath of air. 'I don't disapprove of you,' he said grittily.

Honor continued to hold his gaze for several more seconds and he forced himself not to look away. There was nothing else for him to say. He could hardly tell her how much he admired her courage, or how much he desired to hold her slight body in his arms.

'You may have some time to…accustom…yourself to your change of circumstances,' he said hoarsely. 'Then I'll arrange your journey.'

'I had no idea you had such a passion for administrative tasks,' Honor remarked, walking to the door. 'I always imagined you were more at home leading patrols deep into enemy territory.'

'I am now in the infantry,' Cole reminded her.

'I know.' She smiled slightly. 'But don't you miss the freedom your previous duties allowed you? Joe told us so much about your exploits in the dragoons.'

'Joe wasn't with me then,' Raven said brusquely. 'He only joined me shortly after I transferred to the 52nd.'

'You mean the stories aren't true?'

Cole was startled to realise that Honor was gently teasing him. 'Since I have no idea what Newton told you, I'm not in a position to say,' he replied gruffly.

Honor smiled. 'Goodbye, Major.' She held out her hand to him. 'I am grateful—'

'I'll have Newton escort you back to your billet,' he interrupted her. 'Goodbye, Mrs O'Donnell.'

A few minutes later he closed the door on her and wondered why the devil he'd let her talk him into allowing her to remain in Spain. The only honest answer he could come up with was that, in his heart, he didn't want her to leave.

He walked over to his writing case and took out the most recent letter from his fiancée, Miss Bridget

Morton. They had been betrothed for four years. If not for the fact that Bridget's mother had died shortly after their betrothal, they would have been married for over three years.

Cole had left for Spain before Bridget's period of mourning had ended, and had not returned to England during the intervening years. As soon as he did so, he and Bridget would be married. He read Bridget's letter and tried to conjure an image of her in his mind—but the only face he could see was Honor's.

He set the letter aside with a raw curse and hit the table with his clenched fist, filled with anger, frustration and guilt at his unruly desires.

'Now, why won't you let the Major send you home?' Joe asked, as he escorted Honor back to her billet.

'I'm not ready to leave yet,' Honor replied, wondering how many times she would parrot the same answer to that question.

'Why not?' Joe asked reasonably. 'There's nothing to stay for—is there?' He shot her a sideways look.

Honor sighed. 'It's not so much what there is to stay for,' she said reluctantly.

'And what do you mean by that?' Joe challenged her, when she didn't continue. 'Are you saying there's someone in England you're trying to avoid? The Duke of Selhurst, perhaps?'

'Oh, no!' Honor exclaimed, before she could stop herself. She hadn't given the Duke a thought but, if she'd been more alert, he would have made a good excuse for her foot-dragging, at least as far as Joe was concerned.

'Then who?' Joe persisted. 'Surely your mother would welcome you home again?'

'My mother disowned me when I married Patrick,' said Honor, unable to hide her bitterness. 'I don't think she'll be waiting with open arms.'

'Ahh.' Joe nodded wisely. 'But people change. Perhaps she's thought better of her action since then.'

'Oh, I dare say she'd take me in,' Honor agreed wearily. 'She told me I'd beggar myself if I stayed with Patrick. If I go home now—if Major Raven delivers me to her like a piece of lost property, as he seems to intend—she'll think she was right. I couldn't bear to hear her tell me so.'

'Hmm.' Joe pursed his lips together. 'Not so good. I see your point. But she's not the only person you know in London. Isn't Lady Durrington still writing to you?'

'Yes, she is. But I'm not turning up on her doorstep like a stray mongrel either. Whatever would she think?'

Although Honor enjoyed corresponding with Lady Durrington, she'd never quite understood why the older woman had sought her friendship. Her ladyship had approached Honor quite soon after she'd become the latest rage of Drury Lane. Honor had been surprised. At first she'd been polite but wary, but it hadn't taken her long to decide that Lady Durrington was sincere.

Honor liked the older woman immensely, but it had always been a purely private friendship. Honor had never met Lord Durrington, though she'd heard a lot about him, and she'd never been introduced into the Durringtons' social circle. She had wondered whether her marriage to Patrick would change things, but Lady

Durrington's friendship had remained steadfast. She'd even offered her husband's influence to extricate Patrick from the army, but both Patrick and Honor had been too proud to accept such help.

'If she's a true friend, she would be pleased you thought of her in your hour of need,' said Joe robustly.

'I'm not in need!' Honor protested immediately, hating to be cast in such a pitiful role.

'Ah well, then, if you're too proud to go back to London with your tail between your legs—you'll just have to stop here, and battle it out with the Major,' said Joe phlegmatically.

'I don't wish to battle with anyone,' Honor said, frustrated. 'Least of all Major Raven. I never met anyone so high-handed—'

'Didn't you?' Joe interrupted, sounding startled.

'What? Oh, you mean Mother?' Honor couldn't help grimacing. 'Patrick must have told you about her. I hadn't noticed any similarities between them before. Actually…' She frowned, considering the situation. 'Perhaps you're right. My experience with Mother does make me resistant to being told what to do. But Major Raven has no business giving me orders. I'm not his daughter—nor one of his men.'

'I think he knows that,' Joe remarked, suppressing a small smile.

'I beg your pardon?' Honor was still preoccupied with Joe's earlier comment and didn't notice his expression.

'Nothing important. Here we are.' They'd reached Honor's billet. 'I'll visit you in a day or so,' Joe told her.

'Thank you.' Honor impulsively hugged him. 'You're a good friend.'

'That's all you know,' said Joe gruffly, briefly and awkwardly returning her embrace. 'You're a good needlewoman. Who else will I get to do the Major's mending once you've left?'

Honor laughed. 'I might have known you'd have a mercenary motive,' she teased him.

'You can be sure of that.' He took his leave of her.

Honor watched him go, but her thoughts were with Raven. She'd been sick with anxiety before her meeting with him—so nervous that she hadn't been able to sleep the previous night. But the encounter had been less distressing than she'd feared.

Raven *had* been brusque and autocratic, but he'd tacitly accepted her apology, and he hadn't ridden roughshod over her wishes as she'd anticipated. She'd even seen a brief lightening in his mood, though he hadn't let her thank him for his kindness towards her.

He was, she thought, a very difficult man. He was so unpredictable in his responses that every time she opened her mouth she was afraid she might inadvertently provoke his temper. Talking to him wasn't a relaxing experience—but it was certainly invigorating.

It was a cold, foggy evening and she hugged herself in her shawl. She had an elusive memory of being held in warm and comforting arms, but the comfort wasn't at home in England, it was here in Spain—and it had something to do with Cole Raven.

Honor shook her head, wishing she didn't have such a fanciful imagination. There was nothing about the fierce, hard-muscled Major that was the least bit soft or comforting.

She sighed. She knew she'd have to leave Spain soon, and when she did she'd have to face her mother. But the memory of her mother's rejection still chilled

Honor's heart. She needed more time before she would be brave enough to confront Annie Howarth.

Cole Raven came to see Captain Williams the next day. When Honor first saw his broad shoulders in the doorway her immediate thought was that he had come to see her—but beyond offering her a brief greeting, he devoted all his attention to the Captain.

Honor felt relieved, disappointed and curious in varying amounts. As far as she knew, the two men had not formerly been friends, but Raven made himself at home in the Captain's billet as the two talked endlessly about various masculine pursuits.

She served them with a hearty stew made from local pork, and wondered in bewilderment how anyone could have such an inexhaustible interest in fox-hunting, hare-coursing or shooting woodcock. Dolores obviously shared Honor's feelings, because shortly after she'd finished eating she murmured something about being tired, and disappeared into her room.

Honor dealt with her domestic duties as inconspicuously as possible. When she was finished she lingered, trying to appear busy without drawing attention to herself. She knew she ought to leave the two men alone, but she liked listening to Raven talk, even when she had no interest in what he was talking about.

She glanced up, and realised his intense blue eyes were watching her. She knew instantly that he'd seen through her little charade. She flushed with embarrassment and caught up her shawl. She hurried out of the cottage with a muttered comment about firewood before either Raven or Captain Williams could say anything.

Once outside, she tried to regain her composure.

Almost inevitably she was drawn to the barn where Raven had left Corvinus. It was a long time since she'd had the opportunity to see the horse without his master also being present. Corvinus was pleased to see her and she made a fuss of him, comforted by his undemanding company.

She'd been controlling her emotions from the moment she'd woken after Patrick's death. For the first couple of days it had taken an effort of will not to succumb to her grief. After that she'd been too emotionally numb even to want to cry. Then she'd been distracted by her argument with Raven.

But now she was alone with Corvinus. He was warm and solidly comforting. She leant against his shoulder, her face pressed against his glossy black hide, and finally allowed her guard to drop. Hot tears scalded her eyes and burned her cold cheeks. She clung tighter to Corvinus as she cried out her pain, loneliness and uncertainty.

Raven had visited Captain Williams because he wanted to ensure the man treated Honor with appropriate respect. He allowed the conversation about hunting to continue for a few more minutes, then he came straight to the point.

'Mrs O'Donnell's husband was a good soldier,' he said abruptly. 'When he was dying he asked to me take care of his wife.'

'How did he expect you to do that?' Williams enquired, raising his eyebrows in mild amusement.

'I am arranging for her safe journey home,' Raven said curtly.

'And deprive Dolores of her maid!' Williams exclaimed. There was an edge to his humorous tone.

Raven was aware that the other man didn't like the interference in his domestic arrangements.

'Mrs O'Donnell was devoted to her husband. She is still strongly attached to his memory,' said Raven evenly. 'At the moment she is reluctant to leave the place where he died. I am sure she will continue to perform her duties while she comes to terms with her loss.'

'She'd come to terms with it soon enough if she had a better offer,' said Williams cynically. 'Not much left for her in England now, I don't suppose. But if—' he broke off as he met Raven's cold gaze.

'Mrs O'Donnell is under my protection,' said Raven, his voice soft but deadly. 'If she wished it, I would arrange for her return to England immediately. Currently she prefers to support herself, rather than accept any form of charity. While she is working for you, I will hold you responsible for her safety.'

'If you want the woman, take her!' Williams exclaimed, flushing angrily. 'She's nothing to me.'

'Good,' said Raven. 'I trust Mrs O'Donnell will remain secure while she works for you.' He stood up, ready to leave. He'd made his point. He had no desire to antagonise the Captain unnecessarily. 'Thanks for your hospitality. I hope you enjoy some good runs after the hounds this winter.'

'I'm sure I will,' the Captain replied. His anger had been replaced by a speculative expression as he watched Cole's face. 'It will be interesting to see which of us enjoys the better sport.'

Cole didn't bother to reply. He inclined his head in a brief gesture of farewell and left the cottage. He'd known all along that his warning was likely to arouse Williams's curiosity—but he didn't give a damn what the other man thought of him. As long as the Captain allowed Honor to do her job in peace until she returned to England, Cole would be satisfied.

It was late in the day, and dusk was falling. Cole paused briefly, wondering where Honor had gone. Despite himself, he wanted to see her before he left the village. Then he smiled, guessing where he was likely to find her.

She was indeed with Corvinus, but he was amazed by the sight that confronted him.

Honor was leaning against the stallion, one hand on his withers, her other arm curving beneath his proud neck. Her face was buried in the black's shoulder— and when Cole heard her pain-racked sobs he realised she was crying.

He froze in surprise, both at the intensity of her emotion and the stallion's patient response to it. For the most part, Corvinus was a good-tempered beast, but neither Cole nor Joe Newton took liberties with him. Yet here was Honor treating the stallion like an old, familiar friend.

He'd seen this connection she had with the horse before but, although it still surprised him, he was too concerned about her to give it much thought.

Honor's distress was very real, and it disintegrated the last of his anger with her. He'd always admired her fortitude, but he had thought her unwomanly when she'd restrained her grief so ruthlessly immediately after Patrick's death. Now he wondered how he'd ever thought he had a right to judge her behaviour.

He hated to see her in such distress but, strangely, her obvious grief helped ease his own crushing sense of guilt. The fact that Honor had not cried in his presence, nor turned to him for help when she clearly needed comfort, somehow reassured him that his unruly desires had not sullied the purity of her devotion to Patrick.

Cole was able to console himself with the thought that she really did regard him only as one of her husband's more overbearing, interfering officers. That was not how he wanted her to respond to him in his undisciplined dreams—but it was certainly what he hoped for in his rational mind.

He hesitated, unwilling to intrude upon Honor's private grief. Then he heard men talking as they approached the barn. He stepped outside and recognised several of his fellow officers. He raised his own voice in a loud, cheerful greeting, and stood talking to them for several minutes. By the time he finally entered the barn, Honor had gone.

Cole didn't see Honor again for over a month. He knew Joe visited her every few days, and he trusted his servant would tell him if she needed anything.

Wellington, who'd set up headquarters at Frenada, seventeen miles from Ciudad Rodrigo, went to Cadiz for several weeks over Christmas. The rest of the army and its camp-followers settled into their winter quarters and entertained themselves as well as they could.

Cole took his shotgun out after woodcock, hiking for miles through the rugged countryside. He enjoyed the physical challenge of pitting his strength and endurance against the wild terrain. The mournful howls of the plentiful wolves in the region didn't trouble him; instead, their song stirred a desire within him to explore their wild kingdom.

He relished his solitary forays into the wilderness, but he was restless. He wanted to see Honor again.

Towards the end of January he gave in to his craving and rode Corvinus over to her village. It was time to see whether she was ready to go back to England. He was determined that, however obstinately she protested, she would leave Spain before the next campaign season began.

He dismounted outside the barn, then paused at the sound of voices coming from within. He recognised Honor's voice immediately. She was talking to a man, though he couldn't immediately place the fellow.

'Lawyers!' she exclaimed energetically. 'I hate lawyers!'

'Nay then, we will not wait for their lingering forms,' her companion assured her earnestly. 'But instantly procure the licence, and—'

'The *licence*!' Honor was clearly incensed at the suggestion. 'I hate licence!'

'Oh, my love! Be not so unkind! Thus let me entreat—'

Cole was first stunned, then furious at what he'd overheard. Some jackanapes was forcing his attentions on Honor! He strode forward—then stopped short as Honor spoke again.

'Pshaw! What signifies kneeling, when you know I *must* have you?' she demanded scornfully.

'Nay, madam, there shall be no constraint upon your inclinations, I promise you. If I have lost your heart—'

Cole had heard enough. He stalked into the barn, determined to put an end to this nonsense. As long as he was there to protect Honor she didn't *have* to do anything—certainly not submit to the whims of…

…Lieutenant Gregory?

Cole recognised the younger man immediately. Patrick O'Donnell and the lieutenant had both served in the same company. Cole knew Gregory had thought well of O'Donnell, but that was no excuse for him to take advantage of his widow.

'What the devil are you doing, Lieutenant?' Cole rapped out, his blistering gaze sweeping over Gregory's flushed countenance.

'M-Major Raven!' Gregory stammered. 'W-what…?'

'Good afternoon, Major,' Honor said smoothly. She was as shocked as the lieutenant by Raven's unexpected appearance, but she recovered her wits more quickly.

Her heart raced, partly from sheer surprise, but mainly from excitement at seeing Raven again. He was as tall and formidable as ever. And right now he was furious with the unfortunate Gregory. One look at Raven's grim expression and she knew exactly what he thought was happening. She didn't have time to wonder how she felt about his fierce response—her immediate instinct was to save him from unnecessary embarrassment.

'I didn't know you were such an exacting theatre critic, Major,' she said lightly. 'I thought the lieutenant's performance was very convincing.'

'Th-thank you, Mrs O'Donnell.' Gregory's face flushed with gratification, though he still watched Raven warily.

'Performance?' Raven said wrathfully.

'I'm sure you recognised that scene from *The Rivals*,' Honor said, walking over to lay her hand on Raven's arm.

She touched him without a thought except to calm him, but she was instantly conscious of the tense, corded muscles beneath his sleeve. For a moment she forgot everything except the impact of his powerful masculinity upon her senses.

He stared down at her, his eyes searing her with their intensity. She caught her breath, disturbed by the way her whole body leapt in response to that limited contact with him. She forgot what she'd meant to say.

'I didn't recognise the scene,' Raven said baldly, ignoring her attempt to spare his embarrassment. 'I've never had much time for the theatre.'

'But surely you'll attend *our* performance?' Gregory burst out, sounding both shocked and disappointed that Raven could be so boorish.

'The Light Division's performance of *The Rivals*?' Honor explained breathlessly, seeing that the lieutenant's hasty comment had only caused Raven's already thunderous expression to darken even more ominously.

'Are you taking part in this entertainment?' Raven demanded, ignoring Gregory as he pinned Honor with a diamond-hard, disapproving stare.

'Of course not!' she exclaimed. Her stomach fluttered nervously at his fierce gaze, but she was also exasperated by his high-handed attitude. 'I was simply coaching Lieutenant Gregory in his role.'

'I'm playing Lydia Languish,' Gregory offered, clearly anxious to placate his senior officer.

'You did not sound as if you were playing the part of a female,' Raven said, his blistering gaze sweeping over the discomfited young man.

'He took the part of Jack Absolute so he could see how I managed Lydia,' Honor said impatiently. 'I had no idea you were so straitlaced, Major. No doubt you think it's a pity the theatres were ever reopened after the puritans closed them.'

'It's an indisputable fact that playhouses are a hot-bed for every kind of depravity,' Raven said inflexibly.

'Depravity!' Honor forgot everything except her outrage at Raven's insult. 'How dare you accuse me of being depraved!' She prodded Raven's chest with a furious finger. 'I've put up with all kinds of snide innuendo from others—but you're the first man to call me depraved to my face. Who the devil do you think you are?'

'I did not call you depraved!' Raven shot back at her, his brows drawn down in a forbidding frown. 'Misguided and ill disciplined—yes. But I did not call you depraved!'

'Well, I'll just…I'll just…um…excuse me,' Lieutenant Gregory muttered, edging past them and escaping from the confines of the barn, his battered script clutched to his chest. Neither Honor nor Cole were aware of his departure.

'But that's what you think of me,' Honor said hotly. 'You've alluded to your disapproval of me several times.'

'I do not disapprove of you,' said Cole grittily.

'But you disapprove of the life actresses lead—and therefore of the life I led before I married Patrick,' Honor challenged him. 'And you just called me *misguided* and *ill disciplined*. You really don't have much opinion of me, do you, Major?' Her voice cracked on the last few words. She dashed a quick hand across her cheek and abruptly turned her back on him.

Her heart hammered in her chest. She was both angry and upset. Her throat ached with unwanted tears she was too proud to shed. She'd endured all kinds of criticism in her life, but Raven's condemnation hurt far more deeply than most.

'You said Patrick was well rid of me,' she whispered, barely aware she'd spoken aloud as she remembered what Raven had said the night she'd woken after Patrick's death.

She heard Raven draw in a rasping breath, then she felt his hands rest tentatively on her shoulders. She held herself rigid, but she didn't pull away from his touch.

'I don't disapprove of you,' he said hoarsely. 'I think Patrick was a fortunate man to be blessed with you as his wife.'

Honor stared straight ahead at the stone wall of the barn. Tears filled her eyes until she couldn't see. She knew if she blinked they'd overflow on to her cheeks. She swallowed, pressed her lips together and tried to control her overwrought emotions.

Raven's hands tightened on her shoulders, then his grip relaxed, but he didn't release her. She was acutely aware of him standing behind her. She could feel the virile energy radiating from his powerful body. She could hear his quickened breathing. The tension between them was almost suffocating in its intensity.

'I don't…disapprove of you,' Raven repeated. He rubbed his hands stiffly down her upper arms, then moved them back up to rest them on her shoulders.

Honor ducked her head, swallowed again, trying to regain her composure. 'You think I am misguided and ill disciplined,' she whispered. She hated that his opinion meant so much to her, but she couldn't prevent herself from saying the words.

The silence between them lengthened.

'You are not ill disciplined,' Cole said at last. 'Misguided…yes. You would be safer in England.'

'You're so sure of that?' Honor murmured, a little wearily.

Cole gripped her shoulders tighter for a couple of seconds, then spun her round to face him. 'Why would you not be safer in England?' he demanded sharply.

Honor gasped, startled by his sudden action, then she looked down, unwilling to meet his searching gaze.

Cole waited, but she could feel his barely curbed impatience at her continued silence.

'What the devil am I going to do with you?' he exclaimed, his frustration audible.

'You don't have to do anything with me,' she retorted, finally managing to step away from him.

She missed the warm strength of his hands on her shoulders, but she welcomed the opportunity to brush her own hand across her eyes. She refused to let Raven see her cry.

'I can't help you if you won't let me,' he said roughly.

'I don't need your help.' Her denial was automatic and unthinking. She kept her head averted from him.

Cole didn't reply, and a few moments later she heard him walk out of the barn. She spun around to stare after him, pressing her hands against her mouth in dismay. Uncomfortable though she'd found their encounter, she hadn't wanted it to end so unsatisfactorily.

But then Cole came back into the barn, leading Corvinus. 'There's no need for him to stand in the wind while we debate this,' he said brusquely.

'Of course not.' Honor went straight to the horse, finding comfort in him as she always did. She wished she could lean her head against his shoulder, but she wouldn't do so in front of Raven. Instead she confined herself to stroking Corvinus. She couldn't even speak to him because she was afraid her voice would betray her.

She was surprised that Cole remained silent for several minutes, long enough for her to find some emotional balance.

'You'll have to leave before the campaign season starts,' he said at last. 'And if there is nowhere in England you feel comfortable returning to—we will have to arrange something else for you. We can discuss it another time. I'm going to see what adventures Williams has had with his hounds since I last spoke to him.'

'Major.' Honor stopped him just as he reached the door. 'Do you enjoy spending hours talking about hunting?' she asked, hating the uncertain waver in her voice, but wanting to delay Raven's departure.

He hesitated. 'Perhaps not for hours,' he replied, after apparently giving her question serious consideration. 'Why?'

'I…just wondered,' she said, and saw a glimmer of amusement in his blue eyes. Suddenly she didn't feel quite so bad.

'I cannot help you if you resist me at every turn,' he said quietly.

'I didn't ask for your help,' she reminded him, but without heat.

'Your husband did.'

'Poor Patrick.' Honor sighed.

'You miss him very much,' said Raven. It was a statement, not a question.

'We were married for more than three years,' said Honor softly. 'And I'd known him since I was a child.'

'He was several years older than you,' said Raven.

'Eleven years.' Honor focussed her attention on

Corvinus, but she was acutely aware that Cole had moved a couple of steps nearer to her as they spoke—and that he was watching her closely. 'Patrick was driving the London-Bath mail the first time I saw him.'

'Impressive fellows—coachmen,' said Raven stiffly. 'Every young buck wants to emulate their skill with the ribbons.'

'So did I!' Honor said, a hint of amusement in her voice.

'He didn't let you?' Cole sounded scandalised.

'Of course not!' she exclaimed. 'He was very responsible. Besides, Mother—'

'Mother what?' Raven prompted, when she didn't continue.

'Nothing. I forgot myself.' Honor watched Raven warily out of the corner of her eye.

'Why did you become an actress?' Cole asked, surprising her with the change of topic.

'Because I was good at it—at least, I thought I was,' she said after a few moments. 'It was a way for me to earn an independent living without...'

'Without what?'

'It was more exciting than being a governess,' Honor said a little defiantly, risking a brief glance at Cole.

'I dare say,' he replied drily. 'Was that the only alternative?'

'Not the only alternative,' said Honor carefully. 'But it was the only one I was prepared to consider.'

'What do you mean?' Cole frowned at her evasive answer. 'What of your family? I have never understood why they allowed you to take such a disreputable course of action,' he added, a note of censure in his voice.

Honor turned her back on Corvinus so she could look directly at Cole. The horse rubbed his chin on her shoulder and she lifted her hand absent-mindedly to pat his neck.

'What exactly do you mean by that?' she asked.

'You have the manners and speech of a gentle-woman,' Cole said bluntly, after only the briefest hesitation. 'You don't belong among the camp followers of an army—nor on the public stage. I can only assume your family suffered such a serious reversal you had no choice but to seek your own fortune.'

Honor gazed at Cole. 'I'm not sure if I should take that as an insult or not,' she said at last.

'Will they welcome you when you return—or did they disown you after you went on the stage?' Cole asked.

Honor gasped, stunned by how accurately Cole had assessed her situation.

'You think my family have disowned me—for joining the theatre?' she exclaimed.

'Or…perhaps for your marriage?' Cole said softly, his tone carefully neutral, though he watched her intently.

Honor started to laugh out of sheer, shocked surprise. 'You think I was disowned because I married Patrick?'

'I was obviously mistaken,' Cole said stiffly, withdrawing a couple of steps in the face of her laughter. 'Your reluctance to act reasonably invites speculation—but I did not intend to pry.'

Honor was too shaken by his unexpected perspicacity to challenge his insult to her reason. 'You seem to have given a lot of thought to my situation,' she said wonderingly.

'Certainly not!' Cole retorted immediately, frowning at her. 'I have considered the matter only in relation to fulfilling your husband's last request to me. Had you been less obdurate, I would have been spared considerable inconvenience.'

'How flattering!' Honor responded instantly to his disapprobation. 'I'm sure if Patrick had known you would regard me as a disreputable inconvenience he would never have burdened you with his request.'

Raven drew in a deep breath and exhaled slowly, obviously struggling to retain both his patience and his good temper.

'This is a fruitless conversation,' he announced with finality. 'We will discuss your departure when you are in a more amenable mood.'

He moved purposefully towards Honor. Her heart leapt into her throat. She swallowed back her nervous anticipation at what he intended to do—but he reached past her to take Corvinus's reins.

Honor stood aside, feeling a sense of anticlimax as Raven led the stallion out of the barn.

'I thought you wanted to see Captain Williams,' she said.

'I have changed my mind,' said Cole briefly. 'Good day, Mrs O'Donnell.'

'Goodbye, Major.' Honor watched him ride away, struggling with the conflicting emotions he had aroused in her. His perpetual assumption that he knew what was best for her aggravated her beyond measure. His sweeping condemnation of the theatre offended her. She still wasn't sure how favourably he thought of her—but it was clear that he *had* thought about her a great deal.

She knew it was utterly foolish, but she liked the

idea that Cole Raven thought about her in her absence. She just wished he was less pig-headed and more open to compromise.

She sighed, remembering his firm grip on her shoulders. She'd welcomed the wordless reassurance of his touch. But it had stirred a yearning in her for things she would never be able to have.

Chapter Four

The Light Division's performance of *The Rivals* was staged in an empty chapel in the village of Gallegos.

Despite his lack of enthusiasm for such entertainment, Raven was in the audience. Wellington, who'd returned from Cadiz, attended with his staff. Cole glanced around to see who else was present. He immediately spotted Honor sitting a short distance away beside Captain Williams and his mistress, Dolores.

Honor looked poised and serene as she waited for the performance to start. As Cole watched, she inclined her head to hear something Dolores said to her. She nodded and smiled in response, then she turned to the officer sitting on her other side who also wished to speak to her. A few moments later she smilingly replied to his comment. She seemed completely at ease.

Cole's jaw clenched as he tried to control the surge of undisciplined emotions he always experienced in Honor's presence. Seeing her, without touching her, was an excruciating pleasure. It required all Cole's self-control not to thrust aside the impertinent young officer who was talking to her, then sweep her off to a more private location. He had plenty of unfinished business with the obstinate Mrs O'Donnell.

Since abducting her from the chapel would only create the kind of scandal he'd been trying so hard to avoid, he turned his frustrated attention to the stage. It didn't take him long to conclude that he'd never witnessed so much unmitigated nonsense in his life.

'I wrote a letter to myself, to inform myself that Beverley was at that time paying his addresses to another woman,' Lieutenant Gregory declared from the stage, in his role as Lydia Languish. 'I signed it "your friend unknown", showed it to Beverley, charged him with his falsehood, put myself in a violent passion, and vowed I'd never see him more.'

Raven frowned. In his opinion Lydia Languish deserved a severe dressing down for her romantic follies. Instead her suitor indulged her preposterous fancies without protest. He wondered if Honor had once shared Lydia's ridiculous fantasy that living in poverty was intrinsically more romantic than living in comfortable circumstances. Was that why she'd married a coachman? If she had made that mistake, she'd certainly discovered her error, Cole thought grimly.

He was distracted from his reflections by an unusually long silence from the stage. He realised one of the actors had forgotten his lines. Despite his jaundiced view of the entertainment, he felt sorry for the man making a fool of himself in front of his brother officers, not to mention the Commander-in-Chief.

Fortunately, before the situation became too embarrassing, Wellington himself stood up and began applauding.

'Bravo, bravo,' he called.

Raven sensed the release of tension in the audience

around him. Wellington's encouragement also helped the actors to relax, and the rest of the performance passed without a hitch.

The play was followed by a selection of comic songs. Cole sat back, stretching out his legs, and glanced around the makeshift theatre. He noticed immediately that, although Captain Williams and Dolores were still present, Honor had left.

Cole's limited interest in the entertainment vanished. With a muttered apology to the men sitting next to him, he stood and made his way out of the chapel.

'You were very good,' Honor assured Lieutenant Gregory.

'Thank you, Mrs O'Donnell. Your opinion is very important to me!' he exclaimed, still euphoric from his success.

Honor had slipped outside to discuss the lieutenant's performance with him. She had guessed how excited he would be after the show, and she thought he would probably welcome the opportunity to talk about it. In truth, she was proud of the way he'd responded to her coaching.

She had been prepared for a detailed postmortem of the play, but the Lieutenant surprised her. After only a few questions about his performance, Gregory changed the subject.

'Mrs O'Donnell…ma'am…that is to say…um…' he stammered, and fell silent, a flush spreading over his face.

Despite the brutalising experience of war, he was very young, Honor thought indulgently, his chin still quite smooth. In that respect, he'd been a good choice for the part of Lydia.

'I believe my prospects are quite good,' he said hurriedly. 'I hope to be promoted as soon as I am eligible, and my father has promised to purchase a Captaincy if necessary—though, as I say, I hope to succeed through my own efforts.'

'I'm sure you will,' said Honor, encouragingly, a little puzzled by the lieutenant's choice of subject.

'You must know how much I admire you!' he announced desperately. 'You have such courage, such grace...so beautiful...' He got stuck in the middle of his sentence.

A muffled roar of laughter from inside the chapel filled the painful silence. The audience was obviously enjoying the comic performance.

Honor gazed at the Lieutenant, hardly able to believe where he appeared to be heading. She hoped he wasn't about to ask her to be his mistress—but surely he couldn't be considering marriage?

'I wondered...that is...would you marry me?' he gulped. 'Mrs O'Donnell? Ma'am?' He stared at her, his anxious eyes pinned on her face. She'd never seen anyone look quite so nervous or hopeful.

'Lieutenant...' She hesitated, momentarily at a loss.

She had never envisaged such a proposal from the young officer, and she wasn't sure how to reply. She didn't want him to feel patronised or humiliated by her rejection. It would be cruel to remind him that he was five years younger than she was, and that she was probably his first serious infatuation.

'I know that you cannot possibly love me,' he said, with desperate persuasiveness. 'But I have seen that your situation is not...not *comfortable*.' He flushed painfully. 'And I would take care of you. You may have thought I was backward in protecting you before. But I assure you—'

'Protecting me?' Honor echoed, bewildered. 'I don't understand…'

'You have been much…much *harried* by some of our officers,' Gregory stumbled over his explanation. 'I am sorry I was not more…that is…I was taken by surprise by…by Major…but I assure you in *future* I would—'

'I understand entirely,' Honor said soothingly, as she realised he was referring to the incident in the barn, when Raven had interrupted their rehearsal. She'd forgotten the junior officer had witnessed any of her conversation with Cole. 'Really, sir, you have no reason to feel…' She hesitated. She didn't want to hurt his feelings. 'Lieutenant, your good opinion means a great deal to me,' she said honestly. 'Far more than I can say. And I am proud that you think I'm worthy to be your wife—but I can't marry you.'

She saw him swallow violently.

'Any man would…' he began.

'No, not any man,' she corrected him gently, 'and you know that as well as I do. But that's not why I can't marry you. I can't marry you because I loved my husband. I'm still grieving for him. You deserve much more than I could offer you.'

'I…if you change your mind…' Gregory's throat worked.

'If I change my mind,' she agreed, knowing that on this matter she never would. 'Lieutenant, I am so sorry to disappoint you.'

He gazed at her for several seconds, seeing the finality of her refusal in her face. Then he spun round on his heel and strode away, stumbling slightly on the rocky ground. She suspected he wasn't seeing too clearly. Later he would probably be grateful he hadn't tied himself, so early in his career, to a woman of dubious reputation and no influence—but not yet.

'What was that all about?' a voice growled in her ear.

Honor gasped with surprise. She was so startled her heart seemed to leap into her mouth. She pressed her hand against the base of her throat, trying to calm her agitated nerves.

'For God's sake!' she exclaimed, when she finally found her voice. 'You nearly frightened me to death!'

'Really? I didn't think you were afraid of anything,' Raven replied, arching a mocking eyebrow at her.

Honor drew in several quick breaths. Although her initial surprise at Raven's sudden appearance was receding, her heart still beat faster than usual. She was far too conscious of the virile energy radiating from his broad-shouldered frame—not to mention the gleam of satisfied masculine amusement in his eyes as he enjoyed her discomfiture.

'I didn't say I was afraid of you,' she retorted crossly. 'Just that you surprised me. What are you doing, skulking around out here?'

'I wasn't skulking.' Cole corrected her mildly. 'I'm hardly to blame if you were so engrossed in your conversation you paid no attention to your surroundings.'

'The play was good, wasn't it?' Honor said, trying to change the subject. She didn't intend to discuss Lieutenant Gregory's proposal with Raven, but nor did she wish to argue with him.

Cole grunted disparagingly. 'Preposterous nonsense! I never heard such foolishness.'

Honor opened her mouth indignantly, then closed it

again as she realised that what Raven had criticised was not the performance but the play itself.

'You would have preferred a morally uplifting tragedy?' she enquired, unable to resist teasing him a little.

'There is nothing uplifting about tragedy,' Raven said trenchantly.

'I never thought so,' Honor agreed.

Cole looked at her sceptically. 'From my limited experience of young females, they enjoy nothing better than imagining themselves at the centre of a melodramatic tragedy,' he observed. 'Certainly the play we've just seen supports my view.'

'Lydia Languish is not the only character in the play who acts foolishly,' Honor pointed out, refusing to let Raven bait her. 'Some of the male characters, Faulkland in particular, are hardly paragons of sturdy common sense.'

'Popinjay!' Cole muttered, in what she took to be agreement with her. 'Do you *enjoy* acting?' he demanded explosively a few seconds later, studying her face intently. Clearly he found the idea inconceivable.

'Yes,' said Honor, bracing herself for his castigation. She refused to lie about something which had once been so important to her.

'Why?' he demanded.

'Why?' she repeated gazing at him in momentary uncertainty. It wasn't what she'd expected him to say. 'For the freedom it gave me,' she said at last.

'Freedom?' He frowned. 'To flout convention and flaunt yourself before an audience of strangers?'

'No. *No*! Not that at all!' Honor pulled her shawl over her head, hurt and angered by Cole's assumption. She started to walk away from him, but he stopped her with a hand on her arm.

She stood stock still, her heart pounding at his un-expected touch.

'What then?' he asked.

'It would make no sense to you,' she said unsteadily, keeping her face averted. She was acutely conscious that he was still holding her arm. His grip was strong yet gentle. He didn't touch her often but, whenever he did so, it was always the same. Somehow his hands conveyed a message to her that he'd never put into words.

'Then you will have to make allowances for my faulty understanding,' he said, his voice deeper than usual.

She hesitated a few seconds, then turned to face him. 'It's an opportunity to escape from one's self,' she said, watching him warily. 'To be someone else, free from the limitations and expectations of everyday life. No doubt you consider that the height of folly,' she added defensively, lifting her chin as she spoke.

He studied her so searchingly she felt as if his eyes were probing the depths of her soul.

'Do you intend to return to acting?' he asked in a low voice.

'I'm not sure that's any of your concern,' Honor said coolly. She stepped back, trying to create a more comfortable distance between them. He was crowding too close to her, physically and emotionally.

'I was…curious, that's all,' he replied. Honor could see the fire smouldering in his eyes.

'No,' she capitulated suddenly, tired of sparring with him. 'I don't want to go back to the stage,' she added, making her preference absolutely clear.

Cole relaxed perceptibly at her words. It seemed

strange to her that he was so concerned about what she did in the future.

'I've been thinking about your situation,' he said. 'Since you are reluctant to return to…your family, I have been considering alternative arrangements.'

'Oh?' Honor stared at him. Her heart rate speeded up again. She felt breathless. She wasn't sure if she was waiting for Cole's explanation with apprehension or anticipation.

'I've recently had a letter from Malcolm Anderson,' said Cole, taking her hand and slipping it through his arm. He began to stroll away from the chapel. A few other members of the audience had come out for air. Several officers were looking at Raven and Honor with open curiosity.

'Malcolm Anderson?' Honor prompted him, wondering whether to withdraw her hand from Cole's arm. She could feel the strength in his lean muscles, even beneath his sleeve. She enjoyed touching him, but she wasn't sure if she was wise to indulge herself in such a way.

'Malcolm is my uncle. He took care of business on my father's behalf for years. Now he does the same for my brother,' Cole explained briefly.

'I see,' said Honor. She didn't, not entirely, but she was eager for Cole to get to the point. What plans did he have for her?

'My family has estates in several counties,' Cole continued, watching the ground ahead, rather than looking at Honor. 'I know you do not care for the position of governess—and in truth I don't think any member of my family has young children—but there are a number of other possibilities.'

'There are?' Honor swallowed back a rush of disappointment. When Cole had first talked about other arrangements she'd foolishly wondered if he'd meant something more personal. But it seemed that his suggestion for her was going to be both practical and businesslike.

'For example, Great-Aunt Dorothea.' Cole stopped walking suddenly and turned to face Honor. 'She's lonely—according to Malcolm. In need of a companion…'

'You want me to be her companion?' Honor gazed up at him in disbelief.

'It occurred to me as a possibility,' Cole replied. He didn't look particularly happy at his own proposal. 'No doubt there are others. Malcolm will know better than I. He will take good care of you. This seems to me a good compromise,' he added, looking directly into Honor's eyes.

'You want to send me to your uncle, so he can take care of me?' she said, her voice echoing unfamiliarly in her own ears. This was the last thing she had ever expected Cole to say.

'Yes,' he replied brusquely.

Honor gazed at him, ignoring the cold wind whipping tendrils of her hair around her face, as she tried to understand what motivated his offer. As always when she was with Raven she could sense fierce, unreadable emotions concealed just beneath the surface of his rigid self-discipline. She was confused by his suggestion, not sure exactly how she felt about it—but she was comforted by his continuing concern for her well-being.

'My safety means that much to you?' she said softly.

She almost thought he flinched at her words, but the

expression was so transitory she decided she must have imagined it.

'I promised your husband,' he said roughly.

'So you keep telling me,' she said, suddenly realising she had only Raven's word for that.

'Don't you believe me? He asked me to take care of you at the same time he told me you'd carried him,' Cole said harshly. 'Did you carry him on your back? I didn't see that. He was lying in the mud when I found you.'

'I carried him,' Honor whispered. Her thoughts turned inwards and she shivered at the bleak memories Cole had called to mind.

'Honor?' Cole gripped her shoulders. 'You are safe now,' he said, his rasping tone at a variance with the reassurance his words—and hands—conveyed. 'I will keep you safe. Think about the future—not the past.'

She focussed on his face, seeing a mixture of concern, frustration and regret in his fierce eyes. And other emotions she couldn't decipher. Then she realised he had just made her a promise. He had told her he would keep her safe.

She drew in an unsteady breath. From the way her ribs creaked with the effort it seemed like a lifetime since she'd last breathed.

Patrick had once made her the same promise. But Patrick O'Donnell and Cole Raven were two very different men. And Patrick had tried to keep her safe by marrying her—Cole wanted to send her away from him to the protection of his uncle.

'There has to be a better way,' she murmured, unaware she'd spoken aloud.

'I beg your pardon?' Cole frowned at her. 'I assure you that Malcolm—'

'No, no.' She reached out instinctively to touch him, her fingertips brushing over the scarlet cloth of his uniform. 'That's not what I meant.'

She laid her hand flat against his chest, feeling the solid strength and heat which emanated from his virile body. He tensed, his muscles flexing at her touch. It excited her to be so close to such fierce masculine energy. It hurt too. Because he was sending her away.

'I will think about what you've said,' she told him.

'Good.' She thought perhaps he wanted to say more, but he left it at that. 'You've been standing in the cold long enough,' he informed her briskly. 'Do you wish to return to the chapel, or shall I escort you back to your billet?'

Honor choked back an unwary laugh. Her hands were rough from the manual work she'd done since she'd arrived in the Peninsula. She was currently performing the combined duties of lady's maid, housekeeper and cook, yet Raven treated her as if she were a fine lady—at least when he wasn't issuing her with peremptory orders. She wondered if he was aware of the contradictions in the way he behaved towards her. Did he understand them? Because she certainly didn't.

In March, Lord Wellington decided to hold a ball in Ciudad Rodrigo. This was partly to honour the Spanish, who'd made him a duke of the city, and partly to provide him with a formal opportunity to invest one of his generals with the Order of the Bath. There was to be a grand dinner for various important dignitaries, both Spanish and English, followed by a ball and supper. Cole received an invitation to the ball. He had no particular desire to attend, but no good reason not to go. He decided to make the best of it.

The ball was held in the largest house in Ciudad Rodrigo. The band of the 52nd Foot was playing when Cole entered the room. There was a noticeable chill in the air, and he glanced around sardonically. The ceilings and walls were hung with splendid damask satin drapes which made the room look rather like a large yellow tent—and disguised the fact that a cannon-ball had punched a hole out of the roof when the city had been under siege. There was also a sentry standing guard next to a carpet which had been placed over a gaping hole in the ballroom floor.

He smiled faintly, wondering what Honor would say if she could see the decorations. But this was not the kind of occasion Honor could attend, even though the gentleman outnumbered the ladies by more than three to one. He was grateful for the uneven numbers, which fortunately reduced his obligation to dance.

'A fine spectacle, isn't it?' said Captain Williams enthusiastically, as he joined Cole. 'A pity there aren't more ladies.'

'A great pity,' Cole agreed drily, watching the Captain inspecting several of the female guests with an eager eye. Dolores had not received an invitation.

'Everything done in the grandest fashion!' Williams exclaimed. 'The supper was half-cooked in Frenada and brought here in waggons, so I'm told. Nothing but the best for his lordship.'

'As you say.' Cole located Lord Wellington in the throng, dressed up in his best uniform, glittering with all his orders, dancing with the wife of one of his Colonels. Wellington enjoyed a party.

Raven circulated, ate sparingly in the damask-hung supper rooms, and wondered how soon he could leave. He'd never enjoyed this kind of affair. He was a poor hand at small talk and he was an indifferent dancer. He tried not to think about how Honor would have shone at such an occasion. He was sure she was a graceful dancer, and he knew she could be charming company when she wasn't being unreasonably obstinate.

He sipped his champagne, thinking of his last meeting with her. She hadn't yet agreed to go to Malcolm Anderson, but nor had she dismissed the suggestion out of hand. Cole was sure it was only a matter of time before she fell in with his plans. He was relieved, because soon the army would be leaving its winter quarters, but he also dreaded her departure—because once she had gone he knew he could never risk seeing her again. When he himself returned to England, it would be to marry Bridget Morton.

He'd known Bridget for most of his life. Their families' estates adjoined each other in Oxfordshire. Their fathers had been close friends and the marriage had been planned while they were both still in the schoolroom. George Morton had considerable property, but no male heir. As the younger son of an influential family, Cole Raven had a name and useful connections, but a limited inheritance.

George Morton and Sir Edward Raven had planned the marriage between them. As part of the marriage arrangements, Cole would receive the Oxfordshire estate, which would in due course be united with the Morton property. Thus Sir Edward provided for his younger son, and George Morton for his only offspring.

It was to be a union of families and land. Cole had not enjoyed being the make-weight in such an arrangement, and he had resisted a formal betrothal for several years. But at the age of twenty-five he had realised two things: the first was that he had never yet met a lady who fired his blood enough to overthrow the long-standing arrangements; the second was that, since Bridget's family already thought of her as being promised to him, her chance of finding happiness elsewhere was non-existent. While he kicked his heels, she simply grew older and more anxious about her future. So he'd made a formal offer for her.

Two weeks later her mother had died unexpectedly. It was clearly necessary for them to delay the marriage while her family was in strict mourning, and then he'd been posted to Portugal. Four years later, he was twenty-nine and Bridget was twenty-eight, and her prospects were even less rosy if he jilted her. Not to mention the breach it would cause between their families, and the possible lawsuit against him if he reneged on his obligations.

He wondered what Bridget expected from him? Just his name and his protection—or did she want more than that? His wider experience of women was limited. His own mother had died when he was in shortcoats, and he had been in the army since he was eighteen. With the exception of his feelings for Honor, his liaisons had been brief, and focussed on the mutual exchange of physical pleasure. He was sure that Honor would not be prepared to accept a marriage in name only so, if he took her as his yardstick, he could only assume Bridget wouldn't either.

Cole's mood darkened as he contemplated marriage to a woman whose face he could barely remember. He was tired of the merriment around him. He shouldered his way out of the ballroom, into the frosty night air. There was a silver moon in the sky. He could see his breath in front of his face. The music and laughter from the ballroom sounded muffled and distant. He stepped into the street, intending to find Corvinus and go back to his quarters.

'Major?' A soft-voiced shape detached itself from the shadows.

'Honor?' He was dumbfounded to see her there. 'What—?'

'I came to see the spectacle,' she said softly. 'I peeked earlier, when they were setting everything up. So beautiful—and so theatrical, don't you think. All that yellow satin to hide the holes—just like the back-drop to a play. Anything could happen in the middle of a magical illusion like that. You should be inside, dancing.'

'I don't dance,' he said briefly, gazing down at her.

She'd pulled her shawl up over her head to protect herself from the cold. Her eyes glowed in the moon-light. She looked beautiful and ethereal—Cinderella, waiting for her fairy godmother to send her to the ball. Cole wished he could take her back into the ballroom, let her experience the magic which had made so little impact upon him.

'But you could still enjoy the spectacle—watching everyone else dance,' she said, smiling up at him. 'Didn't you?'

'No.' He stared at Honor. She was so delicately beautiful he felt like an inarticulate clod in her pres-ence. 'I fear I'm too dull.'

'Major!' Her hazel eyes twinkled teasingly at him in the moonlight. 'No one could call you dull.'

'Indeed?' He wanted to ask her what she *would* call him, but he didn't. 'I'm sorry you could not attend the ball,' he said. 'You would have outshone all the ladies present.'

Her lips parted in surprise at his compliment, and he saw her draw in a quick breath. Her mouth looked soft and inviting. He wanted to kiss her so badly it hurt. His own breathing quickened as he fought to control his rising desire. Her eyes widened as she looked at him. As he watched, he saw the focus of her gaze shift to his mouth and she moved almost imperceptibly towards him. He put his hand on her arm, drawing her a little closer, and bent his head...

A couple of loud-voiced officers suddenly emerged from the house behind Cole, obviously in a state of good-humoured inebriation. Their unexpected appearance jolted Cole back to reality.

'I'll take you home,' he said gruffly. He caught Honor's hand in his and drew it through his arm. 'You're miles from your billet,' he scolded her, as they began to walk along the street. 'How did you intend to get back?'

'I thought maybe I'd find someone going my way,' she replied breathlessly. 'Possibly Captain Williams. If not, I could always walk.'

'Dammit, woman!' Cole exploded, finding an outlet for his frustrated desire. 'Haven't you got any common sense?'

'Well...' Honor hugged his arm as they walked. 'I found you,' she pointed out teasingly. 'And you're taking me back to my billet.'

Cole was about to give her his unabridged opinion of that piece of folly when it occurred to him that perhaps she'd been waiting for him all along. She must have known he'd never leave her unprotected in Ciudad Rodrigo. He almost asked her if he'd guessed

correctly, but then he thought better of it. His dealings
with Honor were already too complicated for comfort.

Honor had assumed Cole would either put her on a
spare horse, or take her up behind him. He did neither.
He held her in front of him on Corvinus, resting sideways in the cradle of his arms.

Honor thought it was the most romantic thing that
had ever happened to her. She didn't dare comment
on the arrangement in case he changed his mind and
made her sit behind him. She was completely depend-
ent upon him for her security in the precarious position. She didn't feel in the slightest bit nervous about
her safety, but she did feel a continuous flutter of excitement as she savoured every aspect of her situation.
She was in Cole's arms, protected from the cold air
by the heat of his powerful body. She rested her head
against his broad shoulder and allowed herself to relax.
Whatever he had—or hadn't—said to her, the way he
held her communicated its own message.

Corvinus walked unhurriedly out of Ciudad
Rodrigo, over the Roman bridge that crossed the
Agueda river, and through the chilly countryside.
Moonlight glistened here and there on the white frost
which hardened the road and decorated the dark trees.

'See?' she murmured, rousing herself a little. 'The
moonlight makes the whole world look magic.'

'I'm afraid I'm too prosaic to believe in magic,'
Cole replied gruffly.

'Oh, no.' She tipped her head back a little to look
up at his strongly delineated features. 'Believing in
magic is what makes life bearable.'

'Is that how you've survived this country?' he asked
curiously.

'Perhaps.' She laid her hand against his shoulder and pillowed her cheek against it. 'It's a beautiful country. I wouldn't have missed these last four years, not for anything.'

'Except for the way they ended,' Cole said roughly. She felt a sudden increase of tension in his arms. 'I did not mean to remind you of painful memories,' he added, in a low, regretful voice.

She stroked his shoulder in a soothing gesture, accepting his apology. After a few moments she sighed.

'Poor Patrick,' she murmured. 'He didn't like being a soldier, but he made the best of it, poor sweetheart.'

'How did he come to be a soldier?' Cole asked stiffly.

'A recruiting party took advantage of him when he was drunk,' she replied bleakly.

'I didn't know he drank.' Cole was surprised. In an army where drunkenness was endemic among the soldiers and most of their wives, the O'Donnells had been notable for their restraint and sobriety.

'He didn't usually, that's why he was such an easy mark for them,' Honor replied.

Cole caught an odd undercurrent in her voice, almost as if she blamed herself. He didn't know how to ask her that question directly, or even if he should ask it at all.

'But you stood by him,' he said carefully. 'You came to Portugal with him.' He hesitated. 'You loved him very much,' he added steadily.

Honor was silent for several minutes as Corvinus paced proudly along the road.

'I did love him,' she said, so quietly that Cole had to bend his head to hear her, 'but he deserved so much more than I ever gave him.'

'How can you say that?' Cole demanded, shocked. The stallion halted in response to his rider's unthinking command. 'No one could ask more from their wife than you gave Patrick. You cannot blame yourself because you couldn't save him from—'

Honor reached up and laid her fingers gently over his lips.

'Shush,' she murmured. The moonlight silvered her hair and the curve of her cheek. 'That's not what I meant.' She smiled slightly. 'Are you indignant on my behalf or Patrick's?' she teased him gently.

'I…' He tried to reply, but he couldn't think. Her fingers were delicately exploring the contours of his face.

'If you had a choice,' she said softly, 'would you rather have a wife who could nag a harpy into submission—or one who trembled in your arms?'

Cole was stunned by her words. Did she mean…? What did she mean? The intimacy of the moment was both intoxicating and terrifying.

'Didn't you?' he said hoarsely. 'Didn't you tremble in his arms?'

He saw the moment when a mixture of shyness and shame suddenly overcame her. She flushed and drew her shawl up, turning her head to hide her face in his shoulder. Her embarrassment was incredibly endearing, because in her confusion she'd turned towards him, not away from him. Cole felt as exulted as if he'd just seized a French eagle all by himself. She hadn't trembled in her husband's arms!

He urged Corvinus forward again, giving Honor a chance to recover her composure to the steady rhythm of the stallion's hooves.

'Why did you marry him?' he asked at last, when

the excitement blazing through his body made it impossible to stay silent any longer. He did his best to keep his voice as calm as possible.

'I did love him,' she repeated, as if it was important to emphasise that fact. 'I was very fond of him. I'd known him since I was a child, long before I was successful. I knew he was devoted to me—God! I shouldn't have been so weak-minded!' she reproached herself abruptly, stirring restlessly in Cole's arms.

'Shush.' It was his turn to sooth her. He was overwhelmed with pleasure that, after so many months of resisting his help, she was finally confiding in him. 'What happened?' he asked gently.

'The Duke of Selhurst,' she said tensely. 'I got so tired of it all. Every time I turned round he was there—or one of his minions—flattering me, pawing at me. He had…plans…for me I didn't care for.'

Raven held her fiercely, anger raging through him on her behalf.

'Damn him!' he swore.

Honor stroked Cole's cheek, immensely gratified by his protective fury. 'He came to a mortifying end,' she consoled him.

'He did? How?' Cole demanded.

'I…well, um, it wasn't very ladylike,' she said uncomfortably.

'What did you do?'

'I…um, I kneed him in the groin,' she said blushing hotly. 'He sort of…collapsed. I thought I'd killed him. I was only twenty-one.'

'Honor!' Cole burst into delighted laughter, holding her close.

Honor was amazed. She'd never realised he was capable of such uninhibited light-heartedness. She laughed too, intoxicated by his good humour.

'What a virago!' he exclaimed, planting a celebratory kiss on her forehead.

She gasped, her laughter dying, and gazed up at him searchingly. She felt his breath catch. His face hovered above hers for a heart-stopping moment, then he brushed his lips against hers.

'Oh-ohhh.' Honor's sigh was long and soft.

Again, he touched his mouth gently, almost hesitantly, to her parted lips. She reached up to rest her hand on his high collar. His lips were firm, warm, and tantalisingly tender against hers. He tasted her delicately, exploring the sensuous curves of her mouth. She was wrapped in a golden cocoon—protected and cherished. It felt so good when he kissed her. She wanted more. She pressed up towards him almost impatiently. He groaned softly, and deepened the kiss. His tongue teased her lips, kindling fires deep within her, then thrust boldly into the warmth of her mouth.

She was briefly stunned, then an answering passion surged through her, firing her blood. He wanted to be inside her. She could feel it in the fierce gentleness of his embrace. His lips and tongue plundered her soul, then he withdrew slightly, tempting her to her own exploration. She followed his example, her own tongue flickering tentatively, almost shyly against his firm lips, learning the new game he was teaching her with all the passionate eagerness of which she was capable.

He shuddered in response and groaned. He kissed her cheek then pushed back her shawl so he could explore her warm tender neck. His lips were hot, clever and moist against her sensitive skin. He sucked, drawing heat to the surface, claiming her. She melted against him, fluid in her responsiveness.

'I have you now!' he whispered, hoarsely triumphant in her ear. 'Are you trembling, Honor?' he demanded fiercely.

'Y-y-yesss.' She exhaled a long-drawn out hiss of breath. She rubbed her face against his shoulder like a cat, only wanting to be nearer still to him.

'Honor, Honor.' He rubbed his cheek against hers. She felt the rasp of his whiskers against her soft skin. She wanted more, but he held her quietly until the urgent tempo of their passion gradually slowed. At last he lifted his head and signalled Corvinus to move forward.

Honor was amazed. She'd been married for several years. She'd lived in conditions which had made it impossible for her to remain either naïve or innocent, yet she'd never fully anticipated how devastating Cole's lovemaking would be. He could turn her inside out with a single kiss. She was shaken to the core.

So was Cole. He'd promised himself to keep Honor at a distance, yet here she was in his arms. His heart was still thudding with unresolved desire, his body uncomfortably aroused. Honor's passion had matched his—and she'd trembled in his arms! By her own admission, she'd trembled in his arms! He wanted to give a primitive shout of conquest. He was so fired up with pride and excitement he could have defeated the French single-handedly. A pity Wellington was too busy partying to make use of his new secret weapon.

Raven tried to cool his passion, knowing he was heading them both for disaster. Wanting Honor was completely different from being able to have her. Nothing had changed—he was engaged to a virtuous woman he'd known since childhood. He was unable to make Honor any kind of offer that would be worthy of her.

'We left the Duke of Selhurst writhing on the floor,' he said, when he finally trusted himself to speak.

'What?' Honor had been floating in a magical world all her own. The Duke was the last thing on her mind.

'What happened next?' Cole prompted her.

'Oh.' Honor would have preferred another kiss, but she was too shy to say so. She roused herself to answer his question instead.

'I was frightened,' she admitted. 'Decommissioning a peer of the realm is…unnerving. Righteous indignation can only take you so far—I was afraid of his revenge. And I was tired. I enjoyed playing different roles on the stage, but I'd never anticipated how complicated my life would become away from the theatre. I'd known Patrick since I was fifteen. He was eleven years older than me. I think he loved me for a long time, but he was so patient about it. Then I burnt my bridges with the Duke—and Patrick was there when I needed him. He was safe and kind…but I should never have married him. I took advantage of him.'

'Did he ask you to marry him?' Cole asked carefully.

'Of course!' Honor exclaimed. 'I know I'm as brazen as an eight-inch howitzer, but I'd *never* have pushed myself on Patrick if he hadn't wanted me!'

'I know.' Cole brushed his lips tenderly against her forehead. He could feel her distress. He had never before realised just how sensitive she could be beneath her battle-hardened exterior. 'I was just wondering…' He hesitated, not sure if he should voice his thoughts.

'What?' she prompted him.

'You were frightened and tired,' he said slowly. 'And Patrick was eleven years older than you. He seemed safe in a hazardous world. Perhaps he took advantage of your weakness to—'

Honor moved restlessly and he broke off, half-expecting her to launch into a passionate defence of her late husband, but she didn't immediately say anything.

'I don't know,' she said eventually. 'I had a stronger personality than Patrick. Overbearing is the kindest thing that's been said about me. Termagant, vixen…virago,' she reminded Cole, smiling a little. 'I was wrong when I married him. I was too…forceful—and he was too proud not to mind. I cared about him a lot. I tried very hard to be a good wife and not shame him in front of the other men.'

She turned her face into Cole's shoulder, and he realised she was close to tears.

'He knew that,' said Raven gently, unbearably moved by her admission. 'He was proud of you, Honor. When I found you that day, when I lifted him up onto Corvinus and he told me you'd carried him, he was proud of you. And all the years before that, anyone could see how proud he was to call you wife, how…honoured…he was.'

She started to cry in earnest.

'Ah, sweetheart, you've been so battle-tossed,' Cole murmured, pressing his cheek against her hair.

After a few minutes she pulled herself together, drying her face on her shawl. It was too cold to cry.

'I'm sorry,' she said, somewhat defensively. 'I'm not usually this, this…droopy and limp-minded.'

Cole chuckled deep in his chest.

'Ohh!' She thumped him in exasperation, though it was really only the lightest of taps.

'Your boxing skills aren't on a par with your marksmanship,' Cole teased her.

'I thought I should learn to fire the musket,' Honor informed him with dignity. 'Patrick was dubious…he said I reminded him of my mother,' she added uncertainly. 'When I made him get on my back.'

'Don't you want to sound like your mother?' Cole asked. He was extremely curious about Honor's family.

'No. I don't know,' Honor stirred restlessly in his arms. 'It was because of Mother that Patrick got drunk and the army got him!' she burst out in anguish. 'Or because of me. I don't know. Mother doesn't approve of marriage.'

'She doesn't!' Cole exclaimed. 'Good God! Does she think it's a sinful state?' He could only imagine that Honor's mother was so strictly religious she condemned all human unions.

'Oh, no, she just doesn't believe any woman with a modicum of wit ought to waste her time and energy on propping up a man,' Honor explained matter-of-factly.

'Good God!' Cole said blankly. 'Is she a disciple of that Wollstonecraft woman?'

Honor giggled unexpectedly. 'Mother wouldn't dream of being anyone's disciple,' she asserted. 'She's very independent and strong-minded.'

'She disapproved of your marriage to Patrick,' said Cole, assuming Honor's mother's disapproval of marriage was actually rather more specific than Honor had implied.

'Oh, yes,' Honor agreed immediately. 'But she

wouldn't have approved, whoever it was. I told you, she—'

'Doesn't approve of marriage,' finished Cole. 'Your father...' he began, pausing with unusual delicacy.

'I don't know who he is,' said Honor quietly. 'Mother...' She hesitated, took a deep breath, then plunged on. 'Mother has never *been* married,' she said steadily.

In the silence that followed, Raven realised she was waiting tensely for him to pass judgement on both her mother and her.

'Tell me,' he said gently, and felt her relax again at his lack of condemnation.

'I don't know who my father is,' she said in a low voice. 'I know...she was a maid in a nobleman's house. The son taught her to read. He must have had a genuine affection for her, don't you think?' she asked, lifting her head to look at Cole with almost painful shyness. 'The Duke never offered to teach me anything—useful, that is.'

'I'm sure he had affection,' said Cole, guessing that was the answer his tough, self-sufficient Honor needed to hear.

'Yes.' Honor rested her head against his shoulder again, drawing little circles around one of his silver buttons with her finger. 'I used to like to think of them sitting together over the books and ink well—learning a little, flirting a little. Then of course he had to send her away. He gave her as much money as he could. He pawned his pocket watch and the snuff box and signet ring he was bequeathed by his godfather. She never saw him after that. She had to make a life for us all by herself. Mama is *very* brave and strong-minded. *She* never gave in, in a moment of weakness, and married a man she didn't truly love.'

What a legacy, Cole thought, imagining the child Honor must have been, weaving consoling stories about her father's affection for her mother, to assuage her hurt at his abandonment.

'Did she love your father?' he asked, wondering if perhaps the woman's hostility towards marriage was caused by her bitterness towards one particular man.

'Oh, yes,' Honor replied without hesitation. 'She says he is a man of honour and integrity'—Cole could tell she was quoting something she'd heard many times—'who never shirked his obligations to his name or his family. That's why she called me Honor. They were very young at the time,' she added. 'Mama was sixteen, and my father was nineteen.'

'Sixteen!' The woman had been left to fend for herself and her child with only the value of a few trinkets to save them from oblivion when she was sixteen.

'I was seventeen when I went on the stage,' said Honor defensively.

'Did she force you into it?' Cole demanded.

'Of course not. She didn't approve at all,' Honor exclaimed.

'Her favourite tune,' Cole muttered.

Honor laughed, warmed by his unmistakable partisanship. 'You don't approve of me either,' she reminded him. 'And you're so sure you know what's best for me. Sometimes you remind me of her.'

'God forbid!' Cole sounded appalled.

'She sent me to a seminary in Bath, when I was sixteen,' Honor said, smiling. 'For young ladies of quality. Miss Goodwin said I was a corrupting influence. I was no such thing!' Indignation burned in

Honor's voice. 'Just because I took a small part in a play in the public theatre—for a wager. She'd praised me for my performance in private, amateur theatricals.'

'So you left in disgrace?' Cole said in a carefully neutral voice. Despite himself, Honor's indignation was amusing.

'Certainly not,' she said imperiously. 'I went to London and became the toast of the Town. Actually, it took me a couple of years to become an overnight sensation, but it was very gratifying.'

'I'm sure it was,' Cole murmured. 'What did your mother have to say about it?'

'Oh, she said when I left the seminary, if I was determined to go to the Devil, I'd better get on with it my own way,' Honor said airily.

'Very maternal,' Cole commented drily. 'How did you manage?'

'Susannah, Mama's cousin looked out for me—brought me up really. Even she doesn't know who my father is,' said Honor, revealing what was clearly a continuing gap in her life.

He'd said she was battle-tossed, Raven thought, and he hadn't known the half of it.

'Sometimes,' she said, patting his chest uncertainly, 'sometimes, I am too much like my mother. I am too obstinate, and I am too sharp-tongued,' she said with difficulty. 'I say things that hurt, but I don't mean them to.'

'Sweetheart.' He couldn't stop himself, he had to kiss her again.

She slipped her arm around his neck, surrendering to him completely. He dimly realised that, in telling him the truth about her parentage and her marriage, she had given herself to him more completely than if she'd simply given him her body. Her trust over-whelmed him, because life had not taught her to trust easily. He wondered if she would regret her honesty—and sincerely hoped not.

'You don't have to worry about me,' she whispered. 'I know Patrick asked you to take care of me. But I also know better than anyone that a woman doesn't need a wedding ring to survive. I will manage.'

'Honor.' He buried his face in the hollow of her shoulder. 'It will be past dawn before I get you back at this rate,' he said, when he lifted his head.

'I've…enjoyed my ride,' she said, feeling shy again, worrying that she'd said too much.

'So have I.' His grip tightened reassuringly.

Corvinus tossed his head and snorted.

'He agrees with me,' said Raven.

'No, he's just frustrated with our slow rate of prog-ress,' Honor teased.

'I can't think why!' Cole retorted. 'It seems to me we've progressed quite fast.'

Chapter Five

Honor went about her chores in a daze. In the mundane light of day, it was hard to believe her ride in the moonlight with Cole had been any more than a dream. But if she closed her eyes, she could feel his arms around her, and his lips on hers.

It was a wonderful memory, filling her with tingling warmth and the kind of happiness she'd rarely experienced. Now and then the fugitive thought would creep into her mind that she loved Cole. But every time she became aware of the thought she chased it away again.

She didn't know what Cole had meant by his actions—and that made her nervous. The last time he had spoken of her future, he'd been determined to send her to England, to the safe care of his uncle. He'd even suggested she might become companion to one of his elderly aunts. Honor had a sinking feeling that two moonlight kisses wouldn't have changed his mind about that.

Perhaps he'd simply been carried away by the magic of their surroundings. She had good reason to know that men often succumbed to lust without feeling love or even affection for the object of their desire. Perhaps next time they met he would be autocratic and distant, and simply order her back to England.

She wished she'd been more guarded in the things she'd told him. She flushed with embarrassment as she remembered telling him she hadn't trembled in Patrick's arms. She should never have told him that! How would she ever face him again?

She wielded the long-handled brush vigorously, wishing she could sweep out her worries as thoroughly as she swept the cottage floor.

Raven's temper was atrocious.

'If you've got no orders for me, I'm going to watch the wrestling match in the village, sir,' said Joe Newton, eyeing his master warily.

'Very well,' Cole replied curtly.

Joe looked as if he might have said something but, whatever it was, he thought better of it.

When he was alone, Cole slammed the edge of his fist down onto the table and bounced a newspaper, an ink pot, several loose sheets of paper and a pen onto the floor.

He cursed and bent to clear up the mess. A sealed letter fell out of the newspaper and he stared at it blankly for a few seconds.

'Mrs Annie Howarth, Belle Savage, Ludgate Hill.'

He knew of no one by that name and wondered briefly how the letter came to be on his table. Then he remembered Joe corresponded regularly with home and propped the letter up for his servant to find.

He ran his fingers through his hair and cursed again. What the hell had he been thinking of when he'd kissed Honor?

She believed in dreams and magic. Now she was
sure to think those kisses meant more than they ever
could. He wondered if she was even aware of his betrothal.

He stood up, pushing his chair back so violently it
crashed to the floor. He'd allowed a situation to de-
velop which was dishonest and profoundly unfair to
Honor. All because he hadn't been able to control his
desire for her. He had to explain things to her as soon
as possible. And he had to make her to go back to
England.

Honor finished cleaning the cottage. She left the
door open to let the light in and started the stew for
supper. Then she wrapped her black shawl around her
shoulders and sat down to write a letter to Lady
Durrington. It was hard not to think of Cole, but she
managed to describe the splendid, yellow-satin ballroom in Ciudad Rodrigo without mentioning his name.
She only looked up when her light was obstructed.

Raven's tall, broad-shouldered frame blocked the
doorway. He had to duck his head to come into the
cottage. He was holding his shako in one hand. His
back was to the daylight, but Honor thought his expression was unusually grim.

Her heart rate accelerated. She felt breathless with
anxiety. She'd imagined their next meeting over and
over, but she hadn't been able to decide what she
should say or do. She stood up, and realised her knees
were weak.

'Major Raven,' she croaked.

'Hon—' He cleared his throat. 'Mrs O'Donnell,' he
greeted her.

He stood frozen to the spot, staring at her. Honor

was mesmerised by his vivid blue eyes. She wasn't sure which one of them was more awkward but, as his hostess, she decided it was up to her to put him at his ease.

'I'm…glad to see you,' she said shakily. 'How are you?'

'Very well,' Cole growled.

'And Corvinus?' Honor enquired at random, daunted by his ferocious expression.

'You can see for yourself if you wish,' said Cole brusquely. 'I rode him over.'

'Oh. Er…would you like some tea?' Honor enquired desperately.

'I won't trouble you.' Raven shook his head. 'I'll be on my way shortly.'

'You will?'

'I came to discuss the arrangements for your journey,' he said flatly.

'Oh.' Honor felt a hot wave of shame and disappointment roll over her. She tried not to let her emotions show in her expression but, from the look in Cole's eyes, her efforts weren't very successful.

'Dammit!' He came closer to her, dropping his shako on to the table. Then he hesitated, looking around the cottage. 'Where are Williams and…?'

'They went to Frenada,' she said, trying to control her bitter sense of mortification. 'To shop and hear the gossip.'

'Good.' Cole pressed his lips together, his eyes hard with regret as he looked at Honor. 'I'm sorry,' he said curtly. 'I had no business to behave as I did last night. It was inexcusable.'

'Why?' Honor demanded, unbearably hurt by his rejection. 'Surely I'm *just* the kind of woman to dally with in the moonlight. You're not the only officer to think so—'

'What?' Cole seized her upper arms in a fierce grip, staring down at her with blazing eyes. 'Who's mistreated you? Williams? I warned him—'

'Warned him?' Honor gasped, shaken by Cole's feral expression. 'What…? No.' She suddenly decided it was more important to calm Cole than to question him. 'Captain Williams has always treated me well,' she said breathlessly. 'He is a gentleman. Besotted with Dolores… Please…' she begged, urgently. 'Please.' Cole's hands were still locked on her upper arms, but she was able to lift her forearms to touch his chest with her fingertips.

'No one has mistreated me,' she assured him unsteadily.

His grip relaxed a little, but he didn't release her. 'If not Williams, then who?' he demanded tautly.

'It doesn't matter,' she said, trying to smile. It was silly to feel reassured by Cole's fierce partisanship when he was so intent on sending her away—but she couldn't help it. 'It's not important. They simply asked—and I said no. That's all. It's not important. Please.'

Cole's gaze locked with Honor's for several long moments before the rigidity in his powerful body eased a few degrees. He was still far from relaxed, but she thought he was no longer on the verge of hunting down her unwanted admirers.

She was so shaken by the incident that tears welled up in her eyes. One minute Cole was starkly telling her she must leave—the next he seemed to be on the brink of starting a war on her behalf.

'Don't!' he exclaimed, sounding as tormented as she

felt, when he noticed her shimmering eyes. He started to pull her towards him, then set her abruptly aside and turned away from her.

Honor wrapped her arms around her body, in desperate need of the comfort he refused to offer her.

'Do you know that I'm betrothed,' he asked, without looking at her.

'I…betrothed?' Her voice wavered. 'I don't remember.'

'I am. I have been these past four years,' he said harshly.

Honor's throat was so tight with tears she couldn't swallow. She stared at his rigid shoulders, unable to say anything. The painful silence extended…

Raven turned to face her. His jaw was clenched with tension, but the wild tempest of emotions he was fighting so hard to control seemed to fill the cottage.

'Do you…?' Honor whispered, but she couldn't finish the question she wanted so much to ask. 'You would never betray your fiancée,' she said instead.

'I would never betray you,' he replied, his eyes fixed on her face. 'And I have nothing to offer you that is worthy of you.'

'Worthy of me?' she exclaimed bitterly. 'Have you forgotten what I told you last night?'

Raven gestured impatiently. 'Your father's sins are not yours,' he said fiercely. 'You have to go back to England. There's nothing for you here.'

Honor recoiled as if he'd slapped her. Then her shock turned to anger.

'How dare you dictate to me!' she flung at him furiously. 'I didn't stay for you. And you have no control over my actions. I'll leave when I'm ready. Not when you order me to go!'

She picked up his shako and hurled it at him. 'Get out! Get out!' Her voice shook with rage and unshed tears.

He stepped back a pace, but didn't leave.

Frustrated beyond measure, she spun round and grabbed the broom from its place in the corner. She swung the bristles downwards, ridiculously intent on sweeping him out of the cottage.

Raven twisted the broom out of her grasp, wrenching her wrist in the process, and threw it aside with a clatter.

Honor winced. She instinctively wrapped her fingers around her aching wrist, holding both hands against her chest as she bent her head over them. She bit back her tears, but she couldn't stop herself from trembling.

She heard Cole exhale a long, unsteady breath, then she felt his hands on her shoulders, gentle this time.

'Dear God!' he murmured. He sounded as anguished and shaken as she felt. 'I'm sorry.' He pulled her into his arms, holding her against his chest. 'I'm sorry. I'm sorry.'

She held herself stiffly, unwilling to accept his comfort. She felt his lips brush against her hair, his hands gently stroking her back. She wanted to let him comfort her so badly it took all her will power not to lean against him.

But she couldn't lean on Cole. He'd made that agonisingly clear. He wanted to send her away from him. He'd been trying to do so for months.

She forced herself to step away from him. It was one of the hardest things she'd ever done, not made any easier because his arms tightened around her before he reluctantly released her.

'Captain Williams and Dolores will be back soon,'

she said, not looking at him. 'I have work to do. Goodbye, Major.'

'We'll talk again when we are both…calmer,' Cole replied, after a few moments. 'I will do everything in my power to make sure your life is comfortable. That you are not…harassed…in any way.'

'By sending me to your uncle,' Honor whispered.

Cole didn't reply. He bent to pick up his shako, then walked out of the cottage.

Honor covered her face with her hands, struggling to hold back her tears. The Captain and Dolores really would be back soon and she couldn't bear the thought of them discovering her in such distress.

She brushed her hands across her eyes and set about making a cup of tea for herself before her employers returned. It was just another role to play. She would think of her life in those terms, and never admit how much she hurt inside.

'You should come to the dance tonight,' said Dolores as Honor finished dressing the Spanish girl's hair.

'The dance?' Honor was startled out of her introspection by the unexpected suggestion.

'In the officers' mess.' Dolores nodded firmly. 'All the girls from the village will be there. You should come too.'

'Oh, no,' Honor protested instinctively.

The officers had established a regimental mess in a barn, and once a week they held a ball to which they invited the ladies of the village, but Honor had never attended such an affair. As Patrick's wife it had been impossible for her to socialise with officers and, as his widow, she had to be even more careful in her conduct.

'I think you should come,' said Dolores, twisting in her chair to take Honor's hand. 'You are sad. There will be music, and you can dance.'

'I really don't think I should,' Honor replied, smiling. 'But thank you for asking me. You're very kind.'

'I will be your chaperon,' Dolores informed her. 'And now I will do your hair. You will be the belle of the ball. You are so fair and dainty.'

'Thank you.' Honor hesitated, torn by indecision.

All her common sense told her it would be stupid to attend the dance—but she was tired of being sensible. She was tired of being practical, respectable and dowdy.

'I will come!' she exclaimed. 'I will.'

Dolores laughed happily and hugged her. The relationship between the two women had never truly been one of mistress and maid. Dolores had been wary of Honor at first, afraid she might be a rival for Captain Williams's affections. But as soon as she'd realised that the Captain and Honor had no interest in each other, the Spanish girl had treated Honor with genuine kindness.

'I must have taken leave of my senses—but I will dance tonight!' Honor declared recklessly. She picked up her skirt and took several light dance steps across the room.

Dolores applauded and Honor responded with a graceful curtsy, just as Captain Williams arrived.

'Honor is coming to the dance with us tonight,' Dolores informed him buoyantly.

'Is she, indeed?' Williams glanced at Honor assessingly. 'I look forward to an entertaining evening,' he said, a glint of anticipation in his eyes.

* * *

It was nearly eight o'clock when they entered the officers' mess. Honor gazed around the converted barn, fascinated by everything she saw. She'd never attended such an event before, and she knew she never would again. She was hiding a grievous pain deep in her heart, but tonight she sought temporary release in the gaiety of the party.

She intended to leave for England in the next couple of days, but she wouldn't ask Cole Raven for help. She'd once told Cole that she had been paying her own way since she was seventeen, and that was quite true. Just as importantly, she'd always been frugal with her earnings. Patrick had been too proud to let her spend her money on him, so she'd left it untouched during their marriage. During the last few years her financial affairs had been managed by her lawyer in London. A few days after Patrick's death she had written to the lawyer, asking him to send a portion of her money out to her in Portugal. She'd received his reply towards the end of January. Once she'd visited the bank in Lisbon she would have the cash she needed to pay for her passage home.

Her presence at the party caused quite a stir. It wasn't long before she was surrounded by several officers. Cole wasn't among them. Her eyes automatically sought him out, even though she told herself she was glad he wasn't there.

There was a small orchestra composed of a clarinet, a fiddle and a drum. An officer asked Honor to dance and she let him lead her out onto the hard clay floor. That dance was followed by another. She sat out the next dance on a bench beside the wall as yet another officer brought her some wine. It was a long time since she'd received so much flattering attention. She laughed, waved her fan in front of her overheated face, and tried not to think of anything but the pleasure of the moment.

Cole entered the mess just in time to see Honor spinning around on the dance floor, her cheeks glowing with colour as she laughed up at something her partner said to her. The hem of her skirt was coated with dust thrown up from the floor, but she danced with the grace of a princess at a grand ball.

Cole stared at her, stunned speechless to discover her in such a setting. For a few seconds he could not drag his eyes away from her. Her blonde hair had been dressed in fashionable curls and framed her face like a golden halo in the candlelight. Her hazel eyes glowed with life. Her lips were pink, soft and slightly parted as she smiled at the man dancing with her.

Cole forced himself to look away from her and realised almost every man in the room was watching her either openly or surreptitiously. Several of them wore expressions of undisguised desire. There were many pretty girls in the room—Dolores was beautiful—but they were all dark-haired. Honor was the only one who shone like an ethereal, golden angel.

Cole's shock gave way to burning anger. He was furious that Honor could display herself so wantonly in public. He clenched his fists, overwhelmed by a raging desire to knock her smirking dance partner through the wall, then turn his fury on the men watching her with such open lust. Only years of strict self-discipline prevented him from acting on his first impulse.

As the immediate shock-wave of his anger receded, Cole realised it was not his fellow officers who were to blame for the situation—it was Honor. She was the one who was shamelessly provoking the men around her to act like rutting stags.

He strode towards her. He was dimly aware that the music had come to a discordant end. He was acutely aware of the men around him and the intentions their body movements signalled to him. He was less sharply aware of Honor's shocked expression as he closed the distance between them. He would deal with her later.

He seized her wrist and pulled her towards the door, not bothering to say anything. As far as he was concerned, the situation didn't call for words.

Honor followed him willy-nilly for a few steps. Then she dug her heels in, resisting his inexorable progress. He spun round, released her wrist and swept her up in his arms in one swift movement. Honor gave a soft cry of alarm. He could hear her quickened breathing, but she didn't struggle.

He was nearly at the door when his way was blocked by Lieutenant Gregory. The young man was pale but resolute as he faced his senior officer.

'Stand aside!' Cole growled furiously.

'No, sir!' Lieutenant Gregory lifted his chin, managing to maintain eye contact with Cole, even though he was clearly over-matched.

Honor's wits had flown up the chimney the moment she'd set eyes on Cole. His angular face was dark with anger. The wild emotions he normally held firmly in check were boiling dangerously close to the surface. Shock and disbelief had held her paralysed as he stalked across the floor towards her. She had resisted briefly when he started to drag her out of the room, but he had easily overpowered her mild rebellion.

She was overwhelmingly aware of his fierce

strength as he carried her to the door. Raven's aura of silent menace held the whole room in thrall until Lieutenant Gregory intervened.

When Honor heard Cole order the lieutenant aside she knew she had never before heard such a genuinely dangerous note in his voice. The possible consequences of a confrontation between the two men scared her into finding some of her scattered wits.

'It's all right, Lieutenant,' she said shakily. 'The Major just wishes to discuss some, some...travel arrangements...with me.'

Lieutenant Gregory ignored her. His eyes were still fixed resolutely on Cole's face. Honor knew with absolute certainty he was going to utter a further challenge.

'Lieutenant!' Real fear sharpened her voice as she tried to gain his attention. 'I'm honoured by your concern for me—but there is no need to worry.'

'Let him go, lad,' Captain Williams drawled from nearby. 'He promised her husband he'd take care of her—and we all know how straitlaced Raven is about a little harmless dancing.'

'He promised Patrick,' Honor reiterated urgently. To her relief, after a brief hesitation, Lieutenant Gregory stepped aside.

Cole shot Captain Williams a swift, hard glance, but he didn't say a word as he carried Honor out into the night.

Honor's heart raced with apprehension. She'd always known Cole was a physically strong man, but tonight he was demonstrating his superior strength in a staggeringly direct way. He didn't set her back on her feet once they were outside; he carried her through the streets, striding easily over the uneven ground.

She looked up at his face. There was enough moonlight to see the fierce inflexibility of his expression. He jaw was clenched, his mouth pressed into a thin line. The skin was drawn tightly across his prominent cheekbones.

Honor was nervous, but she wasn't frightened. Cole had never hurt her, and even now she felt safe in his arms. She didn't struggle because she knew it wouldn't do any good—and because she needed a little time to compose her own turbulent emotions before she faced Cole's anger. One second she was furious with his brutish behaviour—the next she was exhilarated by his fierce assertion of masculine authority. Once she'd recovered from her initial shock, she even began to feel like a heroine in an Arthurian romance.

'You should have ridden Corvinus into the party,' she said, incautiously voicing her errant imaginings. 'Then you could have carried me off across the pommel of your saddle—just like a knight in shining armour.'

'I've already done that.' He sounded distinctly unamused by her suggestion.

'Oh. Yes. But the first time I was the wrong way up,' she reminded him unwarily.

He growled wordlessly and her stomach fluttered with apprehension.

'I know my experience is limited, but I'm sure this isn't how ladies are normally escorted home from parties,' she said with false brightness.

'You are not a lady,' he said tersely.

'That doesn't mean I want to be treated like a strumpet!' Her temper flared at his insult.

They'd nearly reached Honor's billet. Cole didn't

reply until he'd thrust open the door and deposited her on her feet in the middle of the dark-shadowed room.

'Then you shouldn't have acted like one,' he said brutally.

'*What?*' Honor was first shocked, then hurt, then blindingly furious. 'How dare you! Get out!' She picked up the first thing that came to her groping hand, which happened to be a candle-holder, and hurled it at him.

In the darkness he didn't see it coming and she heard his brief curse as it struck him. He moved quickly, a looming shape in the shadows—and then she was enclosed in his unyielding embrace.

This time she did struggle, kicking and flailing until he finally managed to pin her arms to her sides. He tightened his hold inexorably, until she was locked breast-to-breast and thigh-to-thigh against him.

Honor stopped struggling and held herself rigid. In the darkness she could hear them both panting with exertion. There was no other sound in the room.

She closed her eyes, hating herself because even after Cole had rejected her and insulted her, she still loved the feel of his hard, virile body so close to hers.

Neither of them moved for several long moments. The tension between them was so potent it almost had a life of its own. Honor's heart pounded with excitement. She seemed to have heightened sensitivity for every place where Cole touched her. She knew the instant the mood of his embrace began to shift—from anger to desire—even though he remained perfectly still. She was acutely aware of his arousal, pressed hard against her stomach.

His hands slid possessively over her hips, pulling her even more tightly against him, but he was no longer holding her prisoner of anything except their mutual desire.

Honor felt his lips brush across her hair, then her temple. Two seconds later he buried his hands in her halo of curls and pulled her head back for his fierce, claim-staking kiss. She surrendered instantly to his burning, soul-shattering passion. There was no strength left in her legs. Her whole body had been transformed into a single, liquid, fiery response to Cole's lovemaking.

Then he stopped kissing her, setting her aside so suddenly that she stumbled and fell in the disorientating darkness. She sat on the hard clay floor, dizzy, shaken, and consumed by unsatisfied arousal.

She heard Cole curse and looked up to see his silhouette standing over her.

'Did I hurt you?' he asked, his voice so guttural she barely recognised it.

She shook her head. 'No,' she whispered, too bewildered to be sure what she was saying.

She heard Cole moving around the room, but she stayed where she was, her hands pressed to her cheeks. Nothing in her previous life had prepared her for the violence and confusion of her emotions at that moment.

At last Cole placed a lit candle on the table. She threw a skittering glance in his direction, then looked hastily away.

'Get up,' he said, holding out his hand towards her.

She stood without his assistance. Her legs were shaking and she sank onto a chair beside the table.

'I'm sorry. That was…unforgivable,' said Cole hoarsely.

'What was?'

'Kissing you so...'

'Oh.' Honor covered her face with her hands. 'You mean it was all right to carry me off from the dance as if you're some kind of...of border raider—but it's not all right to kiss me afterwards,' she asked, looking up at him again.

She tried to read the expression in his deep-set eyes, but the candlelight wasn't bright enough.

'It would have been better if that hadn't been necessary,' he said grittily. 'You had no business going into the officers' mess.'

'Why not?' she asked bitterly. 'I've been invited many times before. Why shouldn't I go?'

'Because you're not a camp-following strumpet,' he said harshly. 'Or you weren't until tonight. Now you've declared open season on your virtue. Half the men there wanted you in their bed tonight.'

'None of them would have had me!' she flung at him.

'Dammit, Honor! This isn't Almack's,' he ground out. 'There are no chaperons here to protect you from your own stupidity.'

Honor flinched and turned her head away. 'I don't need one when I've got a self-appointed moral guardian,' she said rebelliously. 'Hypocritical...! You want me in your bed too!'

Cole's breathing was ragged as he stared down at her.

'Oh, yes,' he said, his voice softly feral. 'I want you in my bed. I can protect you from other men. But be warned—I cannot promise I will always be able to protect you from me.'

He turned and strode out of the cottage without another word.

* * *

'Major Raven was truly magnificent last night!' Dolores exclaimed, her dark eyes glowing with excitement as she looked at Honor. 'Is he a good lover?'

Honor gasped, and flushed with embarrassment at the question. 'Major Raven is not my lover,' she stated categorically.

'But he will be,' Dolores asserted confidently. 'He is so masterful and romantic. Every girl at the party envied you. What did he do next?'

'Nothing! I mean…it was just a misunderstanding.' Honor felt far too flustered to project her normal air of calm composure.

'What was the misunderstanding about?' Dolores pressed avidly for details.

'Major Raven feels strongly that I should return to England,' Honor explained stiffly. 'He didn't think it was…appropriate for me to…to…to dance in public while I'm still in mourning.' She was so pleased with the unexceptional excuse she'd invented for Cole's dramatic behaviour she actually smiled at Dolores, although she'd rarely felt less light-hearted in her life.

'He didn't like you dancing with other men,' Dolores cheerfully reinterpreted Honor's careful explanation. 'I thought he would kill Captain Carstairs for dancing with you! He was so *magnificently* jealous and angry!'

Honor flinched. Unlike Dolores, she found the idea of men fighting over her profoundly disturbing. After Cole had left the previous night, she hadn't been able to sleep at all. She knew—beyond doubting—that Cole had strong feelings for her. But she wasn't sure how far he simply lusted after her, and how much of his behaviour towards her was motivated by warmer, deeper emotions. Sometimes she wondered if he knew himself. In the end, it didn't matter. There was only one honourable solution to the problem for both of them. She'd known that all along. It was past time for her to return to England.

'Soon he will make you his mistress,' said Dolores buoyantly. 'He will give you a donkey—and maybe even a little bird in a cage if you wish it. And we can still be friends—even though you won't be doing my hair any more.'

'That's very kind of you,' Honor said unsteadily. 'I must…fetch some water.'

She hurried out of the cottage, desperate to escape Dolores's well-meaning chatter. She knew she should have told Dolores she would be leaving in a matter of days, but she wasn't up to dealing with the Spanish girl's protests.

Unfortunately, she escaped one interrogation only to walk straight into another. Maggie Foster was striding up the street towards her.

'Well, well, well,' said Maggie, when she was close enough to speak. 'You have been making a stir.'

Honor tried to conceal her dismay. Dealing with Dolores's uncomplicated curiosity was one thing—facing Maggie's shrewd, cynical inquisition was another.

'I'm going home in the next couple of days,' she said, trying to head off Maggie's questions. 'I just wanted to tell you—'

'That's not what I heard,' Maggie interrupted, her sharp eyes scanning Honor's face. 'I heard—'

'He didn't make me his mistress—and he isn't going to,' Honor interrupted in her turn, unwilling to hear what the scandalmongers were saying about her.

'Wouldn't take much effort on your part to change that by all accounts,' Maggie said drily.

'I am a respectable woman!' Honor said fiercely. 'I was a good man's wife. I will not demean myself by becoming anyone's mistress.'

'Patrick was a good man,' Maggie agreed hardily. 'But he wasn't—and never could have been—up to Raven's weight. Wouldn't you like to know what it feels like to have a real man in your bed for a change?'

Honor flushed, furious with the insult to both Patrick and herself. Before she could speak, Maggie raised her hand in a gesture which was both an acknowledgement of Honor's right to be offended and an apology.

'I spoke out of turn,' she said roughly. 'You do what you think is best, girl. But remember—life is short and uncertain for most of us. If you get a chance to be happy—take it.' Her eyes dropped to Honor's flat belly. 'After all, it's not as if you're going to get caught out,' she added bluntly.

Honor lifted both hands to her stomach in an instinctively defensive gesture. In over three years of marriage she had not once conceived. She'd been grateful that no child had been born into the harsh conditions of life in the Peninsula, but her barren state had also caused her much sorrow. It hurt to have Maggie fling it in her face so brutally.

Maggie cleared her throat. 'Well, I've said too much,' she said gruffly. 'You'll go your own road. You always do. You're just like your mother in that respect.'

'You know my mother?' Honor said, surprised into prolonging a conversation she really wanted over.

Maggie looked uncomfortable, then grinned to disguise her uneasiness.

'*Everyone* knows your mother,' she retaliated, with

a short laugh. 'I even worked for her once—before Charlie took it into his head to try soldiering.'

'I never knew that.' Honor was startled by the older woman's revelation.

'Wasn't any call for you to know,' said Maggie shortly. 'I wouldn't have left you,' she added abruptly. 'If I'd known there were no wagons coming—I wouldn't have left you. You take this chance, girl,' she concluded forcefully. 'You can have as much fun as you want—you deserve that—and when you get back to England no one will be any the wiser.'

Honor didn't know what to say to that. In the space of an hour, two women she liked had urged her to become Raven's mistress. She pulled herself together and held out her hand to Maggie. 'You've always been kind to me,' she said. 'Right from the beginning. Thank you.'

'Wasn't anything to speak of.' Maggie hunched her shoulders. 'I'll see you maybe,' she said, and stumped off through the village.

Honor stood still, watching Maggie walk away. It had been an unsettling encounter. She'd come closer to having an argument with the older woman than she'd ever done in the past, yet she believed Maggie had her best interests at heart.

She sighed, and started to turn away, knowing that several curious pairs of eyes were watching her. The melodramatic events of the previous night would be equally entertaining to the local people and to the soldiers billeted in the village. Honor thought it was ironic that, after years of taking care to be inconspicuous, she'd managed to turn herself into a prize piece of gossip just before she left army life behind forever.

She was about to go back to the cottage when a

horse and rider caught her attention out of the corner
of her eye. She turned and immediately recognised
Cole coming towards her.

She swallowed, and resisted the urge to run and
hide. It had been difficult facing him after their moonlight kisses, but this was infinitely worse. Why the
devil couldn't he just stay away from her until she was
safely gone? There was nothing left for either of them
to say. She was acutely aware of the watching eyes
and wondered if she should walk up to the barn ahead
of Cole. At least that way he could speak to her in
semi-privacy. She discarded the idea almost immediately. A private meeting between them would only fuel
the scandalmongers' speculations. She would tell him
here, in the middle of the street, that she had the funds
to get herself safely home, and absolve him from any
further responsibility for her.

And that would be the end of it.

She watched as he approached her. He was riding
stiffly, as if he were in pain. Something was wrong.
Her eyes narrowed as she scanned his face for clues.
She saw the stress at the corners of his mouth, the
subtle tension around his deep-set eyes. His gaze met
hers, and she knew instantly that something dreadful
had happened. Her heart lurched with concern.
Forgetting everything else, she picked up her skirts and
ran towards him.

'What's happened?' she demanded breathlessly, as
soon as she was beside him. 'What's wrong?'

He swung his leg over the saddle and dropped down
in front of her. His eyes were shadowed with grief. For
a moment she thought he hadn't heard her.

'Cole, what's wrong?' Honor grabbed his arms and
tried to shake him, anxiety thrumming through her.

'My brother's dead,' he said, his voice bleak and cold.

For another heartbeat Honor stared at him, then she wrapped her arms around him, hugging him fiercely.

He held her close, but his thoughts were elsewhere.

'His frigate was attacked by two privateers in the Caribbean. He was shot by a sharpshooter, perhaps only wounded—but his ship was sunk,' he said unsteadily. 'Months ago. But the news was delayed reaching England, and delayed again reaching me.'

Honor looked up at him, tears shining in her eyes.

'Take me back to your billet,' she said.

'What?'

Honor took a deep breath, strengthening her resolve. 'Don't argue,' she said quietly. 'Just do it. If it'll ease your mind, I'm not planning on seducing you.'

Despite himself, a bare hint of a smile flickered in Raven's eyes. In his grief he hadn't been aware of anything except the need to seek out Honor. He hadn't thought ahead to what he'd do or say after he'd told her his terrible news. Now she'd competently taken over the task of decision-making. For once he was willing to let her do so.

He took her up before him, just as he had when he'd brought her home from Ciudad Rodrigo. He needed the comfort of having her in his arms. Gifford Raven's death meant so much more than the loss of a beloved brother, though that was pain enough to bear—Cole was now heir to a vast inheritance and all its attendant responsibilities.

Chapter Six

In Raven's quarters they at last obtained some measure of privacy, which had been Honor's purpose in suggesting it. He sat down at the table while she made up the fire, then poured him a glass of brandy.

'I remember that you were more clear-headed in this situation than I appear to be,' he said rustily. 'I should be thinking of all the arrangements I must make—instead I keep remembering when we were boys, the jaunts we used to go on. We haven't seen each other often in the past few years—but by God, we were close then. And not just Gifford, Anthony too!'

Honor knelt down in front of him.

'Anthony?' she said softly.

'Our cousin. He grew up with us,' Cole said jerkily. 'Always helping Father with his experiments. When Father died, he sailed with Giff—to see the world. God, I keep thinking of all our foolish experiments— the jokes we played...'

'Then remember those days,' Honor said huskily. 'There is nothing else you can do for them now.' She rested her hands on his thighs, just to comfort him, nothing more. 'The arrangements can wait.'

He stared at her with grief-stricken eyes, then snatched her up into his arms. He had retained his composure in front of everyone else. He was a soldier, used to the sudden loss of friends and companions, but his grief for his brother and his cousin was different. He wept against her hair, and later he lay beside her on his bed, his head on her breast.

She stroked his hair, and thought about how vulnerable he'd allowed himself to be with her. It was hard to remember the man who had carried her out of the officers' mess in such a rage only the previous evening.

Eventually she slipped out of his arms and set about preparing a meal for them. He ate slowly, and with utter disinterest in the food she gave him.

'I must go back to England,' he said wearily, when he'd finished eating. 'Now that Giff is dead, I cannot stay in the army. I've inherited everything. There is no one else—no one to take my place if I die.'

'Sir Gifford was in the navy,' said Honor. 'Who has been taking care of things in his absence?'

'Malcolm Anderson, my mother's younger brother,' said Cole. 'I've mentioned him before. Father died a couple of years ago. Until then, he had his hands tightly on the reins. He was a younger son too.' Cole's lips twisted ironically. 'He married late when his brother died childless. He was seventy when I was twenty—but he was still a bruising rider.'

'Are you much like him?' Honor asked, eager for anything she could learn about Cole.

'Not to look at.' Raven raked a hand through his sun-bleached, tawny hair. 'Except the eyes. He had jet black hair, befitting his name. He was a handsome man, well into his seventies. He was fascinated by astronomy,' Cole added, as an afterthought.

'You don't think you're handsome?' Honor said, smiling a little.

'No one ever said.' He rasped a thumb down his angular jaw. 'No one who's opinion mattered to me.'

She leant over and traced the planes of his face. 'I've always thought you're handsome,' she said softly. 'Distinguished and commanding. You're a very charismatic man, Major.'

He stared at her, momentarily distracted from his worries.

She threaded her slim fingers through his spikily disordered hair.

'You were telling me about the care of the estates,' she reminded him. 'Why didn't your brother go home when your father died?'

'He did,' Cole replied. He moved his head slightly in response to her caress. He had little experience of being petted and soothed by a woman he wasn't already in bed with—but he certainly enjoyed the sensation.

'Giff was on leave at the time,' he continued huskily. 'I didn't go back. We were in the process of driving the French out of Portugal, and I didn't get the letter telling me of Father's death until two months after the funeral. Giff had just been given his first command of a frigate. He wasn't ready to give that up in exchange for running the family estates. Malcolm and Gifford decided that, as long as I was still alive, Giff could remain in the navy. If anything happened to me, Giff would have to leave…set up his nursery. Now the duty falls to me.'

Honor's hand trembled slightly, then she continued

to stroke her fingers gently through his hair. It was only hours ago Maggie had flung her own inability to conceive in her face. She had never harboured much hope that she might have a future with Cole. Now she knew there was a very practical reason why she would never be a suitable wife for him.

'Will Miss Morton enjoy a large family?' she asked steadily.

'Honor…' Cole's eyes were full of silent pain when he looked at her.

'I know what you must do,' she interrupted him softly, laying her fingers against his lips. Her purpose in mentioning the matter wasn't to cause Cole further distress, but to reassure him. 'You've never misled me, or promised me things I cannot have.'

He reached for her, pulling her on to his lap, burying his face in the curve of her shoulder. She stroked and smoothed his hair.

'I'm ready to go to England now,' she said, smiling a little sadly. 'When do you wish to leave?'

Cole's hold on her tightened. A muffled, wordless exclamation escaped his throat. She was warm and soft and loving in his arms—stirring a deep painful yearning for something he couldn't have. But he also felt confused and unfamiliar with himself. He was used to being in control but, by weeping in her arms, he had displayed weakness and vulnerability to Honor. She'd finally agreed to go home, but it was hardly a victory for him. He knew she was doing exactly what she wanted to do.

He lifted his head, hunger for her—and his need to reassert his authority—destroying his few remaining scruples.

He kissed her, his mouth hard and demanding on

hers. He wasn't in the mood for tender love-play. His teeth bit firmly at her lower lip, then sucked on it. She gasped and quivered. He responded by thrusting his tongue into her mouth, unequivocally claiming her as his. She opened for him, trembling and submissive beneath his passionate onslaught. Impatient to claim his full victory, he drew back and started to undress her.

Honor let him, her hazel eyes large and dark in her pale face. She was stunned by the transition in his mood, and the unspoken bluntness with which he'd made his intentions clear. She knew he was motivated by both more—and less—than a simple desire to make love to her. His heart and soul were being pulled in many directions and she was to be his brief respite from the troubles that surrounded him.

A knot of apprehension tightened her stomach and chilled her limbs. Patrick had been her only lover. Cole was a much larger, stronger man than her husband, with an incomparably fiercer personality. His kisses on the moonlit ride back from Ciudad Rodrigo had been magically seductive and last night he had fought against his own fierce passions. Tonight he was intent on conquest.

He gave a raw sigh when he finally held her naked in his arms. Then he laid her on the bed and unceremoniously stripped off his own clothes.

She stared up at him, her heart racing with a confusing combination of emotions. The candlelight threw shadows which emphasised the strong definition of his lean, powerful body. He was a magnificent, virile man. Despite her misgivings, excitement began to overwhelm her doubts. She'd never before had an opportunity to look so openly at a man—and never one so devastatingly well formed.

Her eyes explored him half-shyly, half-eagerly. His shoulders were broad and powerful. His arms and chest firmly muscled. His stomach flat and hard, his hips narrow…

Her eyes lingered and she swallowed, her mouth dry. There was no doubting Cole's desire, or his intentions towards her. She looked up to meet his eyes—and caught her breath at the raging fire which darkened the blue almost to black.

She shivered, telling herself not to be so foolish. She was no longer an inexperienced virgin, and she'd hadn't been this nervous the first time with Patrick! She'd never loved Patrick the way she loved Cole. She'd never dreamed about Patrick the way she dreamed about Cole…

So why was she suddenly so scared?

Fierce consuming need pounded through Raven. He had wanted Honor for so long—wanted her, yet denied himself. Tonight she belonged to him. His hot, possessive eyes devoured her slim, trembling body. He wanted to drive away all thoughts of the problems that beset him. He wanted to banish Patrick completely from Honor's soul. He wanted to hear her cries and moans of surrender to *him*.

Scalding heat blurred his vision and nearly destroyed his self-discipline. He dragged in an unsteady breath, dredged up a measure of self-control—and realised he was looming over Honor like an avenging warrior.

He lifted his gaze to her face, and at first he could not interpret the unfamiliar expression in her eyes. It was not an emotion he associated with Honor, and it took him a few baffled moments to recognise it as apprehension.

Remorse and frustration slammed through him. He didn't want her frightened surrender, he wanted to touch her soul, the way she'd touched his. He took several more ragged breaths and lay down beside her.

Honor wasn't quite sure what she'd been expecting, but not the surprisingly gentle kiss with which he teased her lips. She liked it, so she kissed him back. She laid her hand against the hard muscle of his arm and felt the shudder which shook his body at her lightest touch. She realised then that he was holding his passion in check for her sake, and her fear vanished. She slipped her hand up to his shoulder and pulled him closer.

He dipped his head, tracking warm kisses down the side of her neck, across her collarbone, until he found her breast. He caressed her sensitive nipple with his tongue, swirling around it with provocative circular strokes as it hardened in his mouth. He bit gently, then harder, then soothed it with his lips—except that Honor had never felt less soothed in her life.

Cole was stimulating feelings she'd never known before, creating deep aches inside her body which demanded satisfaction. She clutched at his shoulders, randomly moving her hands against his body.

Raven was in a hurry, but it was a matter of pride as well as love that Honor should be as eager for him as he was for her. He kissed and caressed her breasts until she was whimpering beneath his ministrations, her hands fluttering helplessly against him like butterfly wings. In a corner of his passion-hazed mind he was glad that she was too flustered to touch him more purposefully. Her random caresses aroused him unbearably. If she knew the power she possessed over him, she could strip him of all control. Like hot, dry tinder, he would ignite at the merest spark.

He kissed her stomach, glided his hand along the outer side of her leg, skimming across her thigh. Honor had never felt so hot, so sensitive, so sensually aroused by the lightest touch on her skin. Patrick had never made love to her like this, never propelled her to the same breathless, wonderful heights of sensation. Filled her with such an ache…

Cole's hand brushed teasingly across her blonde triangle of curls, then his fingers dipped lower—and deeper—in the most shockingly intimate caress Honor had ever experienced.

'Ohh…ohhhh…' A moan whispered from her throat.

Her muscles clenched, her legs closing instinctively against his exquisite, outrageous exploration of her most private flesh.

'Hush, sweetheart, let me.' His own voice was thickened by barely contained passion.

He took her breast in his mouth again, teasing her achingly hard nipple with his tongue, then tugging at it with his teeth. Burning currents of glorious sensation pulsed through her body, peaking where his clever fingers and mouth pleasured her. She was storm-tossed with aching ecstasy…painful yearning…

He moved over her, his big body covering hers. She opened passion-hazed eyes to stare up at him. The angular planes of his face were harsh with rigidly controlled desire. She could feel the brutal tension which gripped the whole of his muscular body. Wild emotion blazed in his eyes. He braced himself on his arms and thrust steadily into her, filling her with his fierce, hard masculinity.

'Honor!' he groaned, her name ripped from his lips.

She clutched at him, her fingers digging deep into the muscles of his arms. He held still for a moment longer, then he finally surrendered to his own overpowering need for fulfilment.

She was caught in a swirling maelstrom of overwhelming physical and emotional passion. Every urgent stroke of Cole's muscular body thrilled and stimulated her further. His earlier lovemaking had excited her so much that she matched him thrust for thrust, as demanding and wild in her need for him as he was in his need for her.

Her body clenched in an explosion of stunning rapture, closing around Cole in a deep caress. She cried out in ecstasy, and heard Cole's deep voice mingle with hers, as his own body shuddered in fierce release. He lowered his head and nuzzled her neck—then bit, open-mouthed, at her shoulder.

Her head lolled away from him. She was almost too sensitised and satiated to bear his touch. He had destroyed every preconception she'd had about what it meant to make love to the man she loved.

With a tremendous effort Cole lifted himself away from Honor and rolled to one side, pulling her into his arms. She melded bonelessly against him. He rested quietly, letting his heart rate and breathing return to normal. Gradually he became aware that Honor's skin was slick and damp beneath his idle caresses, and the room was not particularly warm. He manoeuvred them both under the covers and closed his eyes, welcoming the pleasant drowsiness which claimed him. He sensed that Honor was also drifting close to sleep and he was smugly pleased that she had been so thoroughly and satisfyingly exhausted by his lovemaking.

* * *

Cole woke an hour later to discover Honor still in his arms. His erotic dream had not been a midnight fantasy after all. His first emotion was one of overwhelming satisfaction and contentment—but then he remembered the events that had led up to this moment.

Gifford's death was a deep wound that only time could ease. It also had consequences which Cole found almost too painful to contemplate. He had spent his entire adult life in the army. He didn't want to leave it now. It was ironic, he thought bitterly, he'd been so determined to send Honor home before the next campaign season—and now he wouldn't be part of it either.

Honor.

He instinctively tightened his hold on her. She stirred and muttered in her sleep. He relaxed his grip, stroking her shoulder soothingly. She sighed, and settled against him.

He had broken the most important promise he had ever made to himself about Honor O'Donnell. He felt a twinge of self-recrimination—but not as much as he should have done under the circumstances. In the quiet shadows of night he could not regret holding her in his arms, her naked flesh warm against his.

But he wasn't being fair to her.

He stroked gentle circles on her shoulder and, for the first time, seriously considered the possibility of making her his mistress. Such arrangements were common. Captain Williams lived openly with Dolores in Spain, but he had a wife and children at home in England. Many men who'd never ventured so far afield maintained more than one household. As long as the affair was conducted discreetly, no one raised an eyebrow.

Cole contemplated a future in which he divided his time between his estates, his wife—and Honor. His gorge rose at the mental picture he'd painted. Honor deserved better than that. So did Bridget, if it came to that.

He felt the familiar anger and frustration growing within him at his predicament. But as he continued to caress Honor almost absentmindedly, he also experienced a new sense of resolve. Like it or not, he was going back to London and, for the first time in four years, would not be forced to conduct his personal business at long distance.

He drew in a deep breath, careful not to disturb Honor, and exhaled it slowly, welcoming the renewed sense of control.

His thoughts drifted to his father. For the first forty-two years of his life, Edward Raven had been a younger son, content to pursue his interests in astronomy, natural history, and scientific innovation. His dalliances with women had been limited and undemanding, far removed from the rumbustious couplings which had characterised his older brother. Then he'd been thrust into the same situation which now faced Cole.

Sir Edward had taken a young bride with the practical aim of safeguarding his inheritance—and fallen deeply in love with her. He set about exploring every aspect of his sweet Eleanor with the same enthusiastic, dedicated and somewhat innocent curiosity with which he studied the night sky. He'd been devastated when she'd died soon after Cole was born.

For the rest of his life, his cheerful personality had been sustained by his pride in his sons, his fascination with the latest scientific advances—and his absolute certainty that one day he would be reunited with his beloved Eleanor.

Sadness filled Cole as he realised neither his father nor his brother would ever meet Honor. He deliberately increased the pressure of his caresses, seeking the sweet distraction from grief she offered.

Honor woke slowly, warm and languid in her lover's arms. The muscled shoulder beneath her head was both familiar and strange to her. Memory suddenly flooded back. Her skin burned with embarrassment at her abandoned response to Cole's lovemaking. She had lost all control—allowed him to do things to her…wonderful things…

Unconsciously she rubbed herself against him, as she remembered the way he'd made her feel.

Wonderful things—but perhaps she should have retained some self-awareness, a worried voice whispered in the back of her mind. She'd let him master her completely, yet he belonged to another woman. The more she gave to him, the more fully she would be destroyed when he left her.

Cole rumbled deep in his chest and she realised he was awake. He slid his hand, butterfly light, into the indentation of her waist, over the curve of her hip, and along the outer side her thigh. She blushed again as she discovered she'd been rubbing the inner side of her leg erotically against him. He drew her leg up, and she found he was fully aroused. She tried to pull away from him, but he wouldn't let her.

'Ah, sweetheart,' he murmured, 'I thought you were never going to wake up.'

'I…' she wasn't sure what to say to him. 'Cole?' she said uncertainly.

'Mmm?' He rolled her on to her back, kissing her beneath her ear, then on her still-swollen lips. 'You can make me want you just by breathing.'

That was so demonstrably true Honor's mind immediately lost coherence. She wanted a chance to think about what had happened, possibly talk to Cole about it, but she didn't have time. She'd always known he was a man of action, she thought wildly, she just hadn't known exactly how active he could be.

Cole sent Honor back to her billet the following morning. Honor was too proud—and too unsure of herself—to protest. In the dull grey light of morning, Cole had withdrawn into himself, no longer the tender lover of the previous night. Only a few hours ago he had given her the most exquisitely passionate experience of her life—but now he was detached practicality personified.

Honor took herself and her tangled emotions back to her billet with Captain Williams and Dolores. She told them she would be leaving soon, but she didn't tell them Cole's sad news. She knew it would reach them soon enough via the camp grapevine.

Her situation was both awkward and embarrassing. If she'd stayed with Cole, at least her status as his mistress would have been clear to everyone. As it was, she knew she was the subject of an endless round of speculation. Had Raven sent her away after only one night because he found her wanting in some way? Or had Honor O'Donnell demanded too high a price for her favours?

Honor hid her own unanswered questions behind a politely expressionless face. The situation severely tried her fortitude. It was a considerable relief to her when it was finally time to leave for Lisbon.

Cole provided Honor with a riding horse for the two-hundred-mile journey. Compared to her previous experiences in the Peninsula, she considered herself to be travelling in luxury.

'You ride well,' said Cole, after watching her critically for several miles.

'Thank you.' Honor smiled tentatively at him, but he looked away without responding to her friendly overture.

She'd never known him to seem so distant. Always before she'd been able to sense the passionate emotions smouldering beneath his disciplined demeanour. Now he seemed unnaturally cool—like a polite stranger who simply happened to be travelling in the same direction for a while.

The change in him chilled Honor. Even when he'd been angry with her, she'd always felt a strong, even if intangible, connection with him. Now she sensed no warmth in him towards her at all.

They rode for miles without exchanging a word. Honor watched the changing countryside, remembering the many experiences—both good and bad—she'd had during her time in Spain and Portugal. But all the time she was acutely conscious of the silent, stiff-backed figure riding beside her.

They didn't hurry the journey, finding nightly lodgings at suitable places along the route. The first night Honor wondered briefly if Cole would come to her. But he didn't. Her fugitive hope that perhaps he'd simply been protecting her reputation over the past few days withered. They were among strangers now. No one would have known, or cared, what they did. Cole obviously regretted that moment when he'd allowed grief to overpower his declared intention not to have her.

Honor held her head high, and pretended she didn't care.

It wasn't until they'd covered over two-thirds of the journey that Joe prompted Cole to speak of his exploits early in the Peninsular campaign. Raven had carried out a variety of daring missions, including tracking the route of the French army and sending reports back to Wellington. Honor listened to the two men, fascinated by Cole's stories, but hardly daring to join in the conversation herself. She was terrified that, if she did, Cole might once more retreat into silence. But he did appear to be more relaxed and open than he had been for several days.

'I would have been scared I'd get lost,' she said at last, with total honesty.

Cole smiled slightly, his confidence in his own abilities clear. 'Not much chance of that,' he said lightly. 'Sometimes I might not know exactly where I was, but I always knew how to retrace my steps—and usually how to get from where I was to where I wanted to go.'

'You mean we aren't going to end up in Madrid by accident?' said Honor, daring to tease him. She held her breath, but Cole simply grinned and didn't bother to answer the insult.

'Do you naturally have a good sense of direction?' she queried, genuinely interested in the topic. 'Or were you given special training?'

'I had a few…educational…adventures during my boyhood,' Cole admitted. His reminiscent grin suddenly faded. For a moment his eyes were shadowed

with loss, but then he roused himself to speak again.
'The 16th were stationed in Ireland for several years,'
he continued. 'My commanding officer got to hear of
my tendency to…roam, and decided to put me to the
test. He had me sketching the countryside for him.'

'I didn't know you'd been to Ireland,' Honor said,
surprised.

'I was there two years or more.'

'Strange,' Honor murmured. She'd been married to
an Irishman, but she'd never visited his country. 'I'd
never been further from London than Bath before we
came to Portugal,' she said to Cole. 'You must have
more wanderlust than I do.'

'I go where the army sends me,' Cole pointed out.
'Not the same thing at all.'

'But if you hadn't joined the army you'd have been
safely toasting your toes in front of a blazing fire re-
gardless of where the 16th or the 52nd were sent,'
Honor pointed out. 'Surely that suggests you have an
adventurous spirit?'

Cole didn't reply. Instead he looked away from her,
scanning the vast plains of the Ribatejo with hooded
eyes. Honor bit her lip, wishing she could call back
her unthinking words. She was realising exactly how
much Cole had lost with the death of his brother. Some
men might have welcomed a respite from the gruelling
campaigns, but she knew Cole wasn't one of them.

She'd been preoccupied with her own concerns and
fears for the future. Now she tried to imagine it
through Cole's eyes. She knew he wasn't the kind of
man to revel in the acquisition of unexpected wealth.
He was too passionate and too wild to conform easily
to a regulated life of fashionable domesticity. She
wondered briefly if he might be tempted to find an

outlet for his restlessness in the excitement of gambling—or perhaps an even more dangerous pastime. He'd come close to forcing a challenge on Lieutenant Gregory.

Honor's stomach clenched at the memory. She hastily reassured herself that that had been an unusual occasion. She'd never heard any gossip to suggest Cole was particularly prone to quarrelling with his fellow officers. Far from it—he was generally regarded as a disciplined and reasonable man, as he had been throughout their journey so far.

His temper would probably improve dramatically when she was no longer a thorn in his side. She ducked her head to hide the tears that suddenly welled up in her eyes. It was better not to think too far ahead, she decided. She'd just take each day—each hour—as it came.

Lisbon was just as Honor remembered it, surrounded by vineyards and orange groves, full of dogs and priests, and white houses with terracotta roofs. She remembered the steep, dirty streets, most of them too narrow to accommodate a carriage, the iron balconies and the decorative blue tiles on the walls of the houses.

The city was crowded with officers and men from the Allied army. Further downstream at the little town of Belem there were even more men; those who could not fight, and those who would not fight—the so-called Belem Rangers.

'It's strange to be back here,' Honor said, finding comfort in reminiscence. 'When we first arrived, I couldn't believe how many priests there were—and all the garlic and oil in the cooking! Now I think I'll miss that when I get back to England.'

'And the heat and the dust and the mud and the cold,' said Raven, but he was smiling too.

'I wouldn't have missed these four years,' said Honor sincerely. 'We'll win now, won't we?' she continued, wanting his professional opinion. 'I know we had to scuttle back to the Portuguese border last year, but we've made so many lasting advances. The French are out of Portugal now for good.'

'Yes, they are,' Cole agreed. 'I think the next push will drive the French back to their own border—out of Spain. Dammit!' His fists clenched abruptly, but then he forced his hands to relax. 'We'd better find some lodgings,' he said curtly.

They found rooms at an inn which was popular with British officers. Cole was irked to discover they'd likely have to wait several days for the packet boat. He left Honor discussing arrangements for their baggage with Joe and the inn servants and went out, intent on working off some of his restlessness striding up and down the hilly streets.

He felt as if he had an important puzzle to solve, but he didn't yet have all the pieces in his hands. He needed to get back to London, to speak to Malcolm Anderson—and to see Bridget Morton. He also needed to find an unexceptional way of providing for Honor while he dealt with all his other problems. He had no intention of showing his hand by openly setting her up as his mistress before he had a full picture of the situation.

But Honor had been unusually quiet—submissive even—since the morning after their night together. It unsettled him. He was used to her squaring up to him and arguing virtually every point with him. But when he'd suggested she return to her usual billet that morning, she'd gone without a murmur.

He'd made the suggestion only in the rather vain hope that they might have escaped the eagle-eyed attention of the gossipmongers. Once it was obvious that had been wishful thinking, he'd ridden over to see Honor, intending to ask her to stay with him until they left. But she'd been so coolly polite, and so intent on discussing only the practical details of their forthcoming journey, that he'd left his invitation unsaid.

Perhaps she regretted her night with him, and wanted only to forget her fall from virtue. The possibility appalled him—but he was hardly in a position to try to change her mind.

He was not in a good mood when he returned to the inn. His mood didn't improve when he discovered Honor was already on friendly terms with several other guests at the inn. He would have preferred a more anonymous departure from Portugal.

But Honor was chatting happily to an infantry captain and a young lady who, even to Cole's untutored eye, seemed to be dressed in the height of London fashion. It occurred to him for the first time that Honor was still dressed in the same style as the local peasant girls. He'd never been particularly interested in what Honor wore—as long as her clothes were warm enough—but he had a feeling this was the kind of situation most women would find distressing.

He felt bad that he had put Honor into an awkward situation. He should have realised she would need more suitable clothes once they arrived in Lisbon. He knew she would never ask for his help, she was far too proud. But when he scanned her face for signs of discomfort she looked perfectly relaxed.

'Hello, Major,' Honor greeted him with a welcoming smile. 'This is Captain Robert Bell and his wife, Lavinia. Mrs Bell and I both attended Miss Goodwin's seminary in Bath. Major Cole Raven,' she introduced him to her guests.

'How do you do?' Cole forced a smile to his lips as he shook the captain's hand. The last thing he wanted to do was make polite small talk with complete strangers, but Honor quite clearly expected him to be sociable.

'I was so thrilled when I discovered Honor—I mean, Mrs O'Donnell—was staying at the inn,' Lavinia Bell said, with a mixture of shyness and enthusiasm. 'Meeting an old friend makes Lisbon seem so much less foreign.'

'Have you only just arrived?' Cole asked, dredging up a response.

'A couple of weeks ago,' Captain Bell replied cheerfully. 'We'll be leaving to join my regiment shortly.'

'Mrs O'Donnell has promised to give me lots of advice before we go,' said Lavinia eagerly. 'I could not possibly have let Robert leave me behind, but I don't want to be a burden to him on the march.'

'You could never be a burden to me,' Robert declared, smiling at his wife fondly.

Cole observed her with a more judicious eye. He decided she looked like a cross between a sparrow and a kitten. A sweet little doll who wouldn't last five minutes on campaign.

He was just about to point out the hardships that lay ahead of her when Honor smoothly intervened.

'I'm sure you'll adapt very quickly,' she said to Lavinia. 'And Captain Bell will help you.'

'Of course I will,' said Captain Bell lovingly.

Cole frowned, uncomfortable with this public display of mawkishness. To his relief Honor directed the conversation on to other topics. Cole sat back and listened. He'd never before had an opportunity to observe her company manners under what amounted to drawing-room conditions, and he was impressed. She was poised and charming, and she knew how to maintain a light flow of conversation which was neither tedious nor controversial—a skill that Cole knew he lacked. He frowned thoughtfully, then schooled his features into an expression of polite interest before anyone questioned his momentary abstraction.

'Miss Goodwin was very proud of you,' Lavinia said suddenly to Honor.

'Proud?' Honor sounded amazed. 'Of me? Are you sure?'

Goodwin? Cole was momentarily at a loss until he remembered the name had been mentioned in connection with the seminary at Bath. He still knew very little about Honor's early life, but it was highly unusual for a serving maid's illegitimate daughter to attend a seminary for young ladies unless she had some kind of patron. He wondered again about her reluctance to return to England. Was there some particular person she was avoiding? If so, and they meant to cause Honor mischief, they would now have Cole to contend with.

'Oh, yes,' Lavinia said confidently. 'Miss Goodwin *was* proud of you. She never came right out and said so to us girls. But I know she kept copies of all your reviews. And she slipped off to London once to see you perform—I heard her telling Miss Denby about it. She said you were a fine example of what clear-thinking, perseverance, and natural talent could achieve.'

'Good heavens,' said Honor weakly. 'I had no idea.' Cole saw her glance briefly at Captain Bell. It was the first time she had shown any sign of uneasiness during the conversation. To Cole's relief, the captain seemed unperturbed by Honor's colourful past.

'I'm sorry I never had a chance to see you perform,' Bell said to Honor. 'I wonder?' He glanced from Cole to Honor. 'Would you care to dine with us this evening?'

Cole looked at Honor, and realised she was leaving it up to him to make the decision. He accepted as graciously as he could, and was then relieved when the Captain and his wife decided to go for a stroll before eating.

Honor looked at Cole when they were alone, and for the first time in days felt a sense of connection with him. She started to laugh, she couldn't help it.

'What?' He seemed rather affronted by her amusement, although she saw a rueful gleam lurking in his blue eyes.

'You'd rather have faced a French bombardment than a hour of civilised conversation,' she teased him.

'That was hardly obvious,' he replied austerely. 'Was it?' he added with uncharacteristic doubtfulness, and she went off into a gale of laughter which only added to his discomfort.

He sighed, but he didn't look too disgruntled. In fact, she had the strangest impression that he was pleased with her.

'Did you explain how you come to be travelling with me?' he asked, a few moments later.

'Yes.' She sobered quickly. 'I told them you'd promised Patrick you would ensure I got safely home to England. And I said that, since you have to return yourself, you'd decided it would be most sensible for me to travel under your protection.' She hesitated a moment. 'I didn't tell them exactly *when* Patrick died,' she admitted.

Cole raised his eyebrows, but to her relief he didn't make a sardonic comment.

'I just didn't want our stories to conflict,' she said awkwardly.

He grinned wolfishly. 'Don't worry,' he assured her. 'You are undoubtedly the most contrary, self-willed woman I've ever met—but your secret's safe with me.'

'Where are you going?' Cole demanded the next morning.

He'd returned to the inn from an early morning walk, just in time to catch Honor on her way out, clutching a packet of documents.

'To the bank,' she replied briskly, swallowing back her nervousness. She'd been hoping to complete her errand without Cole's interference, but she held her head up and refused to be daunted by his disapproving frown.

'Why?' he demanded.

'Because I need money to pay for new clothes and my passage home,' she replied.

He stared at her through narrowed eyes. 'Who gave you the money?' he growled dangerously.

'I *earned* it!' Honor snapped, her apprehension overtaken by indignation at the implication of his question. She tried to walk around him. 'Excuse me, please,' she said coolly. 'I have business to conduct.'

'How did you earn it?' Cole barked, easily blocking her attempt to pass him.

'By performing that "preposterous nonsense" you despise so much,' she said tartly. 'You're in my way,' she pointed out.

Cole moved aside, then fell into step next to her. Honor walked quickly, although she knew she had no chance of outpacing Cole. She was frustrated by the situation which had developed. She'd known he would be difficult when he found out she had some money of her own. But she'd really hoped to complete her errand at the bank before they had this confrontation. She'd meant to work round to the subject gently, but it was too late for that now.

'You stopped acting years ago,' Cole said tautly.

'But I was always careful with my money,' she replied. 'And Patrick wouldn't let me spend it when we were married. Now it will see me safely home to England.'

When Cole didn't respond, she glanced sideways up at him. He was grim-faced, but apparently had no intention of continuing their dispute in public. She wished he would let her deal with the arrangements on her own, but she knew there was no prospect of that.

An hour later she had to admit that his formidable, uniformed presence had expedited matters. It turned out that Cole had his own business to conduct at the bank, but it aggravated Honor that the bank official handed over *her* money into Cole's safekeeping. Despite her indignation, she didn't debate the matter until they'd returned to the inn.

'Please keep back my fare for the packet boat,' she said, struggling to keep her voice pleasant and reasonable. 'I will take the rest.'

Cole smiled unpleasantly. 'This is a significant sum

of money,' he said. 'What are you planning to spend it on?'

'Clothes,' said Honor briefly. She knew she ought to be more placatory, but she was annoyed by Cole's attitude. She'd respected Patrick's wishes while he was alive, but she'd worked hard for her money and she was entitled to spend it how she liked.

'All of it?'

'Of course not! I don't know why Simpson sent so much. But it doesn't matter.'

'You mean you don't intend to pay for your room here? Or the food you've eaten at my table? Or even the clothes you're currently wearing?' Cole taunted her. 'I seem to remember when I first gave them to you, you were determined to repay me for them. What happened to your all scruples about accepting charity?'

Honor stared at him, wondering how she could disentangle this situation.

'Some things are gifts, not charity,' she said quietly. 'Sometimes it's hard to tell the difference. If you wish me to pay for my room or these clothes, I will do so.'

Cole spun on his heel and took two hasty strides across the small room. He turned again and stared at her, fire flashing in his blue eyes.

'All this time you *knew* you had the funds to get safely home but you let me worry about you…think up alternative arrangements for you…' he accused her savagely.

'No! I mean, I told you I'd paid my own way since I was seventeen,' Honor replied wildly. 'I *told* you I didn't need your help. You just wouldn't believe me.'

'You do need my help,' Raven snarled. 'Having money doesn't mean you're safe—it just makes you prey to even more hazards.'

'I'm hardly an heiress!' Honor exclaimed. 'I have enough money to dress myself and get home. After that, if I'm not to starve, I'll have to find work.'

'You lied to me.' Cole's voice had sunk to a deadly purr.

'I didn't lie. You never asked.' Honor flung up her hands in dismay. 'Why are we arguing?' she demanded. 'What does it matter if I can pay my own passage home? It doesn't change anything else.'

'What else?' Cole growled menacingly.

'You're going home to be married!' Honor cried recklessly. 'You're angry with me because I'm not so poverty-stricken that I have no choice but to become your mistress.'

Dead silence followed her words.

'You presume a lot,' Cole said harshly. 'Have I asked you to be my mistress?'

Honor swallowed and looked down, trying to hide her shimmering eyes.

'Your money.' He put it down on the table. 'I'll pretend you didn't insult me with your offers of payment.'

'I was taught to pay my own way,' Honor protested helplessly.

'It's too bad you didn't remember that months ago and tell me your true situation immediately,' Cole retorted icily. 'Then it would have been a relief to know the truth—now it's an insult.' He strode out of the room, leaving Honor to brush the tears from her cheeks with trembling fingers.

Chapter Seven

Cole strode down to the edge of the Tagus, then turned to walk along the river bank towards Belem. He was furious with Honor. He'd gone back to the inn with the intention of taking Honor shopping for new clothes—and instead she'd floored him with the news that she was going to the bank.

He was outraged with her dissembling—but he was also hurt. He'd worried about her safety, but she hadn't trusted him with the truth. She'd lied to him by omission, and there was still so much he didn't know about her. Sometimes there seemed to be such harmony between them, but other times she withdrew from him as if he were her enemy. He hated it when she did that. His body lusted after hers, but his happiest memory was the night she'd confided in him on the moonlit ride back from Wellington's grand ball. He wanted her to trust him like that all the time.

He emerged from his introspection to discover he'd drawn level with the ornate little fortress of Belem, sturdily defending the Tagus. He stared out at the waves beating against the fort, a symbol of Portugal's past greatness, and felt his eyes burn with a bitter sense of loss. He was grieving for his brother, his cousin, his profession—the future he'd wanted for himself.

He also wanted Honor. And sometimes, even when she was standing right in front of him, she seemed completely out of reach.

Cole spent the rest of the day away from the inn. He wasn't in the mood to make polite conversation with Captain Bell and his wife, or any of the other guests. In the evening he went to the theatre, which he considered to be a form of self-inflicted misery in keeping with his temper.

The entertainment consisted of a play, followed by a ballet and a musical farce, all of which Cole considered badly performed, not that he regarded himself as an expert. He scrutinised his surroundings critically. The building was quite impressive, but dingy and badly lit. It reminded him of Honor's past experiences in the most negative of ways. How could she ever have put herself on public display in such a place? There was no magic here—just sordid and grimy reality.

By the time he returned to his room it was very late, and he was in a foul temper. He summoned a servant to drag off his boots, then stripped and flung himself on his bed.

In the next room, Honor listened to Raven bang around, occasionally swearing to himself, before he eventually fell silent. She knew he was in an evil mood. She felt utterly miserable herself. She hated it when they argued. She'd been trying desperately not to cry, but she couldn't contain her tears any longer. She buried her face in the lumpy pillow to muffle her sobs.

* * *

Matters hadn't much improved between Raven and Honor by the time they boarded the packet boat. Honor had, rather stiffly, tried to apologise for not telling Cole earlier about her money. She'd meant to be more conciliatory than she was, but he was so frozen and aloof that her words withered on her tongue. She had thought he was reserved on the journey to Lisbon, but now she could sense nothing from him but a chilly dislike of being in her company.

The packet boat was designed for speed. The Captain was under official orders to run rather than fight if he spotted a French ship. The quarters were cramped to say the least. Honor was assigned a cabin not much more than four feet by six feet, with no porthole. Like all the cabins, it opened on to a central dining room in which the passengers ate and, at least in theory, relaxed.

It was, thought Honor, a recipe for frayed tempers—particularly when one of the fellow passengers was the morose Cole Raven. Fortunately, he spent most of his time on deck. Joe Newton, whose presence might have helped relieve her sense of isolation, had remained in Lisbon until he could arrange to bring Corvinus back to England.

Cole stood on deck and ran his fingers through his salt-sticky hair. He welcomed the fresh breeze in his face, even though it was seasoned with a fine rain which dripped steadily from his oilskin cloak. He hated being cooped up in the cramped, stuffy conditions below decks. The packet was making good progress. Clouds obscured the stars, but the weather wasn't stormy, and the wind was in their favour.

Cole was soul-weary in a way he had never previously experienced. Honor had made no further attempts to mend the breach between them. Superficially, she seemed calm and at ease with her circumstances, but the dark circles under her eyes were more noticeable every morning. She could not avoid speaking to him completely, because that would have drawn attention to their private dispute—but she confined herself to addressing only the most commonplace remarks to him.

His fists clenched on the wooden rail. He wanted to mend the situation between them, but he didn't know how. He was no longer burningly angry with Honor's deception—but he was confused by it. He understood and even admired her fierce independence. But why hadn't she told him she was not completely impoverished? It would have been an excellent way of curtailing his interference in her life. And then he wondered why she had stayed so long in Spain. He knew from their trip to the bank that she could have left months ago. He'd gained the impression that she wasn't anxious to return home—that perhaps there were even people in England she was trying to avoid. But had she also had a compelling reason to stay in Spain? A reason that no longer existed as soon as she knew that Cole also had to return to England?

He felt a flare of hope at the possibility—followed by a sense of frustration because the cramped, public conditions of the packet boat made any kind of intimate conversation difficult to achieve. He didn't want to wait until they reached Falmouth before he made his peace with Honor.

There was a light, tentative touch on his arm. He spun round, lurching a little with the motion of the boat. Honor was standing in front of him. It was too dark to see her expression, her face was just a pale oval beneath the black shadows of her shawl.

'Cole?' she said uncertainly.

She was so transparently afraid of her welcome that his heart twisted in pain.

'I...I'm sorry,' she said unsteadily. 'Please, I don't know what...'

'Sweetheart,' he growled, unbelievably relieved that she had come to him.

He reached to pull her towards him and realised his oilskin cloak was drenched with rain. Honor had just come up from below, she was still relatively dry. He opened the cloak with shaking hands and hauled her inside, hard against his chest. He closed the cloak around her and stood with his back to the rain, bracing himself firmly so they were both secure. She trembled against him, her head tucked under his chin. He thought she was crying, but he couldn't hear above the creaking of the ship and the waves lapping against the hull.

'I'm sorry,' he whispered brokenly. 'God, I'm so sorry, Honor. I'm sorry. Forgive me, sweetheart.'

He cradled her close, one hand stroking the soft woollen shawl which covered her head, careful not to pull it back and expose her to the cold.

'No, *I'm* sorry,' she murmured against his neck. 'I should have told you...'

'Shh.' He drew her shawl away from her face just enough to kiss her forehead. 'Sweetheart...darling...' His thoughts lost all coherence. The only thing that mattered to him was that Honor was back in his arms, where she belonged. He didn't care about the rights and wrongs of their argument, only that they were re-united.

Honor lifted her head. Cole kissed her cheek, then he found her lips. His face was cold and wet from the rain. She could taste sea-salt on his lips—or was it her tears?

'Honor,' he breathed warmly against her skin.

His lips were so gentle on hers. He was apologising with his kiss, Honor thought, confused, shaken—and so relieved. Her mouth puckered and she started to cry in earnest, racked by so many tumultuous emotions.

'Oh, love…'

He tucked the shawl around her to keep her warm and held her so tenderly she cried even more.

'Raining inside and out,' he murmured eventually, wryly humorous.

She gave a hiccough of laughter. 'I'm sorry.'

'You can cry all night if it'll make you feel better,' he said, his good humour much restored.

She manoeuvred awkwardly and managed to find her handkerchief. She dried her eyes and blew her nose, all within the cramped but wonderful shelter of his arms, and relaxed against him once more.

He took the opportunity to brace his back and feet even more securely against the fittings of the packet boat. Now he was only likely to be thrown if the boat pitched very violently. Apart from the rain it was a calm night, so he didn't anticipate a problem. It wasn't a particularly comfortable position for him, but he didn't care about that. Honor was snug in his arms, and there was nowhere else for them to go. There was no privacy below deck unless they shared a cabin—which was out of the question. At least on deck the darkness and the inclement weather gave them some protection from their fellow passengers. And most of the crew seemed to take their lead from their taciturn captain, who never said a single word when none sufficed.

'I don't like this boat,' said Honor.

'I'm not overfond of it,' Cole admitted wryly.

'And I can't stand the rest of the passengers,' she added roundly.

'They don't seem too bad,' Cole said cautiously. It occurred to him he'd never heard Honor express an open dislike before. Despite her occasionally caustic comments, she was usually far more likely to make the best of a situation.

'That's because you haven't been spending any time with them,' she informed him, sounding more like her old self. 'I spent nearly all of yesterday in my cabin—in the dark—so I wouldn't have to listen to them arguing about the conduct of the war. I wouldn't mind if they knew what they're talking about, but they don't—apart from poor Lieutenant Soper, of course. Wine merchants and orange sellers!' she muttered wrathfully. 'Hah.'

Cole smiled into the darkness and hugged her close, understanding that she was talking herself back into her familiar self-confidence. God, it was good to have her in his arms again. The wind was cold against his rain-beaten back, but Honor was dry and snug against his heart. He adjusted the cloak, so that no stray draughts could destroy her comfort, and relaxed.

Honor closed her eyes. She was so tired. She thought perhaps they ought to go below, but Cole hadn't said anything and she was so cosy in his arms. He'd called her love. He'd never called her that before. She smiled contentedly.

Cole felt her body soften into sleep. He'd positioned himself so that it was possible to support her slight weight, even though they were still standing more-or-less upright. He wasn't about to let her go now.

He loved her and he thought that perhaps she… cared…about him. He wanted to ask her if she stayed in Spain to be near him, but he didn't. He couldn't quite bring himself to say the words—besides, her actions were pretty strong evidence that he was important to her. Perhaps, when they'd had a little more time together, she might even come to love him as she'd loved Patrick.

Cole decided that possession was nine-tenths of the law—and right now, as she slept in his arms, he had possession of her. He knew he couldn't do without her. The mere thought of never seeing her again after they reached England was unbearable. In his first wild grief at Gifford's death, Honor had comforted him with such loving generosity. Now he wanted her support for the gruelling task that lay ahead of him.

Cole knew he would have to learn from scratch how to manage his large inheritance, which included estates and properties in several counties as well as houses in London and Bath. He was confident he could master the practical, business skills required for his new role—but he was daunted by the endless round of obligatory socialising he would have to undertake. With Honor by his side it would all be so much easier. She would make a beautiful and gracious lady of the manor.

But first he had to deal with Bridget Morton. Cole set himself to think about the problem logically. If he withdrew from the betrothal he knew he would almost certainly be faced with an action for breach of promise. Bridget's father was not the man to leave such an insult unavenged. The scandal would rebound on both Bridget and Honor.

Cole's knowledge of polite society was limited by the years he'd spent overseas with the regiment; but he was sadly aware that, even if he married Honor without a scandal, there might be places in his world where she wouldn't be welcome; hostesses who might not be prepared to receive her into their refined and respectable drawing rooms. He wasn't sure. She'd been a respectably married woman for several years, but she had also been a well-known actress. Her success might depend not only on her own deportment, but on whether she was sponsored by one of the fashionable leaders of the *ton*. Cole had no desire to cut a dash in society, but he had no idea how Honor felt on the subject. He didn't want to spoil her social prospects by making a mess of disentangling himself from the Mortons.

He was also concerned about Bridget. He could barely remember what the woman looked like, but he'd effectively taken ten years of her life. Her family had considered her promised to him since she was eighteen. Now she would be denied the husband and family she had counted on and, at the age of twenty-eight, she would be thrust back on to the marriage mart. It was a cruel position for any woman to find herself in. Cole didn't care about the probable law suit, but he did care about his responsibility to Bridget. He listened to the creak of timber and sail and tried to think of some way he could make restitution to her.

What did women want? he wondered. He'd always assumed it was obvious—a husband and children. But his experience with Honor was teaching him not to take the obvious for granted. Perhaps Bridget didn't

really want a husband. It would have been perfectly
reasonable if she'd asked him to take leave of absence
after her period of mourning had ended. There had
been opportunities during the past three years when he
could have returned to England to marry her. But she'd
never asked him to do so. Perhaps she was no more
eager to marry him than he was to marry her. Perhaps
he could arrange for her to have what—or who—she
really did want.

Unfortunately, he barely knew her. He was bad at
writing letters, and hers were so dull he usually did no
more than skim through them—just to make sure he
didn't miss anything awkward like the fact that someone had died.

'Honor?' he murmured. She was more than half-
asleep. He hoped she'd stay that way while she an-
swered his question. 'Sweetheart?'

'Hmm?' she roused drowsily.

'If you could have anything you wanted, what
would it be?' He thought if he asked Honor, it might
give him a clue about Bridget. They were both female,
after all.

'What?' she tensed a little. 'Why?'

'It's all right, you can say anything,' he assured her,
suddenly nervous and regretting he'd spoken. Perhaps
he wouldn't like her answer. He'd been thinking about
Bridget, he'd forgotten he hoped for a different kind
of answer from Honor.

'Really anything?' she hesitated.

'Really anything. I won't get angry,' he promised,
although his apprehension was growing. 'Pretend
there's a magical moon in the sky,' he suggested, remembering her comments on the night of the ball in
Ciudad Rodrigo, and hoping the memory would put

her in a romantic mood, 'lighting a path of silver for the packet boat to sail along to take you to your dreams.'

'Ohh,' she sighed wonderingly. 'You said you were too prosaic to believe in magic.'

'But you're not. Tell me, sweetheart,' he urged.

'Oh.' She still hesitated and he had to squash his growing anxiety. Unconsciously his arms tightened around her, silently compelling her to speak.

'If I could have anything I want,' she said tentatively. 'I'd…I'd marry you. And you'd take care of me…and—and I'd take care of you…' There was a hint of defensiveness in her voice, as if she expected him to argue the point with her. 'And we'd…love each other, of course and—if I could really have anything I wanted—we'd have babies.' She whispered the last words almost inaudibly.

Cole was tremendously, gloriously happy. He grinned into the rainy darkness like a fool. He didn't care that water was dripping down his neck, or that cramp was threatening to strike in his right leg any minute. Honor wanted to marry him and have his babies. The erotic images her words conjured up, not to mention her warm body pressed closely against his, aroused him so much he was instantly ready to try and fulfil her wish.

She stirred against him, obviously aware of the direction his thoughts had taken.

'Shush.' He held her close. 'Don't wiggle about like that, sweetheart, you'll only make things worse,' he teased her, amusement and tenderness mingling in his voice.

'Cole!'

Her face was covered by the shawl, but he suspected

she was probably blushing within its protective shadows. He'd forgotten how shy she could be sometimes.

'Go back to sleep,' he soothed her.

'You can't be very comfortable,' she protested softly.

'I've never felt better in my life,' he assured her.

'You liked my answer then?' she whispered.

'Yes, love.'

'I wish there really was a moon,' she murmured.

Cole thought wishing on moonlight was unlikely to produce a satisfactory solution to their problems, but he didn't say so. Unfortunately, gratifying though Honor's answer had been for him, it hadn't got him any closer to solving the problem of Bridget Morton. In fact, if Honor was anything to go by, it seemed women really did want a husband and children. How the devil was he going to find Bridget a replacement husband—one who would take care of her properly?

Cole's father had intended Cole to receive the family estate in Oxfordshire on his marriage to Bridget. Now Cole had inherited everything, he decided to give Bridget the Oxfordshire estate as her dowry, as recompense for the years she had spent waiting for him. That was all very well and good, but he could hardly palm her off on some half-pay officer looking for a comfortable billet. Cole wanted to find Bridget someone who would love her as much as he loved Honor.

The rest of the voyage continued more happily for Cole and Honor. Cole didn't tell Honor about his plan to marry her and find a substitute husband for Bridget Morton. It didn't seem quite right to discuss marriage with one woman while he was still betrothed to another. And he also wanted to present Honor with a complete solution to their problem—like a magician pulling a rabbit out of a hat. Fortunately, she seemed reasonably content now that the rift between them was healed, and as disinclined as he was to talk about the future.

'Well, really, this is more pleasant than the voyage out,' said Honor the following afternoon, retracting her comment about not liking the packet boat.

'God, yes!' Cole winced at the thought of the misery she must have endured on the troopship.

The soldiers would have been crammed into the transport with eighteen inches of space each, wives along with their husbands, and no privacy for anyone. There was rarely adequate ventilation or even enough water to clean the decks on the ships. Cole, like many officers, was incensed by the foul conditions in which his men were forced to travel. He couldn't bear the thought that Honor had been exposed to such horrors.

'How did you manage?' he asked tightly.

'Well, it was a terrible shock. I'd never stayed in the barracks with Patrick—I couldn't bear to,' she confessed. 'They were so grim. I found lodgings nearby.' She sounded guilty. 'But when we knew Patrick was going to Portugal, of course I had to go with him.'

'You drew a ticket "to-go"?' Cole asked.

Only six wives per hundred men were officially allowed to accompany their husbands abroad.

'Yes.' Honor smiled a little at the memory. 'We were all crowded in the pay-sergeant's room. All the wives had to pull a ticket out of the hat to see if we were "to-go" or "not-to-go". It's strange, but you could tell if people liked a wife who was going—or if they didn't. There was a groan when Maggie Foster pulled her "to-go" ticket.'

'I'm not surprised!' Cole exclaimed. 'That woman's voice could saw through oak—and she drinks more than three men put together.'

'She was always kind to me,' said Honor quietly. 'When I pulled my ticket, no one knew whether to groan or be pleased,' she continued, smiling wryly. 'They didn't know me, you see.'

'If you hadn't pulled the ticket, you'd have stayed behind,' said Cole. And I'd never have known you, he thought.

'Of course not,' Honor replied briskly. 'I'd have taken a berth in a packet boat and followed Patrick. The army couldn't have turned me away if I'd made my own way to Portugal. I wasn't,' she added quietly, 'quite like the other wives who couldn't afford that option.'

She lifted her chin, almost as if she was waiting for Cole's criticism.

'The transport?' he prompted her, not wishing to pursue the subject of her financial independence. He also wasn't sure he wanted to hear about her misery on the outward journey but, at the same time, he wanted to know everything about her.

'Oh. It was horrible!' She shivered, wrapping her black shawl more tightly around her.

Cole had been ridiculously pleased that she'd gone on wearing the shawl he'd given her, even though she had bought clothes in Lisbon more suitable for travelling in England.

'I'd never seen anything so…so *vile*,' Honor continued, her eyes clouded as she remembered the filth and stench on the crowded decks.

Cole wanted to put his arms around her and tell her

she didn't need to tell him any more, but she was
locked in her memories.

'Patrick was seasick, poor dear,' she said, gaze focussed on the past. 'I was beside myself. I didn't know
what to do.'

'But you made it to Portugal,' said Cole tautly, torn
between his irrational jealousy at Honor's undoubted
affection for her late husband, and his distress at the
idea she'd been so upset she hadn't known what to
do—in his experience Honor *always* knew what to do.
She should never have had to endure such indignities,
he thought fiercely.

'Well, yes.' Honor threw Cole a cautious glance. 'I
did a deal,' she confessed, as if she was admitting to
a serious crime. 'Every day I gave all our rum ration
to the ship's cook, and he lent me a tarpaulin we could
throw over one of the ship's boats. That's how we
travelled to Portugal, in relative privacy and luxury.
And,' she added, determined to make a clean breast of
everything, 'I did some mending and made some
money on the journey.'

She looked sideways at Cole, not sure what kind of
reception her confession would get. She'd always been
proud of her ability to cope, but now her pride was
less important than her need for harmony between
them. Their time together was so limited. She didn't
want it to end with an argument.

He grinned and pulled her towards him, giving her
a quick, hard kiss. Even though it was years ago, he
was relieved she'd had a reasonably comfortable voyage to Portugal.

'Cole!' She pushed him away, embarrassed at being
kissed when others might see them.

'I'm *glad* you managed things so well,' he declared cheerfully.

He didn't mind her taking care of Patrick, he'd spent years watching her do so. But when Honor was his wife, *he* would take care of everything. He was quite certain he would never need Honor to protect him— because he would be protecting her. Still…

'Would you carry me—if I was wounded?' he asked suddenly, and immediately wished the words unsaid. It was a stupid, weak-minded question that made him sound like a sentimental fool.

He regretted asking it even more when she didn't respond with the unequivocal 'yes' he'd expected.

She studied him carefully, little tendrils of hair blowing around her face where they'd escaped from the shawl. He tucked them back inside. Black wasn't her colour. It drained her complexion and made her look paler and more fragile than she was.

'Your legs are so long,' she said at last. 'I'd need a hatchet.'

'To cut my legs off?' He thought she had to be joking, but she looked so serious.

'No, to make a pallet,' she responded seriously. 'What do they call it? A travois. To drag you. I don't think I could carry you, Cole,' she said earnestly. 'Patrick was shorter than me, and you're so much taller— and heavier. But I'm sure I could drag you. Horses can pull much heavier weights than they can carry. I'd have to rig up some sort of harness to go around my chest, only…I haven't got a hatchet.'

Her hazel eyes were wide with anxiety that bordered on panic.

Cole couldn't believe how devastated she was by her lack of foresight. He'd done no more than ask her a hypothetical, slightly ridiculous question, yet it was as though she really was back on the muddy retreat from Salamanca, desperate to find some way of transporting him to safety. He was unbearably moved by her evident distress.

'Sweetheart.' He pulled her into his arms, heedless of witnesses. 'We're in the Bay of Biscay,' he reminded her gently. 'You don't need a hatchet.'

'No.' She pushed back a little, still in his embrace, so that she could look up at him. 'If it seems as if we're about to sink, you must instantly come and find me,' she instructed him fiercely.

She was so solemn and intense it didn't occur to him to laugh.

'Yes, love,' he agreed tenderly.

'If we're involved in a skirmish with a French ship, you will naturally want to take part in our defence,' she informed him. 'But if there's a storm in the night, you must come to my cabin. I would come to you, but you're sharing with Mr Fuller. I don't want to drown with Mr Fuller,' she concluded, frowning fiercely.

'Sweetheart!' Cole just managed to suppress an inappropriate grin. 'We're not going to drown, we're going to Falmouth. But, if the worst comes to the worst, I promise I won't let you drown with Mr Fuller,' he assured her.

'Thank you.' Honor leant against him for a moment, then she gave a horrified gasp. 'Oh, Cole, I'm so sorry!' she exclaimed. 'I forgot about Gifford.'

'That's all right.' Cole stroked reassuringly the black shawl which covered her head. 'Luckily Giff didn't have to drown with Mr Fuller either.'

There was a pause, then Honor said uncertainly, 'That's a terrible thing to say.'

* * *

Cole didn't miss his brother on a day-to-day basis—
he hadn't seen him for several years—but he missed
the idea of Gifford being somewhere in the world. He
wished his father and his brother could have known
Honor. He was sure they would both have loved her.

He was still amazed by how earnestly she'd an-
swered his hasty question about carrying him. And she
didn't want to drown with Mr Fuller! It wasn't her
preference in drowning companions which surprised
him, it was the fact that she'd given so much thought
to the various situations they might encounter. He'd
known she sometimes had romantic ideas about magic,
but could she really visualise all kinds of possibilities
so clearly she could almost be living through them?
Cole couldn't imagine what that might be like. He only
knew Honor had said that believing in magic made life
bearable.

At one time he'd been impatient with her fanciful
notions, but now he knew they were an integral part
of her character. And they were also part of the reason
he loved her so much, even when she was driving him
crazy with her wayward opinions. He decided it was
understandable that she worried about the future, but
he promised himself he would give her the security
and happiness she needed to dream of her magic in
peace.

Honor found a bittersweet pleasure in the rest of the
trip to England. Cole had held her in his arms and
called her 'love', and he'd asked her what she wanted
most in life—but he hadn't talked about their future.
She couldn't believe that she'd unwarily told him she
wanted to marry him and have his babies. The memory
mortified her—and thrilled her, when she recalled his

very positive physical response to her wish. There was
no doubt her words had pleased him. She was sure if
they had been in a more comfortable, private location
he would have made love to her—as tenderly and passionately as he'd made love to her the first time.
Sometimes she dreamed of his lovemaking and woke
hot and aroused to find she was alone. Other times she
couldn't sleep at all, but simply lay wakeful, her body
aching for his touch.

She thought Cole probably meant to keep her as his
mistress after his marriage. It wasn't a role she'd ever
intended to play for any man—but she knew it was
the only way she could be part of Cole's life. He
needed a woman who would give him heirs, and she
couldn't do that. The knowledge hurt her bitterly.
She'd regretted her childless state when she'd been
with Patrick, but then it had only been a dull back-
ground sadness. Now she yearned to have Cole's
baby—and the knowledge that she couldn't was a constant, grinding pain.

She didn't ask him any questions about the future
because she was afraid of his answers. Instead she
lived only for the moment. But she was careful what
she said. She didn't want to provoke his anger again
when they had so little time together.

One day Cole asked Honor if she was ill. She looked
at him in surprise.

'No,' she replied immediately 'Why?'

'You haven't seemed yourself,' he said frowning.

'Oh. No, I'm fine,' she assured him.

He scowled worriedly at her. He could sense a difference in her, despite the fact that they were no longer
at odds with each other. She was quieter, more sub-

dued. Perhaps she was worried about their future. He
wanted to tell her he'd sorted it all out, but he hadn't
yet, so he didn't.

He stroked her hair back from her face. 'We'll reach
Falmouth soon,' he said.

'I know.' She smiled at him.

He glanced round quickly, checking to see if there
was anyone close by. Then he pulled her into his arms
and kissed her. When he released her he was pleased
to see the glow of colour in her cheeks and a new
sparkle in her hazel eyes.

'Everything's going to be fine,' he assured her.
'You'll feel much better when you've got solid ground
beneath your feet again. And I'll feel much better
when I can...kiss you...as slowly and as often as I
like.'

Honor blushed at his unmistakable meaning and
lowered her eyes. Cole found her shy self-
consciousness so endearing he kissed her forehead, his
lips gently caressing her skin.

Later he got out Bridget's letters. If only he could
stay awake long enough to re-read them, they might
give him a clue as to what kind of husband she would
like.

'December...we went to the Pump Room yesterday
to drink the waters. Mrs Howarth introduced me to Mr
Sedgeworth, a gentleman from Derbyshire who is trying to breed an improved sheep. He was most interesting on the different kinds of wool required for different purposes. I had no idea...'

Cole skimmed through a tedious description of sta-
ples and sheep breeds.

'This morning I bought a new hat. Mrs Howarth

says it is most becoming. I trust you are comfortable in your winter quarters…'

'January…this morning I bought a new pair of gloves…'

'February…I bought a length of beautiful muslin…'

Bridget needed a rich man who'd enjoy taking her shopping, Cole decided, exasperated.

'March…I visited Hookham's circulating library in Bond Street. I wished to read one of Mrs Radcliffe's romances, but Mrs Howarth says it is better to live one's adventures, rather than to read them…'

Good for Mrs Howarth, Cole thought. Who the devil was Mrs Howarth? The name sounded familiar. He decided she was probably the woman Bridget's father had hired to be her companion after her mother's death.

Cole laid the letters aside. Bridget clearly hadn't known of Gifford's death when she last wrote. Even now her next letter was probably on its way to him in his winter quarters.

He had little more sense of her after reading her letters than he'd had before. She drank the waters in Bath. She went to Almack's. She visited fashionable shops and libraries in London. She did a lot of shopping. The best he could come up with for her was a man who enjoyed Town life and had a high tolerance for boredom.

But he knew that wasn't fair. No one trying to get a sense of him from his letters would be able to deduce much more than that he could read and write and he was in the army.

For the first time it occurred to him what a difficult situation Bridget had been placed in, trapped in an endless engagement to a man she hardly knew, who had been unflatteringly slow to tie the knot. Had he inadvertently made her the object of pity or gossip? Perhaps he was fortunate that her letters were dull rather than demanding. He decided he must find her a man of wealth, influence and position to salvage her pride.

The sound of the packet's gun signalling for the pratique boat woke Honor early in the morning. She dressed hurriedly and went on deck. Cole was already there, looking towards Falmouth in the grey dawn. Several other passengers joined them, as they waited for the medical inspector to declare it was safe for them to proceed.

Honor gazed at Pendennis Castle and hugged her shawl tightly against the wind. It was the beginning of May, but the early morning air was damp and cold.

'I'll be glad to get off this damn boat,' Cole muttered, and she felt even more chilled.

Cole had made it plain he wanted to make love to her at the first opportunity. But the closer they got to London, the more worried Honor was about allowing him to do so.

The Peninsula had seemed like another world. It had been easy to believe that what she and Cole did there couldn't hurt his fiancée. But now they were back in England, and any gossip which touched Cole would also touch Miss Morton. Honor knew she would have hated it if her husband had kept a mistress. In the cold—very cold—light of dawn, she finally accepted that once they were on English soil she must say goodbye to Cole. She would find her own way back to London.

* * *

The morning was well advanced by the time they
landed at Falmouth. Honor took no part in the arrangements, she simply followed Cole's lead. For the first
time in her adult life, she allowed somebody else to
make her decisions for her. She could imagine the
scornful comments her mother would make if she
knew, but Honor didn't care. She would be fending for
herself soon enough.

'Thank God we're shot of that lot.' Cole breathed a
sigh of relief when they'd finally seen the last of their
fellow passengers. 'I didn't fancy rattling around in a
mail coach all the way to London with any of them!'

Honor forced a smile. She'd been impressed by the
efficiency with which Cole had separated them from
their erstwhile travelling companions. She was grateful
for the privacy of the private parlour he'd arranged for
them in a comfortable inn.

'I think you're being a bit hard on poor Lieutenant
Soper,' she said placatingly, guiltily aware that her
only real grudge against her fellow passengers had
been their unwitting intrusion into her limited time
with Cole. 'Besides, I don't think he can afford the
mail.'

'I can't imagine why anyone would want to,' said
Cole frankly. 'The only time I ever travelled in one of
those contraptions it made me ill!'

'And you a hardened campaigner!' Honor tried to
match his bantering tone, but she found it difficult to
speak at all. She was numb with awareness of what
she must soon say to him. Would he accept her decision—or would their time together end with another
argument? She couldn't bear it if the last words Cole
said to her were angry.

Cole grinned. 'Fortunately I was never asked to go

into battle under the Post Office colours. I'll hire a post chaise and we'll travel to London like civilised people. It's not as if we're in a hurry.'

'No.' Honor's throat tightened so much she couldn't swallow.

His joke about the Post Office colours heightened her sense of alienation. Cole was no longer wearing his uniform. It was strange to see him in a sober black coat and neatly tied cravat. He had already taken the first steps towards his new life. She looked away because she didn't want him to see how upset she was. This parting would be hard enough without her tears to make it worse for both of them.

'Sweetheart?' Cole crossed swiftly to her side. He took her cup and saucer away from her and dropped on one knee beside her chair.

She looked down at his strong hands holding hers in a comforting grasp and blinked quickly.

'Everything will work out,' he promised her earnestly. 'Don't worry, love. I'll take care of everything.'

He'd called her love again, Honor thought distractedly. How could she say goodbye to him when he called her love?

'I can't share you with Miss Morton,' she said jerkily. 'I don't think Miss Morton would want to share you with me. It's not right for you to take me to London, Cole. If Miss Morton finds out, it will hurt her. It would hurt me,' she whispered. 'I will make my own way to London,' she concluded, in a firmer voice. 'It's time we said goodbye.'

Chapter Eight

'No!' Cole's response was emphatic and immediate. 'Under no circumstances! You're coming to London with me.'

Honor shook her head, trying to keep her lip from trembling. She couldn't bring herself to meet his fierce eyes. 'You made a promise to Miss Morton,' she whispered doggedly. 'I've been thinking and thinking…when we were together in Spain and Portugal, that was a different place and time—perhaps what we did was excusable. But now you're home. Now you have to honour your obligations to Miss Morton and your family.'

Cole stared at her without speaking. She risked a glimpse at his austere, angular face. She knew he was in the grip of strong emotion, but she couldn't read the expression in his eyes.

'I don't mean to criticise you,' she said anxiously, suddenly afraid he thought she was condemning his behaviour, when she knew she was as much to blame as he was, 'only to make sure that you understand that I know that from now on things will have to be different.'

His stern expression relaxed into a smile. 'That was a very complicated sentence, sweetheart,' he said tenderly. 'You look tired. I think you ought to rest before we set off. We'll spend the night here, and leave in the morning.'

'Cole!' Honor was exasperated, frustrated, and perilously close to tears. 'Weren't you *listening*? We can't do this any more. *I* can't…' Her voice faltered.

In one smooth movement Cole rose, picked her up and sat down with her on his lap. She was startled into forgetting what she'd been saying. He lifted her so easily. She loved the feel of his arms around her, his muscular thighs beneath her—but she was annoyed at how easily he'd dismissed her heartfelt concerns.

He kissed her cheek. 'I won't ask you to share me with Bridget,' he murmured against her sensitive skin. His lips teasingly caressed the corner of her mouth.

Despite herself, her pulse began to race and she turned her head to meet his kiss. As she did so, she felt passion rise within him. They were alone now, just as Cole had wanted them to be on the packet boat.

His mouth was hungry as he found hers. One hand cupped the back of her head, the other rested on the curve of her hip, holding her possessively against him. She clutched his lapel like an anchor, so overwhelmed by the force of his desire she felt dizzy. But this was *not* what she'd planned, and his patronising response to her painful effort to do the right thing frustrated her.

She dragged her mouth away from his and wrenched herself out of his arms so forcefully she nearly fell on the floor. She stumbled upright and turned to face him.

'Don't!' she gasped, her cheeks blazing with indignant colour.

'What the devil...?' He thrust to his feet, shock and anger in his own angular features.

'Don't treat me as if I'm half-witted and vaporish!' she snapped at him.

'I did not!' Cole was caught up in a furious maelstrom of confusion and thwarted arousal.

'Yes, you did!' she interrupted him fiercely. 'You acted as if neither my opinions nor my morals are important to you. *"That was a very complicated sentence, sweetheart"*,' she mimicked bitterly. 'How pea-brained do you think I am?'

'Don't be so melodramatic!' Cole retaliated irritably, fighting to control his temper. His physical frustration, combined with his awareness of the problems which beset them, threatened to boil over into furious words, scalding them both in the process.

He clenched his fists, bit back the hasty words he was about to utter, and glared at Honor.

She was standing at bay on the other side of the parlour, defiance, anger and hurt in her hazel eyes. Her blunt announcement that they must part had shaken him, and the determination with which she'd wrenched herself out of his arms felt like the most bitter rejection.

'I can't be your mistress,' she said breathlessly. 'I won't! And you made a promise to Miss Morton...to your father. You have to honour that.' Her mouth twisted at what she was saying. She was, after all, named for such honour.

Cole watched her for several long minutes as he battled to clear his mind and control his emotions. He struggled to calm his ragged breathing and reminded himself that, despite her apparent rejection of him, Honor loved him and wanted to be his wife. A breach between them would drive her close to despair. He knew that, if he walked out of this room before they'd resolved their quarrel, Honor would be gone by the time he returned.

'I did not intend to belittle your worries,' he said stiffly, as he realised that was exactly what he'd done.

He hadn't wanted to admit that he still didn't know exactly how he was going to extricate himself from his engagement, so he'd brushed aside her anxieties instead.

'But you did,' she said steadily. 'And you behaved as if my integrity wasn't important to you.' She touched her slender fingers to her lips, still swollen from his kisses.

Cole opened his mouth to point out she hadn't objected to his lovemaking before, but left the words unsaid. He dimly remembered she seemed to think it made a difference that they were back in England. He thought the distinction was spurious. Morally it made no difference where they were, but on a practical level she had a point. Gossip about his conduct in England might be potentially more damaging to his cause than rumours about his activities in the Peninsula.

'I've never doubted your integrity,' he said quietly. 'Or your courage, or your determination to do the right thing.'

He saw her eyes suddenly glisten with unshed tears and a knife twisted in his gut. This whole mess was hurting Honor badly, and it was his duty—his eagerly embraced duty—to take care of her. The trick, he thought suddenly, might be to take care of her without offending the fierce independence he'd always admired in her. Like a man taming an unbroken horse, he must coax her to submit to his will without breaking her spirit.

'What are your plans?' he asked calmly.

He knew he ought to tell her his own intentions, relieve her of some of her anxieties, but he still hoped to present the solution to her on a platter, gift-wrapped and be-ribboned—Bridget Morton's marriage to a rich and eligible bachelor.

Honor drew in a deep breath.

'I must…Patrick wanted me…' she began.

Cole tensed. He still suffered occasional moments of jealousy when Patrick was mentioned.

'My mother,' Honor said more strongly. 'I must make peace with my mother.'

'Peace?' Cole questioned sharply.

'I have not spoken to her, or had contact with her, since Patrick was coerced into the army,' said Honor steadily. 'She condemned me for marrying him, I blamed her for…' She didn't finish.

'I see.' Cole's eyes narrowed. 'You mean to stay with her?' Honor's mother was a rather shadowy presence in his mind. 'Is she… Will you be welcome?' He'd been about to ask whether the former maidservant was respectable, but decided it would be unnecessarily provocative.

Honor smiled without amusement. 'Susannah will be pleased to see me,' she said. 'She'll be *so* pleased to see me,' she whispered, and her lips twisted.

She was very close to breaking down, Cole realised, and pressed on quickly with his questions.

'Is your estrangement from your mother the reason you didn't want to come home?' he asked gently.

Honor swallowed convulsively, and then nodded. It was clearly hard for her to speak.

'Is there anyone else?' Cole asked. 'Anyone else you could stay with who would make you welcome?'

He'd meant to ask Malcolm Anderson to find somewhere suitable for her to stay while he sorted out his affairs, but it might be better for all concerned if Honor wasn't living under the protection of his family while he dealt with the Mortons.

Honor brushed her hand across her eyes.

'Lady Durrington,' she whispered. 'She's been writing to me ever since I left England. I have an open invitation to visit her...'

Cole scoured his mind for any memories of Lady Durrington. As far as he could recall, she was a respectable woman, married to a man of unimpeachable integrity. Lady Durrington would do nicely, Cole decided.

'Very well,' he said firmly. 'We'll go to London. You'll make peace with your mother, but it would probably be best if you stay with Lady Durrington—'

'I couldn't impose upon her!' Honor protested, interrupting.

'I'm sure she won't find it an imposition,' Cole assured her, his voice softening.

'I'll have to find something to do,' Honor said distractedly, taking a few paces around the room. 'I must find work.'

'As an actress?' Cole kept his voice calm. He'd wondered if Honor's love of the theatre would be another bone of contention between them. He didn't want his wife performing on the public stage.

'No, no,' she said impatiently. 'I enjoyed acting, but the rest...'

She stopped pacing and turned to gaze at him, the energy which had briefly animated her dissolving.

Strands of her sun-bleached hair fell in disarray around her slim face. She looked lost and bereft, and very fragile.

'I want you to be happy,' she said, her voice faltering. 'I know you'll be a good landlord and…husband. And I'll be fine, too. There aren't any wolves in England.' She tried to smile.

'Honor.' He closed the distance between them, careful not to provoke her into withdrawing. He put his hands gently on her upper arms. She stood frozen for a heartbeat, her eyes wide, her nostrils flaring slightly—then her self-control melted. She wrapped her arms around him, holding him tightly.

Cole closed his eyes, unutterably relieved to have her back in his arms, and praying she wouldn't push him away again. He stroked her hair, careful not to turn the comforting embrace into something more passionate.

Honor knew it was foolish to cling to Cole this way, but she couldn't help herself. When he'd calmly asked her to tell him her plans she'd felt as if her world had crumpled around her. She'd expected him to argue with her, not let her go so easily. It wasn't reasonable to expect him to love her as much as she loved him, and it was certainly better for him that he didn't—but it hurt so much.

Perhaps he'd never meant to make her his mistress, now they were back in England. She went cold at the thought. She'd made a complete fool of herself over him yet perhaps, even now, he was growing impatient with her clinging-ivy behaviour. She loosened her grip on him and tried to step away, but he wouldn't let her.

'Sweetheart…' he brushed his lips across her forehead '…I won't ask you to be my mistress, but that doesn't stop me loving you—or wanting to care for you.'

She sagged against him, so limp with relief she would have fallen if he hadn't supported her. He'd never before told her he loved her so explicitly.

'I thought…'

'What?' He cradled her tenderly.

'I don't know,' she admitted, resting her head on his shoulder. 'I've never felt so confused.'

'Trust me,' he murmured. 'I'll try not to compromise your principles, but I can't let you go, love.'

'You must.' She lifted her head to look at him.

'Shush.' He glanced around, then guided her to the chair he'd located. He made her sit down, then dropped on one knee beside her. 'You love me,' he said confidently. 'I know you do. You'd rather drown with me than Mr Fuller.'

Honor smiled waterily. 'Don't make fun of me,' she begged.

'I'm not.' He held her gaze steadily, his eyes very serious. 'Sweetheart, I know what sacrifices you are prepared to make for me. I am now a wealthy man. It is no sacrifice at all for me to provide for you. No—' he squeezed her hand as she started to protest '—I know how independent you are. But I want—I need you to realise that this is just as important to me as your independence is to you. I can't bear to hear you talk about finding work, or wondering whether your mother or Lady Durrington will make you welcome in their homes. I will give you a home of your own. And you will never have to worry about scandal, because you will never have done anything to provoke it.'

Honor stared at him, hearing the absolute sincerity

in his voice. Her immediate instinct was to reject his offer, but then she hesitated.

'It would be cruel to deny me this,' he said quietly. 'You would drag me to safety on a travois if I were wounded. Even if we never make love again—even if we never see each other again after we reach London—let me provide for your future.'

Honor gazed at him, caught in the intensity of the moment. Her father had pawned his watch for her mother, she remembered suddenly, and her proud, independent mother had accepted the gift. Love meant taking, as well as giving.

'Yes,' she whispered.

'Thank God.' Cole's response was soft and heartfelt. He leant forward, briefly resting his head against her slight breasts. In his own mind, she'd just agreed to be his wife—he had no intention of providing a home for her he wouldn't share—but he wasn't yet ready to tell her that.

She looked down wonderingly at his dishevelled hair and smoothed it gently with her fingers. It was a curiously intimate moment, even though she was sure they'd just said goodbye. She wondered if this was how it had been for her parents. Feeling so unimaginably close, yet knowing they had to part.

Cole lifted his head. 'We'll go—' He broke off, suddenly perplexed. 'Does your mother live in London?' he asked, realising again how little he knew of the woman.

Honor smiled slightly. 'Yes,' she said. 'So does Lady Durrington.'

'Good,' said Cole briskly. 'We'll travel to London by easy stages. You can speak to your mother, and either stay with her or Lady Durrington, while I make arrangements.'

'I'm not sure if we should travel together,' Honor protested, although her fingers tightened around his. 'Miss Morton…'

'Patrick asked me to take care of you,' Cole reminded her, ruthlessly disposing of her objection. 'I don't think he'd want me to abandon you in Cornwall. We don't have to draw attention to ourselves, sweetheart.'

'Well…' Honor hesitated.

'Let me worry about Bridget,' said Cole firmly. 'Now, you do look tired, love. I think we should stay here tonight, and set out tomorrow morning—unless you're in a hurry to talk to your mother.' He smiled at her.

'Let's leave tomorrow,' said Honor, after a few seconds' thought.

The journey to London tried Cole's self-control to the limits. He was alone with Honor in the privacy of the chaise for hours, yet he felt honour-bound not to take advantage of the situation. Of course, if he told her he was going to marry her, that would put things in a different light—but what if it took him a while to extricate himself from his betrothal to Bridget Morton? He was looking forward to Honor bearing his child, but not before he'd got his ring safely on her finger. On the other hand, perhaps it wasn't absolutely necessary to deal with Bridget before he married Honor.

He sat watching her, opposing arguments scrambling around in his tormented mind, as they trundled on their way to London.

* * *

He was so close, Honor thought, twining her slim
fingers together in her lap. She was breathlessly aware
of his virile body only inches from hers. She could
feel his burning gaze resting on her face. She risked a
quick glance at him, flushed scarlet at the intensity in
his vivid blue eyes, and turned to stare blindly out of
the window. How on earth would they make it to
London? Even on the packet boat she hadn't been this
aware of him. But she hadn't been truly alone with
him since the day he'd told her Gifford was dead, since
the night she'd spent in his quarters—in his bed.

Her heartbeat quickened as she remembered the way
he'd made love to her—and her own abandoned response to him. Her fingers locked painfully as she tried
to control the direction of her thoughts. It was only
safe to think of such things when she was alone—not
when she was sitting less that three feet away from the
man who made her blood burn.

She was so hot, her skin felt as if it were on fire.
Her mouth was dry. She licked her lips and heard his
quick intake of breath. Sensuous heat began to throb
in her body. Her breasts tightened, her knees trembled.
She was glad she was sitting down, if she'd been
standing she would have melted in a pool of desire
beside his glossy boots. Which would have put her in
an excellent position to admire his powerful thighs
and—

She bit her lip, desperately trying to hold back the
hysterical giggle which threatened to overcome her.
She was on her way to London, to give her beloved
to another woman—why on earth was she dangerously
close to being overcome by rampant lust?

She kept her gaze firmly on the passing countryside
but, out of the corner of her eye, she saw him move

closer to her. A flame of excited desire leapt through her. She caught her breath, her body coiled with eager anticipation of his touch…and the coach rolled sedately into an inn yard.

Honor could have screamed with frustration. Cole's muffled curse as he sat back suggested he felt the same way.

They delayed at the inn long enough to eat a midday meal. Honor chewed thoughtfully on a mouthful of delicious pie, and decided she'd better come up with a distraction if they were to reach London with their integrity even minimally intact.

'I could have a small shop,' she announced, when they were once more sitting in the chaise.

'A *what*?' The words shot out of Cole as if from a gun.

'A shop,' she repeated, glancing at him cautiously. His expression was so stunned she decided it was safe to look at him more fully.

'Why?' he demanded tautly. 'I said—'

'I know,' she interrupted, a conciliating note in her voice. 'But I thought…that is…you said you'd give me a house,' she said tentatively, stroking her dress smooth across her lap in a nervous gesture. Then she saw Cole's eyes following the movement of her hands and hastily folded them demurely. 'If you gave me the means to set up a shop, I would feel less beholden,' she continued, 'and, if I made a success of it, you might even get some return on your investment. Profit, I mean,' she said brightly. 'But, of course, it would take me a while to establish a successful business,' she added warningly.

She looked up and discovered Cole was staring at

her with his mouth open. After a few seconds he closed it and swallowed.

'What—what kind of shop?' he croaked.

'A dress shop.' She smiled at him, already warming to the idea. 'I'm an excellent needlewoman, and in the past I always designed my own gowns. I don't know much about business, and it would take a while to build up a fashionable clientele, but I'm sure Lady Durrington would be pleased to recommend me.'

'You want to become a modish dressmaker?' Cole said disbelievingly.

'But, Cole, I can't be your pensioner for the rest of my life,' Honor said earnestly, responding to an objection he hadn't yet made explicit.

'I don't want you to be my pensioner!' he declared passionately, then stopped abruptly, as if he'd caught himself short before he said any more.

'I know...I know you want me to live in comfort and security,' said Honor quickly. 'I understand, and I'm so grateful. But I wasn't brought up to be a well-dressed ornament, Cole. I must have rational occupation to fill my time—especially since...especially...' Her voice faltered.

Especially since she believed she would be alone, Cole realised. His rising anger abated. Sometimes he found Honor's determination to be self-sufficient frustrating, but he also respected her for it. He had no intention of letting her set up her own business, but he was quite happy to play along with her for now.

'Are you sure you want to be a dressmaker?' he asked, frowning at her. 'You would have to flatter your empty-headed customers. Not an easy task for someone of your...outspokenness.'

'I can be tactful!' She flushed indignantly. 'And not

all women are empty-headed!' She rose to his bait as he'd known she would. 'And I've met many gentleman who cannot cope with anything more taxing than the set of their coat and the latest scandal.'

'So have I,' Cole agreed, aggravatingly unruffled.

She glared at him. 'You are deliberately trying to provoke me!' she said accusingly.

'Certainly not,' he denied, schooling his angular features into an expression of innocence. 'I merely wondered, since you are so at home with horses, whether you might not find blacksmithing more to your taste.'

'You think I should become a lady *blacksmith*?' Honor gasped, stunned at his suggestion. 'Getting hot and dirty in a forge? Just because I waded through the mud in Spain, doesn't mean I *like* being filthy and smelly and—'

Her eyes narrowed as she saw Cole was trying to suppress laughter.

'You beast!' she exclaimed indignantly. 'You needn't think you're going to divert me from my plans with your ridiculous suggestions. I'll be the most successful dressmaker in London. Just you wait!' She folded her arms crossly and glared out of the window.

Cole grinned. 'How will you set about it?' he asked, willing to indulge her because she'd responded so exactly as he'd known she would.

Honor looked at him suspiciously. 'I know you aren't taking this seriously,' she said.

'If it's important to you, it's important to me,' he replied soothingly.

Honor hesitated, not entirely happy with Cole's patronising manner. She was tempted not to reply to his question, but then she decided it would be more dignified if she dealt with it in a businesslike way.

'I will need to familiarise myself with the latest modes,' she said slowly, organising her thoughts. 'Then,' she began to tick points off on her fingers, 'premises in a fashionable area of London. Reliable seamstresses. The patronage of one or two influential ladies—the kind who set trends, not follow them. And the kind who pay their bills,' she added drily. She frowned. 'Men have gone out of business, waiting for the Quality to settle their debts,' she observed, tapping her fingers together consideringly. 'Perhaps I would do better to aim at a less modish and more reliable clientele. When we get to London I must look around and see what opportunities there are,' she decided.

Cole studied her, fascinated by the changing expressions that played across her face as she stared out of the window with unfocussed eyes. She was deep in contemplation, planning her future as a dressmaker. He felt a mixture of respect and discomfort at the single-mindedness with which she set about the task. He didn't like the way she could so easily exclude him from her future, yet, if he didn't tell her his true intentions, he could hardly blame her.

He comforted himself with remembering the way she'd rested in his arms on the packet boat—and the wish she'd made that night on an imaginary moon. To marry him, take care of him…and have his babies. That was what she really wanted.

Honor tried to concentrate on the practical details of her scheme, but she couldn't stop thinking how empty she'd feel when Cole was no longer part of her life. He would be married to Miss Morton. Perhaps Miss Morton—Lady Raven as she'd be then—would even come to buy a dress from Honor. Honor closed her eyes against the hurtful vision and struggled not to let her feelings show in her face.

They weren't in a hurry, and it took them three days to reach the borders of Hampshire. Three days of travelling in close proximity to Honor without touching her were enough for Cole. It was more than flesh and blood could bear to have her sitting so close and not drag her into his arms and out of her clothes. At least during the years of torment in Spain and Portugal he hadn't known exactly how rewarding it would be to make love to her. Now he knew—he remembered in excruciatingly wonderful detail at the most inopportune moments—and he wanted it again. Right now.

Unfortunately, Honor knew that, and she'd taken a moral stand not to let anything improper happen between them. Occasionally she even mentioned Miss Morton when she was particularly afraid he might be overcome with ardour.

He'd gritted his teeth and acceded to her determination to distract him. They'd talked about anything and everything—Honor knew all about Cole's childhood exploits with Gifford and Anthony, Cole knew about Honor's acting career and some amazing details about her projected dressmaking plans—but enough was enough.

'I think I'll ride beside the chaise today,' he said at breakfast on the fourth morning.

'Ride?' Honor echoed, looking at him in bewilderment. He seemed tired and on edge. 'Why?'

'Dammit, Honor!' he growled. 'I'm not used to being cooped up in a box all day. I'd rather ride.'

'*You'd* rather ride!' she exclaimed, immediately roused by his words. 'What about me? You want me to be shut up in that horrible carriage while you enjoy yourself?'

'It's a very luxurious carriage!' Cole briefly allowed himself to be sidetracked. 'Much more comfortable than the mail coach.'

'But the choice is apparently not between the chaise and the mail, but the chaise and horseback,' Honor pointed out. 'I think it's an excellent idea. Why don't you see what's available while I finish getting ready?' She stood up and whisked out of the parlour.

Cole grinned at the closing door. Until this trip with Honor, he'd had no idea how devious he could be. Before breakfast he'd already hired two fine riding horses and made arrangements for the chaise, loaded with their baggage, to meet them at an inn within easy marching distance that evening.

Honor put on the new riding habit she'd bought in Lisbon and looked at herself in the mirror. It was very plain, almost severe in its styling, but the soft moss green enhanced her hazel eyes and flattered her more than the black shawl. She smoothed her hair self-consciously, then pulled a face at herself in the mirror. It was foolish to feel so jittery and excited at the prospect of riding with Cole. They'd ridden from Ciudad Rodrigo to Lisbon without anything untoward happening, and now they were headed towards Cole's fiancée in London. It was definitely no more than an opportunity to shake off the cobwebs from the post-chaise.

She quickly packed some essential items to take with her. She was far too old a campaigner to set off, even for an innocent ride through the countryside, without at least a minimum of equipment.

* * *

It was a beautiful May morning. The blue sky was clear and the sun was warm and comforting. Honor smiled with pleasure at the lush green leaves all around her. Dew still sparkled on the grass and jewelled a spider's web in the hedge beside the road.

'I can hear a blackbird!' she exclaimed delightedly.

Cole smiled at her. Even though he had a foolishly sentimental attachment to her black shawl, he was pleased she was wearing something more warmly colourful. She looked poised and elegant on the grey mare he'd chosen for her.

'What a beautiful day,' she said, lifting her face to the sun. 'What a beautiful way to come home.'

'I didn't realise how much I had missed England until I came back,' Cole admitted.

'It seems odd that you're not riding Corvinus,' Honor observed. 'I hope he doesn't mind the sea passage.'

'Joe will take care of him,' Cole replied easily.

'Oh, yes,' Honor agreed. She threaded her fingers idly through the grey mare's mane. 'Perhaps I should breed horses instead,' she said thoughtfully.

'Instead of pandering to the whims of fashionable matrons?' Cole enquired, raising his eyebrows.

'I'm not completely set on that plan,' said Honor.

'I thought you were.' He was surprised.

'I was trying it out in my mind,' she said, with dignity. 'Clothes are something I know a lot about, but I also know quite a bit about horses. I could do it, I think. I have to consider all the possibilities,' she added, seeing the dubious expression in his eyes.

'So I see,' he replied drily. It suddenly occurred to him that perhaps she could contemplate such wildly different futures for herself because she didn't really want either of them. The idea cheered him enormously.

In the chaise he'd talked about his boyish pastimes with his brother, but now he started to tell her about his family estates. Eventually he admitted he knew next to nothing about land management, and he was gratified by her unhesitating confidence in him.

'I believe you'll be an excellent landlord,' she said positively. 'You know how to command men, and you know how to use each man to take the greatest advantage of his particular strengths. I often noticed it in the regiment.'

'You did?' Cole was enormously pleased, and slightly bashful at her praise.

'Yes.' She frowned thoughtfully between her horse's ears. 'I'm not sure the men felt they knew you—not the way they understood some of the officers.' She smiled mischievously and Cole suddenly realised she had an entirely different perspective on his fellow officers than he did. He was greatly intrigued but—almost—too dignified to question her further on the subject.

'They didn't know me?' he prompted her, as casually as he could.

'They did know you,' she corrected him. 'They knew the important things. They knew you were consistent and fair in your discipline and punishment. They knew you led from the front, not the rear. They knew you'd never turn sick soldiers out of their billet so you could have a comfortable night's sleep,' she added in an acid comment on one of his fellow officers. 'They knew you appreciated their efforts and their pain and suffering. That's why they gave you their loyalty and obedience.'

She turned to look at Cole, the May sunshine gilding her blonde hair.

'You don't need to know the details of tenancy agreements to be a good landlord,' she said quietly, reaching out her hand to him. 'You need to know how to deal honestly and fairly with other people. You need to be clever enough to realise when they're trying to cheat you, but you should also be compassionate when they are genuinely suffering hardship. You have all the qualities you need to be successful in your new life.'

Cole took her hand, very moved by her heartfelt testimonial.

She smiled at him. 'Another man might be contemplating what a dash he was going to cut in Town with such a grand inheritance,' she teased him gently, 'not worrying about his unexpected responsibilities.'

'Perhaps.' Cole nudged his mount closer to Honor's mare. He was enchanted by the picture she made in the spring sunshine, earnestly assuring him of his worth.

Honor felt Cole's fingers tighten around hers. The light in his eyes was warm and very intimate. She caught her breath as his gaze focussed on her mouth. He wanted to kiss her. He was going to kiss her—but it really wasn't right. They'd been talking about his inheritance. Miss Morton was part of it.

She silently urged the mare to move forward, forcing Cole to relinquish her hand. Their separation filled her with disappointment, but she was sure she'd done the right thing. Miss Morton wouldn't like it if she knew Cole was kissing another woman in the Hampshire countryside.

'What does she look like?' Honor asked abruptly.

'I can't remember,' Cole admittedly sheepishly, knowing exactly who Honor was talking about.

'You can't remember?' Honor echoed in amazement.

'It's a long time since I last saw her,' said Cole defensively. 'She's got brown hair, I think.' He hesitated. 'She's just an average female,' he said helplessly, aware his description hardly did justice to Bridget, but unable to improve upon it.

'Average female!' Honor exclaimed, torn between laughter and heartbreak. Cole was going to spend the rest of his life with a woman he could barely remember. 'What colour are her eyes?'

He scowled thoughtfully for a few moments. 'Damned if I know,' he admitted eventually. 'Can't picture them at all.'

'Perhaps you just aren't very observant of such things,' said Honor, looking away from him. 'What colour are my eyes?' she burst out, cursing herself for asking such a stupid question.

'Agate green and gold, with flecks of russet,' he said instantly, smiling at the back of her head.

Honor swallowed a sob at his unexpectedly poetic description of her hazel eyes. Given his prosaic description of Miss Morton she'd expected…she didn't know what she'd expected.

'What colour are my eyes?' he asked softly.

'Blue,' she whispered, still not looking at him, unable to put into words the light his vivid blue eyes illuminated in her soul whenever he looked at her. 'Schools,' she said unsteadily to change the subject.

'Schools?' Cole immediately pictured a bevy of blue-and gold-eyed children but decided that, in the present circumstances, Honor probably wasn't talking about their future offspring.

'Lady Durrington wrote to me that Lord Durrington had set up schools on his estates for the children of the farm labourers,' Honor said more coherently. 'He pays them a small allowance to attend, though of course they have to demonstrate a genuine desire to profit from the experience. He believes that everyone should have an opportunity to better themselves.'

'He's an unusual man,' said Cole slowly. 'And somewhat out of step with the rest of the world. I look forward to meeting him.'

'Meeting him?' Honor was surprised.

'Sweetheart, I'm delivering you into his wife's care,' Cole reminded her. 'It's quite likely I'm going to meet the man.'

'Oh.' She hadn't thought of that. 'I've never met him,' she said. 'I always wanted to, but somehow it was never convenient. Cole, I really don't think I should stay with Lady Durrington. I mean, I know I haven't been on good terms with Mama for a while, but I'm sure she'll offer me house-room. And if she doesn't want me, I can go to another inn. I don't want to embarrass the Durringtons or cause a scandal for you and Miss Morton.'

'Your conduct has never been scandalous,' said Cole quietly. 'Whatever scandal may arise from our situation in the future, you are not to blame, Honor. And you are not to take the weight of it upon your shoulders. Promise me.'

'I...'

He reached over and brought the mare to a standstill beside his mount. Then he looked deep into her eyes.

'Promise me,' he repeated, his voice very deep.

'Honor, I will not keep a wife and a mistress at the same time. And I will do everything I can to resolve this entanglement with as little pain and public embarrassment as possible for everyone concerned, but whatever remains is my burden—not yours or Bridget's. And I will not permit you to stay in a public inn,' he added autocratically. 'It may be best if I ask Malcolm to arrange things after all.'

Honor barely heard his last words, she was too busy struggling to divine the meaning behind his earlier declaration. Was he really implying he might end his betrothal to Miss Morton? Surely not. But.. 'resolve this entanglement'…? That sounded much more complicated than simply making her his pensioner and marrying Miss Morton.

She blinked and looked away. She ought to ask him to explain his meaning, but she lacked the courage. Surely he wasn't intending to marry *her*? He was already committed to Bridget. Bridget who was respectable, suitable, and could give him the heirs he needed. Even if he were free, Honor knew she couldn't marry him, because she couldn't bear him children.

'Promise me,' he insisted.

'Yes,' she whispered, not at all sure what she was promising.

Soon after midday they found a pleasant inn and ate a leisurely meal. In the afternoon they abandoned the road for less-frequented paths.

'Are you sure we won't get lost?' Honor said dubiously.

Cole raised his eyebrows at her. 'Are you doubting my sense of direction?' he asked imperiously. 'Wellington thinks quite well of it.'

'I know that,' she said, flustered. 'But I haven't got any, so if you *do* get lost, we'll probably be stuck in Hampshire for ever.'

Cole stared at her, his grin broadening as he contemplated her admission.

'You haven't got a sense of direction!' he exclaimed. 'Good God, woman! You're a seasoned campaigner. You must have some. Otherwise you'd have lost the regiment when you went out foraging for food.'

He knew that, like most of the soldiers' wives, Honor had been adept at discovering and purchasing food from the local people. There were a number of army regulations restricting the practice, but Honor had always managed to escape the sharp eye of the Provost Marshall.

She sighed. 'I did—twice,' she admitted ruefully. 'Once Maggie Foster found me, and once one of the goat boys rescued me. Why do you think I stuck to the regiment so tightly?'

'Honor!' Cole had been joking, but now he was thoroughly shaken at the possibility she might have been cast adrift in hostile surroundings. 'I didn't know…'

'Of course not!' She laughed at herself. 'I wasn't going to advertise my stupidity. After the second time I did a deal with Luis. Whenever I needed to forage, he delegated care of his goats to Pedro and came with me. He's a natural scout—and he has a wonderful sense of direction.'

Cole looked at her, remembering how often he'd seen her in the company of the ragged Portuguese goat boy. They'd made a formidable team. Until the last retreat to Ciudad Rodrigo, Honor had always managed to find food for Patrick and herself.

'Do you know how to read the stars?' he demanded abruptly.

'No,' she admitted.

'Have you got a compass?'

'No.' She bit back a smile at his frown.

'Can you read a map?'

'I don't know,' said Honor cautiously.

'Our maps of the Peninsula were very unreliable at first,' Cole observed, 'but you should have some idea of how to use one. Good God, woman!' he said forcefully. 'What is the point of rigging up a travois, if you don't know which direction to drag me in?'

'I was hoping you'd regain consciousness long enough to tell me,' Honor murmured, secretly delighted that he'd entered so fully into her imaginings.

'I'll start teaching you about the stars tonight,' said Cole decisively. 'In the meantime...' He paused, momentarily stumped at the prospect of teaching Honor a skill he instinctively possessed.

'Which way's London?' he asked.

'Um...that way,' Honor pointed hopefully along the narrow track they'd been following. 'Then why are we going that way?' she demanded, when she saw the negative response in Cole's eyes.

'Because otherwise we'd have to walk on water,' he replied, a teasing light in his eyes as he nodded to the stream that meandered on their left. 'We're taking a slightly circuitous route,' he added carelessly. 'Now, the sun's in the sky and it's about three o'clock. Which way's north?'

Honor just looked at him.

'You must have some idea!' he exclaimed. 'Within ninety degrees, say.'

'What's ninety degrees got to do with anything?' Honor asked, confused.

'It's a quarter of a full circle—or the compass,' he explained. 'I was allowing you forty-five degrees of error in either direction.'

Honor opened her mouth, then closed it again. She'd rarely felt so bewildered in her life.

'Goodness,' she said inadequately.

Cole grinned and pulled his compass out of his pocket. He flipped it open and laid it in her hand.

She looked down, fascinated by the shivering needle.

'That's north!' she said, pointing triumphantly. 'I still don't know where London is, though,' she admitted.

'No,' Cole agreed easily. 'Unless you've got some idea where we are now, you won't. And it's important to remember the compass doesn't show true north—it shows magnetic north.'

Honor stared at him in consternation and he laughed.

'I'll teach you,' he said.

Cole had inherited his father's natural curiosity, and he was a good teacher. He showed Honor how to use a compass and told her about his father's experiments, recalling some of his happiest boyhood memories as he did so.

Honor became so engrossed in her lesson that she didn't notice the passage of time until early evening—when she realised they were nowhere near any form of human habitation.

'I thought we were spending the night at the King's Head,' she said suspiciously, looking around at the place they'd fetched up in.

'We're headed in the right direction,' said Cole blandly. 'We just haven't arrived yet. What with your navigational lessons, we dawdled more than I'd anticipated.'

Honor looked around. There was an abandoned building, overgrown with weeds and brambles beside a clear flowing stream. A willow sighed into the rippling water, gilded by evening sunlight. Behind her an old, forgotten orchard of apple trees was laden with warmly flushed blossom.

'We could reach the King's Head by nightfall?' she said uncertainly.

'But these horses aren't trained for long marches,' Cole objected. 'They need rest.'

'You knew this place was here?' Honor accused him.

He smiled and refused to admit his culpability. He simply dismounted and raised his hands to lift Honor down from her saddle.

She hesitated, then slid down into his arms. He'd been so patient and relaxed while he'd been teaching her, it made her love him even more, and all afternoon she'd wondered whether he'd truly meant he intended to marry her. Of course, she knew he couldn't—and shouldn't. But even the remote possibility had given an extra glow to the beautiful day.

She looked up at him, half-expecting him to kiss her, but he set her gently aside.

'Time to set up camp,' he said briskly. 'Shouldn't take long for two such old hands.'

They selected a spot near the ruins, then took care

of the horses. Honor was surprised and pleased that Cole didn't object to her looking after her mare.

She was surprised and suspicious when she discovered that, between them, they had all the essential utensils to set up a comfortable bivouac. That morning, she'd assumed it was just habit which had prompted Cole to use his Hussar saddle, complete with valise, for their ride—now she wasn't so sure…

As long as it didn't rain, they could happily sleep in the open. She contemplated the ruin, then decided to investigate it more closely. It only required a short inspection to assure her that the remaining walls and roof were quite secure, and would provide adequate shelter if the weather changed.

She tried to remember if Cole had ever described any boyhood adventures in this locality, because he'd certainly known about this place.

A pistol shot, fired nearby, jolted her out of her musings. She spun round, frantically searching her surroundings for trouble. She'd momentarily forgotten she was no longer in a war-torn country.

'Cole!' she shouted urgently.

'I'm here.' His deep voice was calm and reassuring. A moment later she saw him striding towards her through the twilight, a limp rabbit dangling from one hand.

'Supper,' he announced. 'Will you do the honours, or shall I?'

'You can prepare it,' she said tartly. 'You scared me out of my wits.'

He grinned apologetically. 'I didn't think that was possible,' he teased her.

'I'll collect some firewood,' she announced, ignoring him.

She found brittle, dead wood under the apple trees. When she returned with an armful, she discovered Cole had found dry kindling inside the ruins. She left him nursing his fire into life, and went to collect more wood.

Her emotions were in turmoil. She had no doubt that Cole had planned this night deliberately, but she didn't know how she should respond. She loved this peaceful place he'd brought her to, and she loved him, but she wasn't sure if she should surrender to the fantasy of her surroundings.

Cole was fulfilling a fantasy of his own. For years he had watched Honor make camp for Patrick. But now she belonged to him. He wanted this night with her, in peace and solitude, before he faced the hurdles he had to negotiate to claim her publicly as his wife.

When Honor returned to the fire, the rabbit was roasting and she was unsurprised to see that Cole had also provided them with bread, cheese and tea.

'No milk, I'm afraid,' he apologised, glancing up at her. He seemed relaxed and boyish as he sat by the fire, a far cry from the austere officer she'd first known in Portugal.

'I like tea better without milk,' she said vaguely, her mind on other things. 'I'm not going far,' she murmured, picking up her bag.

'Honor?' Cole twisted round, reaching up to catch her arm as he looked up at her questioningly.

'Just behind the building,' she assured him. 'You'll hear me if I call. I just…please.'

He continued to study her for several moments in the fading light, then his hand slid down her arm to briefly clasp her hand before releasing her.

'Don't go far,' he said.

'I won't.' The temptation to twine her fingers through his tousled hair was irresistible, so she gave in to it. He moved under her hand, almost like a great cat, inviting a caress. She stepped away from him, before he made it impossible to leave.

Chapter Nine

The water was clean, but cold. Honor slipped quickly out of her clothes and stood naked beside the stream in the twilight. The evening air was cool against her vulnerable skin and she shivered. She'd never before been naked beneath the open sky and she was both exhilarated and nervous at her own daring. If Cole found her like this it would be…definitely scandalous.

She sat on the grass beside the stream and dangled her legs into the water. She gasped at the cold and decided she'd better be quick. She slid into the water, feeling gingerly for the bottom. When she moved a little way into the stream, the water level came just above her knees. The current tugged gently, but not alarmingly around her legs. She lowered herself until she was submerged, focussing on the refreshing, rather than the freezing aspect of her preparations.

Then she waded out of the stream, dashed as much of the water off her slim body as she could with the flat of her hands, and dried herself on her ubiquitous black shawl. Instead of putting her riding habit on again, she pulled out a dress from her pack. It wasn't a modish dress—she'd been careful with her purchases

in Lisbon—but it gave her a sense of dressing for dinner.

Finally she brushed her hair, then hesitated, unsure
what to do with it next. It would be too obvious to
leave it tumbling around her shoulders, but she was
sick of the severe style she always wore it in.

'Honor?' Cole called.

'Coming.' She quickly stuffed her stockings and
comb into her bag. Her riding habit was bulkier than
the simple dress she now wore, and she had to drape
it over her arm. She picked up her shoes and shawl
and rejoined Cole. She draped her clothes over the
branches of a sapling and sat down beside him.

The circle of firelight made the night around them
seem darker than it was, and emphasised the intimacy
of their situation.

'I didn't put my hair up yet,' she said breathlessly,
suddenly shy in his presence. 'I didn't want you to
worry I was taking too long. I'll just—'

'Leave it.' He touched her hair gently, then slipped
his fingers beneath it to lift the shining weight against
the back of his hand. As he did so, his fingers softly
caressed the nape of her neck.

She held her breath, snared by the sensuous magic
of his touch. She didn't move, or even look at him,
afraid to break the spell.

'It's much prettier when it's not muddy,' he murmured provocatively, still seductively stroking her
hair.

She threw a startled glance at him and a teasing
smile curved his lips.

'You were not a pretty sight, when I pulled you out
of the Huebra feet first,' he said reminiscently. 'A
sadly bedraggled example of a fighting woman.'

Honor struggled to respond appropriately. It was hard to feel indignant when he was touching her so distractingly.

'You didn't have to haul me over your saddle bow like a sack of corn,' she huffed unconvincingly.

'I could still feel you across my legs for hours afterwards,' he said softly. 'My hand on your waist, your breasts against my thigh—'

'Cole!' Honor had left the top few buttons of her gown undone, and she instinctively clutched the modest opening together. 'You shouldn't say such things,' she scolded him.

He chuckled gently and let his hand slip around her waist to pull her closer towards him.

'Sweetheart.' He lightly kissed her temple. 'You like it when I touch you, why shouldn't you enjoy it when I talk about touching you?'

'Well, because…' Honor leant against him, feeling his breath ruffle her hair as he caressed her with his lips. They were so close, it would be natural if she let her hand rest on his thigh, but somehow she lacked the courage. 'It really isn't proper!'

He laughed again. 'How can you have lived such an adventurous life, and still be such an innocent?' he enquired tenderly. 'Of course it's proper if you love me and I love you.'

His simple, matter-of-fact comment stunned her into silence.

'But…'

'Shush. You don't really think I'd do anything to hurt you, do you?' he murmured, kissing her temple, then her cheek, before moving away from her to check the progress of their supper.

Honor watched in a daze as she considered the implications of what he'd said. She should tell him not to set his hopes in her—but perhaps he was merely intending to make her his mistress after all. No, he'd said he wouldn't. She ought to ask him outright what he meant, but she didn't want to spoil the magical atmosphere of the evening.

'There. I have provided you with both meat and bread,' he said with considerable satisfaction as he handed her supper to her.

'Thank you. You've often provided me with food,' she said, surprised at his comment.

'Not under these circumstances,' he replied.

'You mean you hunted for me?' she asked, unable to resist teasing him a little. 'It's not real food unless you shot it and skinned it?'

'Or ploughed and sowed it,' he retorted, acknowledging her good-natured teasing with a crooked smile.

'What?' Honor asked, impulsively resting her hand on his thigh as a shadow momentarily passed over his face.

He looked into the fire for a moment, then roused himself to smile at her again. 'I always had a notion that when the war was over I might try exploring the New World. Canada, perhaps, or...'

'But...' Honor had been about to say that Miss Morton might not have liked that, but she didn't finish her observation. She didn't want to think about Bridget Morton now. Cole had far more pressing reasons why he had to abandon such dreams.

Instead of continuing the conversation, Cole laid his hand over hers where it rested on his leg. She suddenly became aware of the intimacy of her gesture and tried to draw her hand away, but he wouldn't let her. She felt the tension in the muscles of his thigh as he gently guided her hand inwards and a few inches higher.

Her breath locked in her throat. She couldn't believe how brazen he was. She was even more shocked to discover his action had filled her with pleasurable, though nervous, excitement. She had no doubt how the evening would end, but she wasn't quite ready for such bold games.

He released her hand and offered her another piece of roasted rabbit.

'No, thank you,' she said breathlessly.

She saw that he had also finished and moved with the intention of tidying up, but he forestalled her.

'Sit.' He rested his hand briefly on her shoulder. 'We've established I'm competent, and you should rest, sweetheart.'

She should have protested, but she didn't. It was very pleasant to be cared for so tenderly. She gazed into the embers of the fire, her mind a warm and comfortable haze, as Cole moved around the campsite. He made her tea, and she set it down on the grass to cool.

She sat for some time in an unthinking daydream before suddenly realising Cole wasn't nearby, and hadn't been for a while. She stood up, glancing around, not really anxious about his absence, but mildly concerned. It was colder, and she shivered in the night air. The moon had risen, silvering the stream and casting dark shadows among the apple trees. The quiet horses were silhouetted against the sky. She retrieved her shawl from the branch and threw it around her shoulders, then wandered down to the bank of the small river.

A splash from upstream attracted her attention. She

approached cautiously, expecting to discover a water
bird, or possibly an otter. Instead she found Cole.

He was standing in the water, his powerful body
delineated by bright moonlight and dark shadows, silver ripples circling outwards from his legs. Ever since
they'd made love she'd dreamed of his body; now she
could see that it was as magnificent as she'd remembered. When he turned towards her she could see the
strong, graceful definition of his muscular torso.
Moonlight haloed his hair and highlighted the angular
planes of his face. His stomach was flat and ridged
with muscle. He was unbelievably beautiful to her. It
didn't occur to her that she should accord him the same
privacy he'd allowed her. She couldn't take her eyes
off him.

He looked up and towards her. His eyes were in
shadow, but he didn't seem surprised to see her. He
made no effort to cover himself and, because of his
position, facing partly towards her, and partly in profile
towards the moon, she knew exactly how her presence
affected him. She swallowed, a little embarrassed by
her own daring, but unable to retreat.

He waded towards the bank, silver ripples sparking
around his legs, and stepped easily out of the water,
but he didn't approach any closer to her. They were
alone in the mysterious dark and pearly light. The silence between them was charged with tension. Honor
took a step towards him. He waited, still and unmov-
ing, but emanating an aura of virile power. Honor's
heart thudded in her chest. This was beyond her experience. She didn't know what she was supposed to
do, she only knew she was drawn inexorably towards
him.

She stopped a couple of feet away from him. Still

he said nothing, and made no move to touch her. Moonlight glistened on his wet shoulders. Drops of water gleamed like dewfall in the shadowy curls on his broad chest.

This close, she could see his expression a little more clearly. His lips curved in a sensuous, masculine invitation, but he didn't reach out towards her. Honor caught her lower lip between her teeth, torn between uncertainty and desire. Barely conscious of what she was doing, she pulled her shawl from around her shoulders, and began to dry him with it. She stroked the soft, slightly damp wool over his arms, his chest and his back, caressing him and glorying in his male beauty.

He didn't say anything, but she felt him tremble. She leant forward and almost timidly kissed his water-cooled back, then rested her forehead briefly against his shoulder. She was hot and quivering with her own urgent emotions, remembering the last time they'd made love—anticipating the first moment he would touch her this time.

He moved, turning to face her, and she lifted her head, her lips already parted, open and vulnerable to him.

He bent eagerly towards her, then shudderingly controlled the driving demands of his body to possess her. He brushed his mouth gently against hers, summoning a soft moan from her when he drew back without consummating the kiss. He put his hands on her hips, holding her away from him when she tried to press closer, and started to bunch her dress up in his hands, hitching it higher and higher up her legs.

Cool night air flowed around her calves, then her thighs. She felt wickedly erotic as he slowly exposed her nakedness to the moonlight. When he'd pulled her dress up to her hips, he slipped his hands beneath. His shuddering reaction when he discovered she was wearing nothing beneath it reverberated through her. He paused a moment, his hands on her waist, and lightly kissed her forehead.

'You could tempt a saint, sweetheart,' he murmured hoarsely. 'What chance have I got?'

'I like tempting you,' she whispered, completely surrendering to their mutual seduction. 'You…tempt me.'

She put her hands on his shoulders, delighting in the strong smooth feel of his muscles beneath her fingertips. The water had been cold, and his skin was still slightly cool, yet she could sense the heat radiating from his body.

He slid his palms upwards, until they grazed the sides of her breasts. Her nipples were tight with anticipation. Her body ached and throbbed for his touch, but he made her wait.

'Cole!' she whispered, her fingers digging urgently into his shoulders.

He brushed a kiss across her cheek.

'What do you want, sweetheart?' he murmured huskily in her ear.

'Touch me!' she ordered breathlessly, twisting with frustrated need against his restraining hands.

'Like this?' His hands moved around her ribcage until he was framing her small breasts in the angle between his thumbs and index fingers.

'Ohh!' She sounded so disgruntled Cole chuckled in spite of himself.

'Like this?' he asked softly, teasing her erect nipples with the sides of his thumbs. 'Sweetheart?' He bent his head to kiss the side of her neck, his lips teasing and caressing her warm, sensitive skin.

'Mmm.' Honor's legs turned to water. Cole's touch beneath her dress was sinfully delicious. 'Oh.' Her head fell forward against his shoulder. 'You haven't even kissed me yet,' she mumbled incoherently, heedlessly voicing an errant thought. 'Not properly.'

'Sweetheart.' Cole's lips curved in a smile against her neck. 'There are a lot of things I haven't done yet. Lift your arms.'

'I might fall over,' she protested vaguely.

'I'll catch you.' He slipped her dress neatly over her head, then swept her up in his arms and carried her around the ruined building to the blanket beside the smouldering fire.

'So, you want to be kissed?' he teased her, lying on his side next to her.

'Yes.' She was amazed by her own boldness, but too aroused to be embarrassed. She rolled on to her side so that she was facing him, and brazenly rubbed her breasts against his chest.

He locked his hand in her hair and pulled her head back almost roughly to cover her mouth with his own. His kisses were fierce and possessive, completely overwhelming her. She curled her arm around his side, clinging to him as he ravaged her senses with his lips and tongue. She could feel his erection pressing against her stomach, the urgent need pulsing through his virile body. The certainty of his desire for her aroused her even further.

She rubbed her soft, inner thigh against his hard muscular leg, then tried to roll on to her back, pulling him on top of her. To her confusion, he resisted her efforts. Instead he moved on to his back, and lifted her to straddle him.

'Oh, my!' Her surprise momentarily interrupted the smooth current of their passion. 'What…?'

He guided her carefully, his hands gentle on her slim hips, though his arms trembled with the self-control he was exerting not to go too fast. His breath suddenly exploded out of him at the immense, glorious pleasure of feeling her tightly enclose him.

'Cole,' she breathed, holding herself away from him as she gazed down into his face.

'Did…I hurt you?' he asked jerkily, suddenly afraid he hadn't given her enough time.

'No.' She sounded bewildered, not hurt. 'But—'

'Shush.' He cupped her face in his hands and drew her lips down to his. 'Kiss me,' he murmured.

'Mmm.' She did, but she was distracted by other sensations, and the increasing compulsion to move. She lifted her hips experimentally and was rewarded by the tightening of Cole's embrace, and his barely stifled groan.

'Oh, you liked that!' Her voice was so breathless and thick with arousal she didn't recognise it. For the first time she realised she was not just the recipient of Cole's desire, but an active participant in their mutual arousal and ultimate satisfaction.

'Yes!' Cole's hands followed the curve of her hips and waist to find her breasts. He cupped them in his palms, caressing their hard, sensitive tips, and Honor closed her eyes with pleasure.

Then she experimented some more, concentrating on Cole's delight rather than her own. It was too dark to see his face clearly, but his body's response to her efforts, and his hoarse moans of pleasure gave her the cues she needed. In a distant part of her mind, she was surprised when he slipped his hand between them, but then he touched her intimately, and she was lost to the devastating sensations he conjured in her. Her body contracted, and she cried out as blinding ecstasy pulsed through her, overwhelming all her senses for several long, shuddering moments.

Cole's hands gripped her hips as he thrust up into her and surrendered to his own, soul-quaking release.

She lay on top of him, their hearts beating in unison, as they slowly recovered from the intense experience.

'Sweetheart.' Cole lifted his head to press a kiss against Honor's damp skin, then flopped back on to the blanket, thoroughly satisfied and spent by their lovemaking.

She barely stirred. He was still inside her, and he wanted to stay like that, but the night breeze was cool against her damp, naked flesh. He rolled them carefully to one side, ignoring Honor's mumbled protests, and wrapped them both in a cosy cocoon of blankets.

She snuggled against him, already half asleep. He held her close, enjoying the feel of her relaxed body next to his. It occurred to him that Patrick really couldn't have been much of a lover. Under any other circumstances, Honor's amazement at his reversal of what she'd expected would have been comical. They were, Cole decided, going to have so much fun discovering each other—just as soon as he'd sorted things out with Bridget. The prospect of dealing with Bridget and her father momentarily disturbed his contentment—he wasn't looking forward to his meeting with them. But then he realised his muscles were tensing in anticipation of the encounter and he deliberately pushed his concerns aside. Tomorrow would be soon enough to deal with problems. He drifted asleep, his mind full of Honor and the erotic fantasies that she'd inspired.

Honor woke up in the middle of the dawn chorus. It never failed to amaze her how much sheer noise birds could generate at the first hint of grey light. She lay close to Cole and thought about what had happened in the night. She should have been embarrassed at her uninhibited behaviour, and part of her was—but mostly she was full of happiness because she knew she had made Cole happy. She had known he liked looking at her, touching her, making love to her, but until last night she had never fully comprehended how much she could also contribute to their mutual pleasure. She wished they had more time together, but she resolutely set her mind against their future parting. She wondered if Cole had known there would be a moon last night, and decided he must have done. He knew she thought the moon was magical, and he'd given her a magical memory.

The sun was sending its first warm rays over the horizon when she heard a faint noise from the direction of the old apple orchard. She lifted her head cautiously, anxious in case they'd been discovered, and saw three deer, frozen like statues as they looked towards her. She was enchanted. She watched as they stepped delicately through the trees, then sat up. Cole stirred in his sleep and she tucked the blankets carefully around him.

Then she got to her feet and silently followed in the path of the deer. The damp morning air was cool against her sleep-warmed skin and she shivered, but she didn't bother with her clothes. She was living in a magical adventure where the normal rules had ceased to apply.

She paused beneath an apple tree, unable to see where the deer had gone, and unwilling to go too far from the camp. She heard a sound behind her and turned to smile up at Cole. He was as naked as she was.

'You could be the nymph of the orchard,' he said softly, one hand resting on the branch above her head, 'so beautiful in the dawn.'

'Oh.' She blushed at his praise, self-conscious of her nakedness, and lifted her hands to cover herself.

He caught her wrist and shook his head.

'I like to look at you.'

'I…like to look at you too,' she said daringly.

He smiled. 'That makes me very happy,' he murmured. 'And touching me, sweetheart?' He lifted her hand and placed it against his chest.

'Yes.' She whispered. She stroked her hand across the firm muscles, softened by the mat of light brown curls. She found a flat nipple and circled it gently. Then she glanced down and discovered he was more than happy with her response to him. She looked up at him. He smiled deep into her eyes, and they shared a moment of intimate, sensual awareness.

He shook the branch above her head and apple blossom fell on her like a benediction, lying delicately on her hair, her shoulders and her breasts.

'My Honor,' he murmured, delighted with the picture she made, and bent to kiss her, before carrying her back to their blankets.

'I must be feeding you properly,' said Cole lazily.

'Why?' Honor smiled up at him.

'Your breasts are fuller than they were in Spain,' he replied matter-of-factly.

'Oh.' She blushed.

'And your curves are generally…curvier,' he continued, inspecting them with both his eyes and appreciative fingertips.

'I thought they were a bit too,' Honor admitted, deciding there was no point in being embarrassed. 'Do you like it better?' she asked shyly.

'I like it better that you're healthy and well fed,' said Cole decidedly. 'You were too thin before. The life was too hard for you. No.' He gently laid his fingers over her lips to silence her immediate, indignant protest. 'The life was too hard for many of the men, as well, sweetheart. I know that. I know *you* never collapsed in defeated exhaustion beside the road. And I know you could do it all again if it were asked of you—but I hope to God it never is.'

'I'd do it for you,' said Honor.

'I know.' Cole kissed her, at first gently, then with increasing passion.

Honor threaded her fingers through his hair and held him close. She'd meant to talk to him about their future, but he hadn't let her, he'd been too busy loving her.

'This is such a wonderful place,' Honor said, feeling very sad as she took a last look around at the stream and apple trees before they left their camp. 'Did you know it before?'

Cole grinned. 'I'll show you,' he replied. He led the way downstream until the little river grew broader and shallower. The horses splashed easily over to the other side and, after a few minutes riding, Honor suddenly found herself gazing at the ruined shell of a once-grand house.

'We think the fire was started by a bolt of lightning,' said Cole. 'It was about fifteen years ago. I was at school, Giff was already in the navy, and Father, Malcolm and Anthony were in London—so the stories about how it happened are a bit variable.'

'It's *your* house!' Honor exclaimed, staring in fascination at the fire-blackened remaining walls.

'Mmm.' Cole scanned his surroundings with narrowed eyes against the low rays of the early morning sun. 'Father said he'd leave it up to Giff to decide what he wanted to do about it—the house, I mean. Malcolm's still managing the land and the tenants.'

'Now it's up to you,' said Honor, urging the mare closer to the ruins. 'Will you rebuild?'

'Do you like it?' Cole asked, watching her.

'The grounds are beautiful,' she declared, smiling appreciatively at an old oak tree nearby. 'It feels so peaceful here.'

'I always liked this place,' Cole confessed. 'Not the house, particularly. My grandfather had it built and I thought it was ugly—so did Father. But the countryside, and the view of the hills—they feel like home to me. I can imagine living here.'

Honor suddenly perceived where the conversation might be heading and it made her nervous. The fireblackened house now seemed ominous rather than merely interesting.

'We must catch up with the chaise,' she said quickly. 'Otherwise they might send out search parties for us.' She urged the mare into a brisk trot.

'The village inn is called the Raven's Arms,' Cole called after her, grinning. 'If you keep heading in that direction you could call in for a tankard of ale—but you won't get to London.'

'So where, exactly, are we going?' asked Cole, when they were once more seated in the chaise.

'The Belle Savage, Ludgate Hill,' Honor replied, avoiding his gaze.

'The Belle Savage?' Cole echoed. Honor had just named one of the major coaching inns of London. 'Is your mother a housekeeper there?' he hazarded, frowning. He'd often wondered what had happened to the illiterate chambermaid, but Honor always seemed reluctant to talk about her mother.

Honor's smile didn't reach her eyes. 'Mama owns it,' she said tensely.

'She's the *proprietor*!' Cole exclaimed. 'How—?'

'She worked hard—and she's clever,' Honor replied tightly.

'Of course she is, she's your mother.' Cole drew in a long, deep breath, watching Honor carefully. Why was she so edgy? He decided to proceed cautiously. 'From chambermaid to proprietor of a large coaching inn is a long step up,' he observed.

'Several inns,' Honor corrected him, gripping her fingers tightly together as she recited her mother's assets. 'Mama also owns two other inns on the Bath road, and one on the Brighton road. She has stables near Epsom—it takes thousands of horses to keep Mama's coaches on the road. She owns a coach-building business—which makes coaches for the aristocracy as well as for Mama. And she is the contractor for the London ground of the London to Bath mail. Mr Hasker, he's the superintendent of the mail coaches, is a great admirer of hers. He says if all the contractors managed their affairs as efficiently as Mama, his life would be much easier. Of course...' Honor paused to catch her breath '...Mama's not the only widow woman running a successful coaching business in London—she's just the only one who never had a husband to start with.' She met Cole's eyes rather defiantly as she concluded her speech.

'Well, I'll be damned,' he said softly, watching the complicated play of emotions on Honor's face. He'd always known her feelings for her mother were far from straightforward, now he was finally beginning to see why.

'How did she achieve all that?' he asked after a moment, stunned by the magnitude of the task. Surely the woman must have had some kind of patron—even if not Honor's father?

Honor looked at him cautiously, almost as if she was anticipating his disapproval.

'I share Mr Hasker's respect,' he said hastily. He might feel hostile towards Honor's mother because of the way she'd treated her daughter—but that didn't alter his feelings for Honor.

Honor studied him in silence for a few seconds, then she started to explain.

'First she learned her trade. When I was born, my grandmother was still alive. She had Mama very late in her life—when she was forty-four years old!' Honor sounded awed by the accomplishment. 'So she was already quite old when I knew her. She died just before I married Patrick.'

'You missed her?' Cole said softly, seeing another reason why Honor might have been jolted into her hasty marriage.

'Oh, yes,' Honor agreed fervently. 'She never did

learn to read, but she was the wisest person I've ever
known—and a wonderful cook! She was one of
Mama's most important assets. For the first few years
after I was born, Gran went on working as a cook and
Mama did several jobs in various inns—learning all
the time.'

'Who took care of you?' Cole demanded.

'Susannah.' Honor smiled. 'Mama's cousin. She
was only eleven, but she took good care of me.'

'You were left in the care of a child?' Cole couldn't
help the disapproval in his voice, though he knew far
worse happened all the time.

'She took *good* care of me!' Honor fired up. 'I *liked*
being with her.'

'I'm looking forward to meeting her,' said Cole.

'So'm I,' Honor whispered, wiping her eye with the
back of her curled forefinger, before looking out of the
carriage window.

Cole remembered then how traumatic this home-
coming was going to be for her.

'Your mama learnt her trade,' he prompted, trying
to divert Honor from her worries.

'When she was twenty-one she bought a rundown
old inn on the Bath road. I was four years old. I can
remember the roof leaking and weeds growing through
the cobblestones in the yard. But Mama turned it round
so fast.' Pride shone in Honor's eyes as she recalled
both her own memories and the stories she'd been told
by Susannah and her grandmother. 'She'd already got
the best cook she could have in Gran. She'd met a lot
of good people while she was still hiring herself out,
and some of them were willing to take a chance on
working for her. Lord Sandler's butler came to work
for her when his master died—he knew everything

about wine. Colin Macey kept the stables in apple-pie order. And Mama and Susannah did whatever else needed to be done. It took less than two years before their reputation was so good she was taking trade from the old-established inns nearby.'

'That must have made her popular,' Cole observed drily.

'Mama's tough.' Honor smiled slightly. 'And clever. I don't remember much about it, but Susannah told me someone tried to sabotage the stables once. Mama wasn't having any of it—nor was Colin. He can be a big, fierce man when he wants to be.' Honor chuckled.

'He's still around?'

'Oh, yes.' Honor sounded slightly surprised. 'He's not much older than Mama. He and his wife are still running that first inn Mama ever bought.'

'I see.' For a moment, Cole had wondered whether Colin Macey had had any romantic interest in Honor's formidable mama, but it seemed not.

'When Mama could afford it, she bought another inn,' Honor continued, settling into her story-telling. 'And then another. At her peak, she had several inns on the Bath road, two on the Brighton road, and a couple on the Great North Road, but what she really wanted was a centre in London. About ten years ago she sold off several of the smaller inns to buy the Belle Savage. You could say the Belle is the heart of her empire.'

'It sounds like it,' Cole agreed uneasily. Had Honor inherited her mother's fierce ambition to succeed? 'Is that the kind of thing you'd like to achieve in your own life?' he asked, his voice carefully neutral.

Honor sighed, her brief spurt of energy dying away.

'I don't want to be an innkeeper,' she said wearily. 'I never did. Dressmaking…? I think I'd rather breed horses—but not for Mama,' she added, with a hint of rebellion.

Honor wanted to marry him and have his babies, Cole reminded himself, forcing his tense muscles to relax. But he had to admit, he was quite intrigued by the story of Honor's mother.

What was it like to start with nothing and build it up into a veritable empire? He clenched his fist in a surge of excitement as he realised he didn't have to confine himself to approving tenancy agreements. He could look around and find something to do that really interested him!

'What happened?' Honor sounded bewildered. 'You look so…happy?'

'I am!' Cole exclaimed, leaning forward in the opposite seat and cupping her knees enthusiastically between his hands. 'Honor, I just realised I don't have to settle for being a landlord and gentleman of leisure, after all. If your mama can keep inns, breed horses, build coaches, and run stage coaches and the mail, I'm damn sure I can do more than one thing at a time, too!'

'Oh my God, you're just like her,' Honor breathed, half-horrified, as she stared into his blazing eyes.

'Is that bad?' he asked, momentarily disconcerted by her expression.

'Well…no.' She gave a shaken laugh. 'No, of course not. What are you going to do?'

'I don't know yet.' He sat back, unbothered by the admission. 'I'll find something. Coach-building sounds interesting. Designing a more comfortable coach—that would be worthwhile. Father was telling me about ex-

periments with steam when I was last home. It was
fascinating. I've been out of touch too long.'

Honor gazed at him, loving him, but a little bewildered by this new side of his personality. How could
coach-building be interesting? And what was fascinating about steam?

Cole saw her expression and laughed, pulling her
onto his lap.

'Cole!' She pushed ineffectually at his embrace.
'It's broad daylight.' She lowered her voice, even
though they were alone in the chaise.

'It was broad daylight this morning, too,' he teased
her.

'That was different,' she scolded him. 'We're on a
busy road. People might see.'

'Pull the shades down,' he countered, grinning.

'We'll be changing horses soon.'

'You've got an answer for everything.' He cupped
the back of her head with his hand and kissed her.

'So have you,' Honor gasped, when she could
speak. 'Please, Cole,' she added uncertainly.

She felt confused. She didn't want him to let her
go. She felt safe on his lap, but she knew that soon
they would have to have a serious discussion about the
future. And after that, she would be alone. She closed
her eyes and rested her forehead against his cheek.

'Sweetheart.' His arms tightened comfortingly
around her. 'Are you afraid of your mother?' he asked
softly.

She didn't answer for a long time. Eventually she
sighed.

'Not…exactly,' she said slowly. 'We've had some
horrible arguments. Gran used to say it was because
we're so much alike—but I don't think we are. Not

really. In some ways we are—sometimes we've both got sharp tongues. But Mama always has to have the last word.' She sighed again.

Cole stroked her back reassuringly, but he didn't say anything.

'I never wanted to work in the inn,' Honor admitted. 'I don't know if that's because I don't like innkeeping—or because I just couldn't see myself working for Mama. She said I could be an idle lady of fashion, and sent me to the seminary in Bath—but how could I simper and flirt behind my fan when it was Mama's hard struggle that had made it possible for me to be idle?'

'So you ran away to become an actress,' said Cole.

'Sheridan used to visit the Belle Savage,' Honor replied. 'It's amazing the people you meet when you grow up in an inn—and the scandals you hear,' she added, smiling wryly. 'Then I had all that trouble with the Duke of Selhurst—and I couldn't bring myself to run back to Mama and have her tell me she told me so.'

'So you married Patrick instead,' said Cole.

'And Mama hasn't spoken to me since,' Honor finished. 'And I haven't spoken to her either. Not since Patrick went to see her and she upset him so much he got drunk and the recruiting party got him.'

'Sweetheart.' Cole held her close, determined that Honor's tempestuous relationship with her mother was never going to drive her into doing something foolish again.

Honor let him comfort her for a few minutes, then she pushed herself off his lap.

'I can handle her,' she said flatly. 'I will pay my respects to her, like a polite and dutiful daughter, but

I will not be beholden to her. I will not go crawling back to her like the prodigal daughter. I will find somewhere else to live.'

Cole opened his mouth, then closed it again. He wanted Honor to know she wasn't the prodigal daughter, that she had a secure place in his life. But she'd just pointed out that a large inn could be a hotbed for scandal. He didn't want the scandal of his broken betrothal to reach Bridget before he'd had a chance to speak to her himself. Under normal circumstances, he didn't have any doubts about Honor's discretion, but clearly her relationship with her mother was far from normal.

They changed horses frequently and made good time. Consequently, it was mid-afternoon when they finally reached Ludgate Hill and the post-chaise swept under the arch into the outer courtyard of the Belle Savage.

Honor looked out of the window; the bustle of a busy inn was achingly familiar to her. The coffee room, the booking office, the tiered galleries that surrounded the courtyards, the horses and ostlers, private carriages and her mother's stagecoaches, the ostlers and many-caped drivers...

'Miss Honor! Miss Honor!'

Honor blinked, then smiled in delighted recognition at one of the drivers. 'Jethro!' she exclaimed holding out both hands. 'It's good to see you.'

'Miss Honor!' He seized her hands in his, holding her at arm's length as he looked her up and down. 'Miss Honor, it's so good to have you safe home,' he said, gulping, and looking as if he was too overcome to say any more. 'Ned! Sam!' he called. 'Miss Honor's come home!'

Immediately Honor found herself surrounded by a crowd of her well-wishers, all of whom worked for her mother.

Cole allowed himself to be elbowed aside by people who wanted to see for themselves that Honor was home safe and well.

'Miss Honor—' Jethro began.

'Mrs O'Donnell,' Ned hissed, nudging him in the ribs.

'But Patrick's dead, isn't he?' whispered another man.

Cole suddenly remembered that Patrick had been a coach driver. Had he once been the colleague of these men who were greeting Honor with so much excited, but respectful, affection? It was obviously more comfortable for them to ignore her widowed state and treat her as the unwed daughter of the house she'd been when they'd known her.

Cole looked around the huge courtyard, the hub of the empire Honor's mother had built, and finally realised the enormity of what Honor had done when she married Patrick. It was as if the General's daughter had upped and married a private soldier! Cole suppressed a disbelieving grin. No wonder Honor's mother had been beside herself when she'd found out.

'Honor! Honor!' A woman called from the other side of the courtyard.

Both Cole and Honor swung in the direction of the voice. Cole saw a tall, elegant woman pick up her skirts and run towards Honor.

'Susannah!' Honor met her halfway and they fell into each others arms.

Cole shouldered his way through the crowd to join them. He'd no desire to intrude upon Honor's reunions, but he did want to be close at hand if she needed him. Her mother still hadn't appeared, and he knew that would be the moment of truth for her.

'You look so well!' Honor held her mother's cousin away from her so she could gaze at her, then hugged her tightly again.

'So do you,' said Susannah warmly. 'But I've been so worried about you!' she exclaimed. 'Why'd you take so long to come home?'

'I…wasn't ready before,' Honor said unsteadily.

'Hmm.' Susannah looked straight past her into Cole's eyes.

He was momentarily surprised by how young she was. It was shocking to realise how much of a child she'd been when she'd first taken care of Honor. He wondered what she was doing now. She certainly wasn't dressed as a poor relation, and he couldn't remember the last time he'd been assessed by such a shrewd pair of eyes.

'Major Raven,' she said, obviously needing no introduction for him. He wondered what Honor had said about him in her letters. 'I'm pleased to meet you, sir,' said Susannah, holding out her hand to him.

'And I you,' he replied, shaking her hand.

'Oh, I never introduced you properly!' Honor exclaimed, looking from one to the other in mild consternation. 'This is Miss Susannah Rivers, Mama's cousin and business partner.'

'Miss Rivers,' Cole smiled.

'Let's go inside,' said Susannah, taking Honor's arm. 'Annie's out at the moment,' she added in a lower voice.

Cole saw an almost imperceptible relaxation of Honor's shoulders.

'Annie?' he said questioningly, although he'd already guessed she was Honor's elusive mama.

'Annie Howarth,' said Honor. 'My mother.'

Cole frowned as he followed Susannah and Honor inside. The name sounded familiar, but he couldn't immediately place it.

'Major Raven, I am so grateful for the way you saved Honor's life,' Susannah said sincerely, as soon as they were sitting in her private parlour.

'I think she can take most of the credit for that herself,' said Cole, uncomfortable with Susannah's gratitude.

'Honor has always been brave and determined,' Susannah agreed, 'but even she couldn't have carried Patrick all the way to Ciudad Rodrigo if you hadn't found them.'

'Did she tell you she shot a wolf?' Cole asked, turning the conversation in another direction, quite sure he wouldn't shock this self-assured woman.

'No!' Susannah exclaimed. 'Honor!' She looked at her accusingly.

'I thought it would worry you,' said Honor guiltily.

'Worry me? I'd have taken the packet to Lisbon and brought you back myself if you hadn't come home soon,' Susannah declared. 'Annie's been going crazy with worry about you.'

'Mama has?' Honor sounded as if she didn't believe it.

Cole saw a look of faint exasperation pass over Susannah's face, as if she was tired of being caught in the crossfire. Her loyalties must be uncomfortably divided by the breach between Honor and her mother.

And he suddenly realised why the name Annie Howarth was familiar to him. Before he had time to think through the implications of his realisation, he heard a commotion outside the door.

A few seconds later the parlour door flew open and a slim, flushed woman bounced inside and stopped short, staring at Honor.

'Mama,' Honor whispered, rising to her feet.

Cole automatically stood up as well. His first reaction was one of disbelief. He'd been expecting a hard-faced harridan, but the woman before him hardly looked old enough to be anyone's mother, let alone a woman of twenty-five. Then he remembered that, Annie Howarth being only sixteen when Honor was born, she was barely forty-one now.

Annie Howarth had caramel-coloured hair and blue eyes. Her face was a perfect oval. Her features were less angular than her daughter's; her figure, though slim, was more womanly. It was easy to imagine the pretty child she'd been when she'd caught the eye of Honor's father, and it made her achievements over the past twenty-five years all the more remarkable. The most likely fate for a young, poorly educated girl in Annie's situation would have been a descent into poverty and degradation. Many women in similar circumstances might have exerted their best efforts to find another, richer protector, but Annie Howarth had spurned such tactics. The fact that she had not only survived, but prospered, told Cole that she must be a truly formidable woman.

In the first few seconds after Annie first saw Honor her emotions were reflected, unguarded, in her sapphire eyes. In that instant, Cole had no doubt that Annie Howarth loved her daughter very much—and

he was also sure that his half-formed deduction of only
a few moments ago was correct.

Joe Newton had been writing regularly to a 'Mrs
Annie Howarth' on Ludgate Hill, though Cole had
only occasionally seen the letters. He wondered briefly
how Annie Howarth had established contact with his
servant—and then he remembered that Joe had only
travelled out from England *after* Cole had transferred
from the 16th Dragoons to the 52nd Foot. Cole's previous servant had been unable to stand the rigours of
campaigning and he'd asked Malcolm Anderson to
send him out a replacement. Somehow Annie had
managed to take advantage of the situation to install
her own man as Cole's servant. Annie had been kept
abreast of everything that had happened to her daughter on a regular basis for the past eighteen months.
Probably longer if she had other informants Cole
didn't know about. And given the size of her coaching
empire in England, he thought it was quite likely that
she did.

Not only that, in recent months Bridget's letters had
been full of references to 'Mrs Howarth'. What exactly
had Honor's mother been hoping to achieve by making
friends with his fiancée?

Cole started to laugh out of sheer amazement.

Chapter Ten

Honor stared at her mother. She was overwhelmed by so many cartwheeling emotions that she didn't know how she felt. Annie hadn't changed at all in the four years since they'd last seen each other. She was still perfectly beautiful, perfectly in charge of her amazing empire.

Honor couldn't speak. She could hardly breathe. Her knees were weak and trembling. She gripped her hands together tightly. She would *not* make a fool of herself in front of Annie. This was just a brief, businesslike meeting to re-establish polite contact between them.

Then Cole started to laugh. Honor was startled and disorientated by the sound. She turned her head to look at him, swaying slightly as she did so. He moved quickly to stand behind her, resting one hand reassuringly on her waist as he looked over her head at her mother.

Annie had clearly been surprised by his laughter as well. Her eyes jumped from Honor's face to Cole's.

'Was I ever in danger of being cashiered?' he asked, sounding mildly amused.

Annie raised one exquisite eyebrow in a haughty

expression all too familiar to her daughter. But then, to Honor's amazement, her mother's face softened into a smile that almost seemed to indicate approval of Cole.

'No,' she said.

'I'm glad to hear it.' Cole's deep voice vibrated reassuringly close to Honor's ear. He still kept one had firmly on her waist, but she felt him rub her gently between her shoulder blades with the knuckles of his free hand. She was grateful for the support he was offering, but she was also embarrassed that he should touch her so openly in front of her mother. She thought she ought to step away from him, but she couldn't quite bring herself to do so.

'Mama, this is Major—no, I mean…' She stumbled over the introduction as she belatedly realised Cole's title had changed.

'Sir Cole Raven,' Annie said with assurance. 'I'm delighted to meet you, Sir Cole.'

'The pleasure is all mine,' Cole reciprocated. 'I've heard a great deal about you. I understand you believe it is better to live one's own adventures—rather than read about them in someone else's novel?'

Annie raised her eyebrow. 'I may have said something of the sort,' she conceded. 'Do you disagree with my opinion, sir?'

Honor struggled to make sense of the conversation. She was sure she hadn't said anything like that about her mother to Cole—yet Annie seemed to know what he was talking about.

'No. In fact, I look forward to furthering our acquaintance very shortly, ma'am,' Cole said to Annie. 'But I have another call to make now. If you'll excuse me?'

Honor slowly registered that Cole was leaving. She twisted round to look up at him, dismayed by the prospect of his abrupt departure.

There was an odd gleam of amusement in his blue eyes when he looked down at her, but then his expression softened into one of tenderness.

'I'm coming back,' he said gently. He pulled her shaky, unresisting body towards him and lightly kissed her forehead. She gasped and lowered her head, partly because she was embarrassed to be kissed in front of her mother, and partly because she was assailed by so many strong feelings she didn't know what to do.

Cole didn't try to make Honor look up; instead, he bent his own head and kissed her cheek.

'It's all right, sweetheart,' he murmured in her ear, too softly for anyone else to hear. 'She's pleased you're home. And I'll be back tomorrow. So don't set up in business as a dressmaker before then!'

Honor managed a slightly watery laugh as she drew away from Cole. 'You can't set up an entire business overnight,' she retorted, taking comfort from Cole's assurances. 'Not even Mama could.'

'I don't think a wise man would bet against that possibility,' Cole said, a definite—and very confusing—gleam of amusement in his eyes as he glanced from Honor to her mother. 'Good day, Mrs Howarth.'

'Goodbye, Sir Cole,' Annie replied calmly. 'We will expect to see you tomorrow.'

She stood aside so that Cole could leave the parlour. Honor distractedly noticed that Susannah left with him. She was finally alone with her mother. She couldn't quite meet Annie's eyes. She'd been dreading this confrontation for months.

'Well,' said Annie at last. 'At least this time you've chosen a man with half a brain in his head.'

'I haven't chosen him. I mean—'

'He certainly seems to have chosen you,' Annie cut briskly across Honor's denial.

'He can't. It's not how it looks at all,' Honor replied wearily. She didn't want to discuss Cole with her mother. Her heart was already aching from the pain of his loss.

'You look…thinner,' said Annie, coming closer. 'Your face is…thinner. What happened to your hair?'

The new growth was darker blonde, but the long ends were still sun-bleached from the previous summer.

Honor self-consciously brushed back a stray curl. 'It was the sun,' she whispered.

'You look older.' Annie came a few more cautious steps closer. 'You were a child when you left. Your cheeks were round like a child's. Now…' She tentatively touched one of Honor's elegantly sculptured cheekbones.

Honor gazed at her mother, shaken not only by the gentleness of her touch, but by her hesitancy. Honor had never known Annie Howarth to be uncertain about anything. Then she saw the shimmer of tears in her mother's eyes and her own self-control disintegrated. She burst into tears, and the next minute she was locked in her mother's arms.

Cole went straight to the Mortons' town house. The butler seemed a little flustered when Cole gave his name.

'This way please, sir.' The butler quickly regained his equilibrium and showed Cole into a small downstairs room. 'I will inform Mr Morton that you are here.'

Cole waited nearly ten minutes before his host finally appeared.

'Cole, dear boy!' George Morton strode across the room towards him. 'I was sorry to hear about poor Gifford.' He seized Cole's hand in a hearty grip.

'Thank you.' As ever when he thought of his brother Cole felt a pang of grief. 'You look well,' he told the other man.

'Very fit, very fit,' Morton asserted vigorously. 'You've sold out, I take it?'

'It was necessary,' Cole replied briefly. 'Sir, may I come directly to the point—?'

'Bridget,' Morton interrupted. 'You wish to discuss…sit down, boy! Sit down! Ah, Penge!' He swung round as the door opened and the butler entered carrying a silver tray. 'Brandy. I'm sure you'd welcome a glass, Raven,' he declared jerkily.

'Thank you.' Cole accepted the brandy and sat down, stretching out his long legs. Despite Morton's fulsome welcome, it was fairly clear to Cole that his arrival had unsettled the other man. He decided to leave it up to Morton to direct the conversation.

'No doubt you hoped to see Bridget,' said Morton abruptly.

'Is she not here?' Cole enquired politely.

'No. Cole, I assure you, if I'd had any idea what she planned—!' Morton burst out. He leapt to his feet and began to pace in front of the hearth.

Cole waited, trying not to look as hopeful as he felt. Despite his realisation that Annie Howarth was acquainted with Bridget, he hadn't dared to hope he might already be freed from his betrothal.

'Dammit! I've never been so embarrassed or shamed in my life!' Morton declared. 'Bridget is already married.'

'I beg your pardon!' Cole set down his glass with a sharp click. He couldn't remember the last time he'd heard such good news, but he could hardly say so. 'What the devil do you mean?'

'I mean she eloped.' Morton looked truly miserable as he met Cole's eyes.

'She fled to Gretna Green?' Cole knew it wasn't a very tactful question, but he couldn't resist asking. He'd always thought Bridget was rather dull. He found it hard to imagine her in full flight to the border.

'No, no,' Morton replied impatiently. 'She was far too old to need my consent to the marriage. She was wed by special licence in Oxford. Now she's living with her new husband in—' He broke off, glancing at Cole warily.

'I see,' said Cole drily. He wondered if Bridget's father expected him to chase vengefully after the happy couple. 'When did the marriage take place?'

Morton looked even more uncomfortable. 'A month after we heard the news from your uncle that Gifford was dead,' he said stiffly. 'I knew any letter I sent you would probably cross with you on your way home. We've kept it very quiet. There hasn't been any scandal.'

'Good,' said Cole. He didn't pretend to be heartbroken at the situation, he knew Morton wouldn't expect it of him. It had always been primarily a business arrangement.

'Bridget did not mean to insult you,' Morton said with dignity. 'You know as well as I do that this union was something your father and I hatched between us.

Neither you nor Bridget ever expressed much enthusiasm for it—though you both did your duty by us.
I—'

Cole held up his hand. 'There's no need to say any
more,' he said quietly. 'I was away a long time. I don't
feel my pride or my honour have been affronted. I
hope Bridget will be very happy with her new husband.'

Morton nodded his acknowledgement of Cole's
comment. 'He seems a steady enough fellow,' he replied grudgingly. 'And you'll have the pick of the
Season's beauties now, hey!' he continued, striving for
a more jovial note. 'A wealthy, eligible bachelor. All
the pretty young girls will be throwing their handker-
chiefs for you.'

Cole grimaced at the prospect. 'I'm not exactly a
ladies' man,' he said.

Morton laughed and slapped Cole on the back encouragingly.

In the end the two men dined together. Their families had been neighbours for over a century and Cole
preferred to stay on good terms with his father's old
friend. He let Morton rib him about his new-found
eligibility, but he didn't tell him about Honor. As far
as possible, Cole was determined that no scandal
would be attached to her name. He didn't want Bridget
to experience any unnecessary discomfort as a result
of her impulsive action—but he did prefer news of her
marriage to be generally known before he introduced
Honor to the world as his wife.

He questioned Morton discreetly about the details of
Bridget's affair. To his relief, Mrs Howarth's name
wasn't mentioned in connection with Bridget's elopement. Bridget had met her new husband, Mr

Sedgeworth, in the Pump Room at Bath the previous December. George Morton apparently wasn't aware they'd been introduced by Annie Howarth. Bridget and Sedgeworth had continued their clandestine relationship through letters and occasional surreptitious meetings in London and Oxfordshire until the unexpected news of Gifford's death and Cole's impending return had precipitated them into taking action.

Morton began to question Cole about the progress of the war in the Peninsula, and Cole allowed the subject of Bridget's elopement to drop. He'd question Annie later. He wondered how much Honor's formidable mother would be willing to tell him.

'What kind of business are you considering?' Annie asked Honor.

Honor was momentarily disconcerted by the question, then she realised why her mother was asking.

'I mentioned to Co…Maj…*Sir* Cole,' she stumbled over his correct form of address, and blushed at Annie's slight smile of amusement, 'that I might consider becoming a dressmaker,' she explained.

'A *dressmaker*!' Annie sounded appalled.

'I mean I thought I might have an establishment in Mayfair,' Honor explained defensively. 'I know it would require an initial investment and—'

'What does Sir Cole think of your idea?' Annie asked, arching her eyebrow quizzically.

Honor hesitated. She was having dinner with her mother and Susannah. It was a long time since they'd all eaten together. Honor was unbelievably relieved that she'd made peace with her mother, but she also felt oddly dissociated from her surroundings. So much had happened to her since she'd last stayed at the Belle

Savage, and it hadn't been her childhood home. Annie had only bought the London inn shortly before Honor had gone to the seminary in Bath. Honor had visited for increasingly brief intervals between the ages of sixteen and twenty-one, but after she'd left the seminary she'd lived in the cheapest respectable lodgings she could find. She'd stopped confiding in her mother years ago because somehow Annie always seemed to criticise her plans—but now she sensed a change in their relationship. She decided to put her new-found confidence to the test.

'I did tell Cole about my dressmaking plans,' she admitted, 'but he didn't seem very convinced.'

'I'm sure you would be very successful,' Susannah said loyally. 'You were always an excellent needle-woman.'

'I thought so,' Honor agreed blandly. 'But Cole wasn't convinced. He suggested I might become a blacksmith instead—because I'm so good with horses.'

Susannah looked startled, but Annie laughed. 'A very sensible idea,' she said, without a blink. 'I employ several blacksmiths. If you wish, I could arrange for you to be apprenticed to one of them.'

Honor frowned. Her mother always managed to have the last word.

'Honor shot a wolf, Annie,' Susannah broke in hastily. 'She was so brave.'

'Of course,' Annie said matter-of-factly. 'I never doubted it.'

Honor looked down at her plate, suddenly too full of emotion to swallow, let alone eat the rest of the splendid food before her.

Her whole life was upside down. She was speaking to her mother for the first time in four years, but Cole was gone. She was so tired and emotional. She didn't want to talk about her relationship with Cole to any-one—not even Susannah, who had been her life-long confidante and ally. She just wanted to be alone, to rest and come to terms with her new circumstances.

'Come, I'll take you to your room,' said Annie briskly. 'You've travelled such a long way to get here.' Her voice cracked slightly on the last few words, but she covered her own emotions with a practised smile.

'I am a little tired,' Honor said carefully. She stood and started to follow Annie, then she turned back and hugged Susannah. The older woman held her for a long time before she released her into Annie's care.

'Ring if you need anything at all,' Annie said a few minutes later in the beautifully appointed room she'd assigned to Honor.

'Yes, Mama.' Honor caught her breath as she saw her familiar black shawl laid on the bed. She picked it up and held it against her breast. The shawl embodied so many varied memories for her. 'Mama, do you know a woman called Maggie Foster?' she asked sud-denly, a snippet of conversation floating into her mind.

'Maggie?' said Annie slowly. 'I believe she worked for me once. Why do you ask?'

'I just wondered,' said Honor, feeling a growing sense of curiosity as she noticed Annie's almost im-perceptible uneasiness at the question. 'She didn't mention she'd worked for you until just before I left Spain—but she must have known I was your daughter for the whole four years I knew her. I just thought it was strange.'

'Perhaps the subject never arose before,' Annie said casually.

'You didn't...discharge her?' Honor pressed, fear-ing the worst. 'I know she could be a bit…abrasive, but she was a very good woman. I'm sure…'

'I didn't discharge her, I asked her to look out for you,' Annie exclaimed irritably. 'I assume she did, or you wouldn't be defending her so loyally.'

'But you said you never wanted to speak to me or see my face again!' Honor exclaimed. 'Why—'

'For Heaven's sake, Honor!' Annie burst out, goaded beyond endurance. 'I didn't mean it! You can't possibly have imagined I let you go off to Portugal without taking steps to protect you!'

Honor stared at her with her mouth open. It honestly hadn't occurred to her that her mother would do such a thing. Annie had always been so insistent that her daughter should learn to be strong, independent and self-sufficient.

'And while we're on the subject, why on earth didn't you come to me when Selhurst was making such a nuisance of himself?' Annie demanded in exasperation. 'I admit I was a little distracted at the time because Brown had just set up a rival stagecoach to Liverpool—but I dealt with the Duke as soon as I realised what was happening. And then I found out you'd married Patrick! Good grief, girl!'

'You…dealt with…the Duke?' Honor echoed. She didn't know whether to laugh or cry.

'Of course I did,' Annie said impatiently. 'What did you expect me to do?'

'I don't know.' Honor flung her arm out in a wild gesture. 'Tell me to go to the devil my own way?'

There was silence for a few highly charged seconds.

'I didn't mean that either,' said Annie at last. 'I didn't want you to go on stage. I wanted you to be a lady. I wanted you to be happy.'

'Did you…make me such a success?' Honor whispered, tears clogging her throat. She'd always believed her successful career as an actress was the one accomplishment which was truly her own. Now she wondered.

'No,' said Annie quietly. 'You made yourself a success. I couldn't have achieved that for you. I was proud of you. I *am* proud of you.'

'Oh.' Honor didn't know which way was up any more. She didn't know what to say, what to do or what to think.

'You must sleep,' said Annie. 'In the morning we can talk about your plans. You're safe here.'

'I don't have any plans,' Honor said helplessly.

'But you know what you want to do,' Annie said briskly. 'You've always known what you wanted to do next.'

'No I haven't,' Honor cried. '*You've* always known what you wanted to do next, Mama. I just…*do* things. I don't know—'

Annie put her arms around Honor. She was a few inches shorter than her daughter, although normally her forceful personality made the discrepancy in their heights unnoticeable.

'But you do know what you want now,' said Annie softly.

'You can't give me this, Mama,' Honor's voice was muffled. 'No one can.'

'We'll see.' Annie cupped Honor's face in her hands and kissed her forehead. 'Wash your eyes in cold water before you sleep so they aren't puffy in the morning,' she instructed. 'Goodnight, Honor.'

Honor stumbled through her preparations for bed like an automaton. She curled up in a ball on her side as she waited for sleep to find her. It didn't matter what Cole or Annie said, she couldn't have what she wanted—because she would never be able to give Cole the heir he needed to secure the future of his inheritance.

'Good morning, Sir Cole.'

'Good morning, Mrs Howarth.' Cole had arrived at the Belle Savage a few minutes earlier and asked to see Honor. Instead he'd been brought straight to Annie, sitting in her office at the heart of her empire.

She stood up and walked around the desk, offering him her hand as she did so. He shook it and looked down at her speculatively.

'You have a question, Sir Cole?' she enquired, with a polite arch of her eyebrow.

'Possibly,' he replied. 'How is Honor?'

'She was tired after her journey,' said Annie. 'Please, sit down. Have you come to ask my permission to marry her?'

'No.' Cole sat down. 'Do you object?'

'I object if you're planning to make her your mistress,' Annie said bluntly. 'She deserves better than that.'

'Then we're in agreement,' said Cole calmly. 'Which is rather fortunate since you've just divested me of a perfectly good fiancée.'

'Is that what Mr Morton told you?' Annie's eyebrow rose again.

'No, he didn't mention your name,' Cole replied. 'I wondered about that. Bridget's recent letters were quite full of you—how did you manage to avoid involvement in her marriage?'

'Probably because, after I introduced her to her new

husband, I never mentioned him to her again,' Annie said serenely. 'I did encourage her to take a more energetic approach to her life. Of course, I've known Mr Sedgeworth for years. He always stays at the Belle when he visits London. A very steady and well-intentioned young man, with a romantic streak he has only recently learnt to explore. On a practical level, he has worked hard to improve the condition of his estates.'

'An ideal husband, in fact,' Cole observed, fascinated by Annie's revelations.

'Yes. I wish you to understand—I did not wantonly throw Miss Morton and Mr Sedgeworth together,' Annie said seriously. 'I made Miss Morton's acquaintance months before I introduced her to Sedgeworth—'

'Which you did as soon as you heard the news from Joe that Patrick was dead,' Cole interrupted.

'Patrick was dead and you held Honor in your arms while she slept,' Annie said calmly. 'Joe was most eloquent on the tenderness of the scene. Miss Morton and Mr Sedgeworth are a good match. I believe they will do very well together.'

'I suppose I must resign myself to the fact that, by the time my ring is on Honor's finger, you will have a battalion of your spies in my employ,' Cole said drily. 'In fact, you probably already have—and if I do anything to hurt her…'

'You would very much regret it,' Annie said coolly.

'Well, now.' Cole's blue eyes were as shrewd and unflinching as Annie's as they both evaluated each other across the width of the room.

Cole didn't appreciate being spied upon, or having anyone meddle with his life as Annie had done. But he knew that she had done it for Honor, and the fact

she'd taken care to select a suitable husband for
Bridget was a point in her favour. He'd noticed that
George Morton had made no complaints about his
daughter's new husband. He'd simply been embarrassed at the way the marriage had taken place.

'For Honor's sake—and my own—I would prefer to
be on good terms with you,' Cole said quietly. 'If you
don't hurt her, and drive her away from you, you won't
need to set spies to find out how she is.'

Annie turned her head away. 'You are direct, sir,'
she said tautly.

'Sometimes it's necessary,' Cole replied, a note of
steel underpinning his pleasant tone. 'I will be offended if you continue with your meddling when
Honor and I are married. But if you respect our privacy, I am sure we will get along very well.'

Annie looked at him curiously. 'I think you mean
that,' she said.

'I do,' said Cole. 'May I see Honor?'

'I'm afraid she went shopping with Susannah,
shortly before you arrived,' Annie said apologetically.

'Shopping?' Cole was startled.

'She's very close to Susannah,' Annie explained.
'I'm sure they'll be back soon. Indeed, they may already have returned. Come this way.' She stood and
led the way out of her office.

They found Susannah in the parlour, but not Honor.
At Annie's sharply voiced question Susannah smiled.

'She went to call upon Lady Durrington,' she ex-
plained. 'Apparently her ladyship corresponded with
Honor throughout the time she was in the Peninsula.
Honor wanted to thank her for her kindness.'

'You let her go alone?' Annie's voice sounded un-
characteristically harsh.

'I've never met Lady Durrington.' Susannah frowned in surprise at Annie. 'And Honor wanted me to return home, in case Major Raven should call. So that I could—'

'Lady Durrington died two weeks ago,' Annie said grittily, jerking on the bell pull to summon a servant.

All the colour drained out of Susannah's face. 'Oh, dear, I didn't realise,' she whispered. 'Poor Honor! She was very fond of Lady Durrington.'

'I want a carriage and driver ready immediately,' Annie informed the servant who'd responded to her summons. Then she spun round to face Cole.

'Go and get her back,' she ordered tensely.

Cole didn't waste time taking offence at Annie's peremptory tone. His first consideration was Honor. He noted the address Annie gave him, and went straight there.

Honor realised there was something wrong as soon as she arrived at the Durringtons' Piccadilly town house. It was years since she'd last visited Lady Durrington but, to her surprise, the sombre butler seemed to remember her.

'This way, if you please. I'll inform Lord Durrington of your arrival,' he said solemnly.

'No, I came to see *Lady* Durrington,' Honor corrected him breathlessly.

'This way,' the butler repeated.

Honor followed him into an elegantly furnished drawing room. She'd set out to make a brief social call, but now she was filled with apprehension. The house seemed to echo with dark sorrow. The room was cold, despite the fact that it was a sunny May morning outside. She shivered, and wished she hadn't come.

She heard the door open and turned to see a tall, sombre-faced gentleman dressed in mourning come into the library.

'Forgive me for keeping you waiting,' he said. His voice was pleasant and softly spoken, but not quite steady. 'I'm Arthur Durrington.'

Even in the midst of her own discomfort, Honor thought he sounded oddly unsure of his welcome, which was strange, considering they were in his house. She suddenly realised she hadn't given her name to the butler, and he hadn't asked. She hastened to repair the omission.

'I'm…'

'Honor,' said Lord Durrington, a strange note in his voice.

'Yes.' She was surprised by his familiarity; she'd been about to introduce herself as Mrs O'Donnell. 'I suppose Lady Durrington may have mentioned me to you,' she guessed.

'Once or twice,' he agreed, his eyes still fixed on her face. The intensity of his scrutiny made her feel very unsettled.

'Lady Durrington asked—' she began.

Lord Durrington cleared his throat. 'I regret…I am sorry to tell you my wife died suddenly two weeks ago,' he said hoarsely.

'Oh! Oh, dear. I'm so sorry.' The news was a shock to Honor, even though she'd been afraid something was seriously wrong. 'I had no idea,' she said in distress. 'I only arrived in London yesterday. I shouldn't have intruded…'

'No, please, sit down,' Lord Durrington said quickly. 'My wife talked about you frequently. I have

often wished to meet you. Please, sit down,' he repeated.

Honor hesitated. She didn't want to stay. She was
sad for Lady Durrington, but Lord Durrington made
her uncomfortable. She didn't like the way he stared
at her so intently, or his eagerness to keep her with
him. But it would be rude not to stay a little while
when he was being so hospitable.

'Thank you.' She sat down on the edge of her chair.
She would stay a few minutes, she decided. Then she
would claim a prior appointment and make her escape.

When Cole arrived at the Piccadilly house he had a
brief conversational tussle with the butler before he
established that Honor was indeed visiting Lord
Durrington.

'I'm sorry, sir,' said the butler frigidly. 'His lordship
gave strict orders he didn't wish to be disturbed. If you
would care to leave your card—'

Cole solved the impasse by pushing past the butler
into the hallway and lifting his voice.

'Honor!' he shouted. 'Honor?'

A few moments later a door burst open and Honor
ran out straight into his arms.

As Cole gathered her against him, he discovered she
was trembling uncontrollably.

'Are you all right?' he demanded fiercely, filled with
anger that he'd found her in such overwrought state.

'Yes,' she said, but she still clung tightly to him.

Cole looked up to find they were being observed.
As soon as he saw Lord Durrington his suspicions,
aroused by Annie Howarth's distress at finding where
Honor had gone, were confirmed.

The man watching them had the same green, gold

and russet eyes as the woman Cole loved. Not only that, but Lord Durrington and Honor also shared the same distinctive bone structure. When Honor was happy and well-fed she looked elegantly slim, but when she was hungry and anxious she looked as gaunt and hollow-cheeked as Lord Durrington now appeared. The shape of their eyebrows, their mouths—even the colour of their hair—were all very similar. If Lord Durrington had spent four years under the Iberian sun, his dark-blond hair would be as sun-bleached as Honor's. No one in the same room with the two of them could be in much doubt as to Honor's parentage. No wonder Lord Durrington had always avoided meeting her in the past.

'Honor.' Lord Durrington's voice cracked with emotion. 'I didn't mean to upset you. It just…it seemed such a miracle that you came to see me.'

'Perhaps you would be kind enough to give us a few minutes alone, Lord Durrington,' Cole said coolly.

'Of course, sir,' said Lord Durrington, stepping to one side and gesturing to the room he'd just vacated. 'I'm afraid you have the advantage of me.'

'Cole Raven,' Cole curtly introduced himself.

'Ah, yes.' Lord Durrington's mouth curved in a brief, crooked smile. 'You rescued her from drowning. I should have guessed.'

Lord Durrington's comment irritated Cole. It appeared that Annie Howarth hadn't been the only one who'd been keeping track of their activities. Had Lord Durrington relied on his wife's correspondence with Honor for his information—or had he had spies of his own in the Peninsula? Cole decided there and then that, in future, no one was going to play devious games with Honor's life.

* * *

'He says he's my father,' Honor said a few minutes later, when her trembling had subsided and she felt safe in Cole's presence.

He nodded, apparently unsurprised, and tenderly brushed her hair back from her face.

'Did you know?' she asked in amazement.

'Not until I saw him just now,' Cole replied reassuringly. 'You look very much like him. But your mother was upset when she heard you'd come here. She sent me to fetch you. That did make me suspicious.'

'Oh. I never told Mama I was friends with Lady Durrington.' Honor twisted the material of her skirt nervously between her fingers. 'I don't understand it,' she said. 'Do you think Lord Durrington made Lady Durrington be friends with me so she would tell him about me? I don't like this. I feel so, so...*lied* to. It's horrible.'

'I'm inclined to agree,' said Cole tautly.

Honor looked up at him, distracted from her bewilderment by the censure in his tone. 'I don't know what to think about anything any more,' she admitted shakily. 'What are you doing here?' Tears suddenly started in her eyes, though she hadn't cried at her father's news. 'Miss Morton won't like it.'

'Bridget is already married to Mr Sedgeworth and no doubt living happily in Derbyshire,' Cole said, smiling at her encouragingly. 'There's nothing to worry about any more, sweetheart. I'll take you home and you can speak to Lord Durrington another time, when you've had a chance to get accustomed to his news.' He took Honor's cold hands in his, squeezing them reassuringly.

'Oh.' Honor swallowed. She was on the verge of

giving way to a tidal wave of tears, but she struggled to maintain her composure. 'I'm being stupid,' she whispered. 'I shouldn't be making such a fuss. Mama won't approve. She says you should always appraise every situation in a properly businesslike way.'

'But this isn't a business matter,' Cole pointed out gently, giving her his handkerchief.

'No.' Honor dried her eyes, but more tears welled up to replace the ones she'd wiped away. 'I'm so sad for Lady Durrington,' she whispered. 'It was such a shock...I thought everyone in London was safe—so far away from the war that nothing bad would happen to them. And then...and then he told me...' Her voice quavered and failed.

Cole had been sitting on a low stool in front of her. Now he shifted to sit beside her on the sofa. He put his arm around her comfortingly.

Honor drew in several careful breaths, exhaling slowly as she tried to assimilate all the new information she'd learned. Lady Durrington's death. The identity of her father. Bridget Morton's marriage to someone else...

She put her hand up to touch her hair. 'I must look a sight,' she said distractedly. 'Am I very dishevelled?'

'You look beautiful,' said Cole simply.

'Don't say that!' she exclaimed, feeling more tears threaten. 'I must be calm and composed. You must say practical things. Is there a mirror in here? I don't think you're a reliable witness.'

'I assure you I can be extremely practical,' Cole replied, a hint of indignation in his voice. 'Stand up, I will inspect you.'

Honor's smile was a little watery as she did as he ordered. She didn't let herself meet his eyes as he looked her over, then stroked a curl of blonde hair back from her face.

'Hmm,' he said consideringly. 'Not enough mud for a truly soldierly appearance—but you'll do. Are you ready to leave?'

'Yes.' She took the arm he offered her. 'I will tell Lord Durrington that I will speak to him another time,' she said firmly. 'But I wish…' she faltered. 'I don't want him to visit me unexpectedly,' she said in a more uncertain voice. 'Do you think that seems fair?'

'Yes.' Cole's response was immediate and unhesitating. 'You will not have to speak to him again until you are ready to do so.'

In Cole's opinion, Lord Durrington had shown an appalling lack of consideration for Honor. The man had abandoned her before she'd even been born. To claim her as his daughter only moments after he'd broken the news of Lady Durrington's death seemed both precipitant and unnecessarily cruel. Cole had no doubt Annie would protect Honor from her father while she was staying at the Belle Savage. He made a mental note to give appropriate instructions to his own servants.

'I will talk with you again,' Honor assured Lord Durrington, a few minutes later. He'd obviously been hovering nearby, because he'd appeared in the hallway as soon as Cole opened the door. 'I'm sorry Lady Durrington—' Honor broke off mid-sentence, and Cole felt her stiffen beside him.

'Did you *ask* Lady Durrington to befriend me?' she asked Lord Durrington croakily.

'No! On my honour,' Lord Durrington replied quickly. 'She saw you on stage and…forgive me, she saw the likeness between us. I did not know she'd made your acquaintance for several months. I think…she couldn't have children. You were the daughter she couldn't…' He didn't complete his explanation.

'My letters,' Honor said raspily. 'Would you return them, please?'

Cole saw the surprise and hurt in Lord Durrington's eyes at Honor's unexpected request. But he also understood why she was so shaken by the situation. She'd told him once she'd never met Lord Durrington. All the time she'd been writing to Lady Durrington, Honor would have assumed her letters were of no interest to anyone but her friend. She'd just discovered Lord Durrington had no doubt been perusing them as eagerly as his wife. Lord Durrington might be her father, but he was still a stranger to her.

'Send them to my house in Berkeley Square,' Cole told Lord Durrington.

Honor's father nodded, looking defeated.

'If you wish to be my friend, you will have to start from the beginning, the same way all new acquaintances start,' said Honor. 'I don't wish…that is, Mama always told me you were an honourable man. Lady Durrington told me only good things about you. But I must learn for myself. I'm sure I will discover that they were both right,' she added, in a softer tone.

Cole was proud of her. Her voice was steady, and contained no hint of anger or bitterness at her father's betrayal. Lord Durrington might have harboured dreams of a tearfully joyous reunion, but first he would have to gain Honor's trust.

'I will look forward to our next meeting,' said Lord Durrington huskily.

Honor nodded, and let Cole escort her out of her father's house.

'Do you think I was too unkind?' she asked, as soon as they'd gained the privacy of the carriage.

'No,' Cole replied immediately. 'He abandoned you. It's up to you if you wish to receive him.'

'Mama always told me he was an honourable man,' Honor said, chewing her lip. 'He couldn't help it. He had other responsibilities. He looked so sad…'

'I'm sure he is,' said Cole. 'But you've spent your whole life not knowing the name of your father. I think you need a little time to collect your thoughts before you speak to him again. When you do, I'm sure you'll have many things you want to say to him—and to ask him.'

'Yes.' Honor let Cole draw her against his side as the carriage trundled through the busy London streets. She rested her head on his shoulder and closed her eyes. So many, many thoughts whirled around in her head.

Her father.

Cole.

Miss Morton—who was already married to someone else… ·

Chapter Eleven

'Where are we?' Honor had expected Cole to take her back to the Belle Savage. Instead the carriage stopped outside a large house in Berkeley Square.

'This is my home,' Cole replied.

He helped her out of the carriage, then gave the coachman instructions to return to the Belle Savage.

'It's a very fine house,' said Honor politely, as Cole led her up the steps to the front door.

'Thank you.' Cole smiled slightly at her comment. 'Morning, Kemp. This is Mrs O'Donnell,' he introduced her to his butler. 'Please bring us some tea in the library.'

'Yes, sir.' Kemp's sharp eyes darted from Cole's face to Honor's. She knew he was curious about her, but that was the least of her concerns. Cole had brought her to his home. He'd already told her that he was no longer betrothed to Bridget Morton.

Honor gripped her hands together as she worried about what Cole might be about to say next. And what she would have to tell him…

'This was always our favourite room,' Cole said a few minutes later, as he gazed around the library.

Honor heard the sadness in Cole's voice and abruptly remembered the circumstances of his return home. She was appalled that she'd forgotten.

'I'm so sorry,' she said unsteadily. 'This must be so difficult for you.'

'Last night was the first time I'd been in this house since my father died,' Cole said distantly. He revolved slowly, his eyes roaming up and down the library shelves until his gaze came to rest on a large portrait.

There were four men in the picture. An older man, sitting in a chair, surrounded by three youths. Honor immediately recognised one of the lads as a young Cole. She saw that he shared the same vivid blue eyes as the older man. But Cole's father smiled upon the world with cheerful friendliness. He lacked the fierce intensity of his younger son which was visible even in the portrait.

Cole was standing on his father's left side. The young man standing at their father's right hand possessed the same vivid blue eyes, but jet black hair.

'Gifford?' Honor murmured.

'Yes.'

'It's easy to see you're brothers,' Honor said. 'You both have your father's eyes. And you are all very handsome.'

Cole's lips twitched in a brief smile.

Honor continued to study the portrait. She was fascinated by the picture of Cole as a younger man, but also by the images of his father and brother. At first sight she'd imagined the black man standing behind Cole's father was a favoured servant—but then she looked again. Her eyes narrowed as her gaze flicked from one man's face to another. There was a resemblance between all the men in the portrait.

'Who—?' she began.

'Anthony,' Cole replied. 'My cousin.' She sensed him stiffen beside her, but she kept her eyes on the portrait.

'He died with Gifford,' she said softly. 'You grieve for him also.'

'I do.' Cole sighed, and she felt him relax. 'Gifford is—was—five years older than me. It does not feel unusual for me to come home and he not be here. But Father and Anthony—they were always here. Working on Father's experiments...' He glanced around the library, almost as if he expected to see the familiar figures of the two men sitting in the well-worn chairs.

'How is it that Anthony is your cousin?' Honor asked.

'His father was my father's older brother,' Cole explained. 'His mother was a runaway slave Uncle James rescued. Not that I ever knew my uncle. If he hadn't died unwed years before I was born, Father wouldn't have married and I wouldn't be standing here today.'

'But Anthony grew up with you?' Honor prompted.

'He was two years older than Giff,' Cole replied. 'But his mother died in the same carriage accident that killed Uncle James. My parents took care of him, and when Giff and I were born we were all raised together.'

'Even though he was...not legitimate,' Honor whispered, seeing how Anthony gazed out of the portrait with the same self-confidence that Gifford and Cole displayed. He looked sure of his place in the world.

Honor could rarely remember feeling such certainty about her own situation. Cole had told her once she had the manners and speech of a gentlewoman. Annie had raised her daughter to be a lady, yet Annie herself had never made any attempt to enter the fashionable world for which she'd carefully prepared Honor. And Honor had spoiled all her mother's plans by running away to join the theatre.

'I don't think my father cared about that.' Cole slipped his arms around Honor from behind, drawing her back to lean against his chest as he looked up at the family portrait. 'Anthony was his nephew. He was part of our family.'

'Your father was a very fine man,' Honor said shakily. 'Some men don't recognise their own—let alone someone else's—mistakes.'

Cole didn't respond for two heartbeats, then he spun Honor round to face him.

'You are not a mistake,' he said fiercely. 'Any more than Anthony was. I was proud to have Anthony as my cousin. I am proud—'

He broke off, cupping Honor's face between his hands. He smiled at her—the sweetest smile she'd ever seen on his lips.

'I will be proud to call you my wife,' he said softly.

Tears filled her eyes and overflowed onto her cheeks. She could see him only through a distorted haze as she tasted salt on her tongue.

'I can't,' she whispered brokenly. 'I *can't*!' She dimly saw Cole's shocked expression, then she began to cry in earnest.

He pulled her into his arms, holding her with such fierce possessiveness she cried even harder. She tried to stop. She knew she had to stop. But she'd been fighting to control her turbulent emotions for too long. The calm she sought was far beyond her reach.

Cole was first shocked, then alarmed by Honor's wild tears. He'd seen her cry before, but he'd never seen her in such uncontrollable distress. He stroked her hair, trying to soothe her, but it made no difference. He resisted an urge to shake her—or even to order her to stop crying. Cold water was supposed to be good for hysterics, he thought distractedly. But he recoiled from the idea of throwing cold water over Honor. Besides, after everything she'd endured, not to mention the shocking information she'd learned from Lord Durrington, she was entitled to a few tears.

Cole sat down on the sofa and drew Honor on to his lap. He fumbled in his pocket and found his handkerchief. He pressed it into her hands, then he held her comfortingly and waited for her to stop crying.

Honor rested her head against Cole's shoulder, feeling utterly miserable. Her face was hot and swollen. She couldn't breath properly. Her head ached. Her heart ached. And now she had to tell Cole what was wrong.

She felt him stroke her hair back from her damp face, then kiss her forehead. She turned her face towards him, trying to hide in the space between his neck and shoulder.

'I'm sorry, I'm sorry,' she whispered brokenly.

'Sweetheart, what's wrong?' She heard the worry in his voice.

'I'm sorry,' she whispered again. She moved in his arms, trying to get to her feet. He tightened his hold momentarily, then he let her stand up.

She turned her back on him immediately, drying her eyes and blowing her nose. Never in her life had she had to tell anyone something this painful. Part of her had hoped she'd never have to tell Cole. Part of her had hoped for a miracle. Either way, she'd always meant to be calm and in control when they had this discussion. Now she was so overwrought she could barely speak.

She heard Cole get up, and braced herself for his touch. She was afraid she might start crying if he touched her again. Instead he went over to the door. She wondered where he was going. He went out for a few moments, then returned, closing the door carefully behind him. She threw a quick glance in his direction and saw that he was carrying a tea tray.

'Kemp can be very discreet,' he explained cheerfully. 'He left the tea tray on the hall table. Father trained him not to interrupt at crucial moments in his experiments.'

'Or w-when he had hysterical women to t-tea,' Honor said, trying to make light of her outburst.

'Bread and butter and cake as well,' Cole said approvingly. 'I meant to ask if you were hungry.' He poured two cups of tea. 'Come and sit down,' he said gently.

Honor hesitated, then sat beside him on the sofa. If she'd chosen a more distant chair she would have had to look straight into his questioning blue eyes.

She could sense the tension in Cole's large body, but he waited while she tried to compose herself. It was hard to swallow her tea. She was only just in control of her emotions. But at last her teacup was empty.

Cole took it from her and put it back on the tray. Then he took her hand in his.

'Why can't you marry me?' he asked tautly. 'On the packet boat—'

'I *wished* on the packet boat,' Honor interrupted him before he could repeat what she'd said then. It was far too painful to hear those words now.

'But I'm *free*,' Cole said with fierce impatience. 'There's nothing to stop our marriage. I don't give a damn whether your father was married to your mother—or a bigamist ten times over. It's *you* I want to marry.'

'I...' Honor swallowed and stared down at her lap. She began to pleat her skirt with nervous fingers. 'I...'

She could feel Cole's tension increasing with every second she delayed. She *had* to tell him.

'I'm barren,' she whispered, her eyes filling once more with tears.

'What?' The word exploded out of Cole.

'I'm barren,' she repeated more loudly, finally raising her head to look at him. 'I can't give you children,' she added desperately as she saw he was staring at her in disbelief. 'I *can't!*'

She saw his chest expand as he drew in a deep, deep breath. He exhaled slowly, then drew in another deep breath. She could hardly bear to look at his face. She was braced for his disappointment, perhaps even his anger. He would surely feel she had betrayed him.

He drew in another deep breath and let it out slowly. His tense muscles relaxed. And he smiled at her.

'Is that all?' he asked quietly.

'All?' She couldn't believe she'd him heard correctly. 'Don't you understand what I just said?' she demanded, her voice rising with distress and frustration. 'I can't have children.'

'I know what you just said,' he replied steadily. 'I still want to marry you.'

'No!' Honor exclaimed. She leapt to her feet and paced about the room in her agitation. 'I admire your sense of honour—but that's just folly. You *can't* marry

me. You came home to set up your nursery. You told
me so yourself.'

'Yes.' Cole watched her stride around the room,
flicking her skirts nervously with agitated fingers.

She came to a brief pause. 'Then it would be stupid
to marry me,' she informed him curtly, and resumed
her restless pacing.

'You think I'm only determined to marry you now
out of some foolish sense of honour?' Cole enquired
coolly, playing for time.

He hadn't been sure what to expect after her bout
of frenzied weeping, but he'd seen Honor cope with
too many disasters to assume her worries would be
insignificant. He'd been prepared for her to tell him
almost anything. Even so, her news had come as a
profound shock to him. His mind teemed with questions.

How could Honor be so sure she was barren? Why
hadn't she said anything before? How was he going to
protect his inheritance now?

But he didn't blame her for her condition. His father's rational yet uncomplicated teaching ran too deep
in him. Cole's father had never attributed unexpected
illness or other infirmity to God's punishment. He'd
simply said there was a physical explanation which
men had not yet discovered. Cole wanted to know why
Honor believed she was barren, but he didn't judge her
for her state.

It took him a few moments to absorb all the implications of her announcement. He briefly considered
setting her aside as she insisted he must—and knew
immediately that he couldn't do it. No matter how
many difficulties might lie ahead of them, he could not
imagine his life without Honor.

He stood and moved to stand in front of her. She lifted her head. Her face was pale and blotchy, her eyes puffy from crying. She watched him warily, as if anticipating his rejection. He put his hands on her shoulders, tightening his grip in an instinctive attempt to reassure her.

'I want to marry you because I cannot imagine living my life without you,' he said, his voice very deep and sure. As he spoke he felt his last remaining tension drain away. He knew beyond doubt that this was the right thing to do. 'I want to marry you because I love you. Because you are the woman my heart and soul have chosen...'

'But you must have *heirs*!' Honor cried in desperation. She shook her head at him. Her hair fell around her face in damp, untidy strands. 'I can't give them to you. You must find a woman who can!'

Cole pulled her into his arms, holding her close against his chest despite her rather feeble efforts to escape. 'Easier said than done, love,' he said almost teasingly.

'What?' Honor abandoned her attempt to resist his embrace. It felt too good to be in his arms. She'd been so certain he would be disappointed or angry—though she'd hoped he would hide the worst of his unhappiness with her. She couldn't credit how calm he was. He probably hadn't understood the importance of what she'd told him. She braced herself to explain more fully. He had to realise that, if he married her, he would never be able to fulfil his duty to his family name.

He brushed his lips against her temple.

'The only way I could guarantee a fertile bride would be to marry a young widow who has already had a child,' he pointed out gently. 'Alternatively, I suppose I could try impregnating one of this year's debutantes. I could draw up some kind of agreement with the lucky lady's father to that effect.' A hint of amusement crept into his voice. 'She only gets my ring on her finger when I'm quite certain that she's already carrying my child.'

Honor tensed even as she allowed herself to lean against him. 'Are you taking this seriously?' she asked sharply, on the verge of losing her temper. She couldn't bear him to make fun of her at such a time.

'Oh, yes,' said Cole. His reply was simple and heart-felt. 'In this life there are no guarantees for any of us,' he said quietly. 'The only certainty I have is that I love you, and you love me, and that it would be a sin to deny that love.'

Honor tilted her head back and gazed up into his eyes. 'You really mean that,' she breathed, over-whelmed and humbled by the love and conviction she saw in his face.

'I was going to give Bridget the Oxfordshire estate as her dowry, after I had told her that I wouldn't be able to marry her,' Cole said.

Honor was momentarily confused by his change of topic, but she listened anyway.

'It turns out I didn't have to tell her anything,' Cole continued. 'Instead her father apologised to me for her elopement.'

'You were going to break off your betrothal?' Honor whispered, understanding dawning. Cole was telling her that he'd always meant to marry her—that he hadn't proposed to her just because he'd unexpectedly found himself free to do so.

'Yes.' Cole confirmed her realisation.

'Lady Durrington couldn't have children,' Honor said, her thoughts going off at another tangent. 'It was a great sadness to her. She said…that is, I understood it caused a—a coolness—in her relations with Lord Durrington.' Honor couldn't bear the idea that one day Cole's feelings towards her might change.

'I think there may have been other reasons for that coolness,' Cole said gently.

'Me?' Honor looked up at him anxiously.

'Perhaps. He didn't forget you, sweetheart. And I doubt very much whether he forgot your mother. He could have done.' Cole hesitated, she thought he was choosing his words carefully. 'A man might lie with a woman and forget her the following day,' he said slowly. 'Men do. Women too, sometimes. But I will never forget you. If you sent me to another woman, she would get the worst of me. You would always be in my heart and head.' He smiled crookedly. 'It's quite possible your mother has been in Lord Durrington's mind for the past twenty-six years,' he said. 'From all I've seen and heard of her, I don't think she'd be easy to forget.'

Honor laid her palms flat against Cole's chest as she considered what he'd said.

'Mama told me she'd never seen my father or spoken to him after he sent her away—before I was born,' she said pensively. 'But her memory might have been a powerful rival. Lady Durrington wasn't very…I mean, well, she was a bit insipid,' Honor revealed guiltily. 'Very kind, but…well…' Her voice trailed off.

Cole had his doubts about Lady Durrington's motives for befriending Honor, but he didn't mention them. He was more interested in Honor's comments about Lady Durrington's inability to have children. He guided Honor back to the sofa and sat down beside her.

'Why are you so sure you can't have children?' he asked gently.

'Well...because I was married for more than three years and I never had any,' Honor replied, surprised. 'The other women noticed. Maggie even said—' She broke off, blushing painfully.

'What?'

'That—that it wouldn't matter if I became your mistress, because I couldn't be c-caught out,' Honor stuttered uncomfortably, refusing to meet Cole's eyes.

Cole bit back a hasty retort. 'You mean your only reason for believing you're barren is because you were married for three years and didn't have a child,' he said carefully.

'Yes.' Honor looked at him warily.

'And did Lady Durrington often discuss her own problems with you?' he asked.

'She mentioned her sadness before I was married,' Honor replied, surprised by the direction of his questions. 'After I was married she discussed it more fully. She said she prayed I would be spared such sorrow.'

'Generous of her!' said Cole drily. 'Sweetheart, forgive me...you spent most of your marriage marching the length and breadth of Portugal. The conditions weren't exactly ideal. And before you went to the Peninsula—didn't you say you couldn't bring yourself to live in the barracks with Patrick?'

'Y-yes.' Honor stared at him with almost painful intensity.

'Forgive me,' he said again. 'But, Honor—were

there many opportunities when you *could* have conceived a child?'

Honor's mouth formed an O as she stared at him in
surprise.

'Honor…sweetheart, you do know how…?' he began tentatively, suddenly wondering exactly how so-
phisticated her knowledge was on this subject. She'd
always been so self-sufficient it was hard to imagine
she might not be well informed. On the other hand,
she'd sometimes surprised him by her sweet naïvety—
especially considering the conditions under which
she'd lived.

'Of course I know!' She nodded her head violently.
Every visible part of her face and neck flushed crimson
with embarrassment and she couldn't meet his gaze.
'Susannah explained. At first I thought…I thought…'
Her voice faded away.

'You thought what?' Cole prompted.

'At first I thought you could get pregnant just sitting
on a sofa at the same time as a man,' Honor mumbled.
'Mama was so strict. But then Susannah explained that
other…things…had to happen as well.'

'Good for Susannah!' said Cole. He was feeling almost as overheated by the conversation as Honor. His
own education on this subject, as on so many others,
had been matter of fact and straightforward. He realised once again how much he owed to his father.

He pulled Honor on to his lap and kissed her temple.
'I'm not trying to embarrass you,' he assured her, kissing her hair, because she still wouldn't look at him.
'But, sweetheart, you're going to be my wife, it's perfectly acceptable for us to discuss this kind of thing.'

'I didn't…I mean, Patrick didn't…' Honor mumbled.

It took a superhuman effort on Cole's part, but he managed to stop himself asking what it was Patrick hadn't done. Fortunately Honor told him before he exploded with curiosity.

'We didn't discuss this…this kind of thing,' she said. 'Patrick and me, I mean. I didn't know…'

'That's all right,' said Cole cheerfully. 'You're married to me now—or you will be, as soon as I can arrange it. And we—you and I—can discuss anything we want.'

'Oh.' Honor leant her head against his shoulder, and rubbed her finger up and down the lapel of his coat as she contemplated his proposal. 'Do you really think I might have been mistaken?' she asked hopefully. 'About children?'

'I don't know,' he said gently. 'I do know that my parents were married for a year before Gifford was conceived, and it was another five years after that before I was born. And my father knew exactly what was involved in producing an heir—and my mother was rested, well fed, well cared for, and miles from the nearest battlefield. I don't want you to worry about having my child. I don't even want you to think about it. I just want you to marry me and be happy. Will you marry me?'

Honor hesitated. She had been anxious about this for such a long time it was hard to let her worries go. She could see so many problems ahead of them. If she didn't give him a son, how would Cole feel in twenty years' time?

'I think you should have longer to think about this,' she said at last. 'It's such an important decision, Cole. I want you to be sure.'

'I am sure,' he said firmly, a hint of impatience in his voice.

'Please.' Honor cupped the side of his face with her hand. 'This means so much to me. I want you to wait a week. If you can tell me then that you believe, with all your heart and soul, that you will be happy with just me—even if we never have children...then I'll marry you.'

'One week,' said Cole, in a voice that brooked no argument. 'Very well. But if you raise any more objections then, I swear I'll drag you to the altar!'

Honor gave him a rather watery smile. Once his autocratic manner had infuriated her—now it sounded deeply reassuring.

'You won't have to drag me,' she promised him. 'I'll be sitting on the altar steps, waiting for you.'

Cole and Honor were married exactly a week later. Cole had used the intervening period to buy the special licence and make the other necessary arrangements. The wedding was witnessed only by Annie, Susannah, Malcolm Anderson—and Lord Durrington. Cole had decided not to invite his more distant relatives. The fact that he was still in mourning for Gifford was a good reason to keep the wedding small and private. Honor had pondered for some time about her father. In the end she had chosen to invite him to her wedding, though he did not give her away and played no part in the ceremony.

Afterwards they all went back to the Belle Savage. Honor looked around the room, still a little dazed by the speed at which her fortune had changed. She had been anticipating the worst for so long—now she had almost everything she could want. Most importantly of all, she had Cole's fierce, abiding love.

Halfway through the toasts the door was flung open.

'Excuse me, sir. Excuse me.' An inn servant tugged fruitlessly, and not entirely courteously, at the intruder's arm. 'This is a private wedding party. Perhaps you might wish to hire a private parlour for yourself and your companion…'

The intruder's appearance was so disreputable that it was easy to understand the servant's evident doubts.

He was a tall, powerfully built man, who easily brushed aside the servant's efforts to detain him. His thick black hair was far too long to meet the dictates of fashion. A long scar ran down one side of his face, above and below the eyepatch which covered one eye. A streak of grey hair indicated where the scar extended across his scalp. His good eye was an intense vivid blue, and he scanned the room quickly, ignoring the servant's protests.

'Dammit, man, stop pawing at me!' he ordered. 'I'm damned if I'll miss my own brother's wedding.'

'Giff?' Cole whispered.

He was not the only one present staring at the man in the open doorway. Honor glanced around to see that all her companions were equally startled by his appearance. Malcolm Anderson looked as shaken as Cole.

But Honor was only concerned about Cole. He was staring at his brother, all colour drained from his face, his muscles tense with shock. She wasn't even sure if he'd drawn a breath since his stunned whisper.

'Cole?' She took his hand, squeezing it, trying to give him the composure and strength he needed to deal with this most amazing and wonderful apparition.

His fingers tightened convulsively around hers, although she wasn't entirely sure he was fully aware of her. All his attention was focussed on his brother.

'Gifford?' he said, his voice unrecognisable. Suddenly he surged to his feet, knocking the table out of his way as he did so. Plates, glasses and cutlery went flying, but he didn't notice.

'I'm not so easy to kill,' said Gifford hoarsely, looking into his brother's eyes. Then they were locked in a fierce embrace.

Honor smiled, and realised she was weeping at the same time, overcome with happiness for Cole. Behind the two brothers, she saw an ebony-skinned man.

Anthony, she thought dazedly. Gifford and Anthony. They'd both come home.

It took a few minutes for Cole to recover from his shock. He turned, seeking her with his eyes, and she walked into his arms. He hugged her against his side as he introduced her to Gifford and Anthony.

'My wife, Honor,' he announced, making no attempt to disguise his pride in her. He was grinning at his brother and his cousin, drunk on happiness and relief, though his eyes were still a little blurred by tears.

'You will never know how glad I am to meet you,' said Gifford sincerely, lifting Honor's hand to his lips in a startlingly graceful gesture.

'Put on your airs for someone else,' Cole protested. 'You look more like an out-of-luck pirate than a fine courtier.'

'But that's the time when fine airs are most important,' Gifford countered, stepping back so that he could sweep Honor one of the most extravagant bows she'd ever seen. 'To fool the innkeeper you can afford the fancy dinner and private parlour you've just bespoken.' He flashed a sideways glance at Annie as he spoke, an irrepressible gleam in his blue eye.

'Have you ever thought of going on the stage?' Honor asked, unable to stop herself.

Cole groaned. 'Don't encourage him,' he protested. 'His whole life is one long performance as it is—' He broke off, his gaze locked with his brother's.

'True enough,' said Anthony, his calm voice releasing the sudden tension. 'We couldn't even get to London without having an adventure. Some fool tried to hold up the mail coach with Gifford on board—can you believe such folly? That's why we nearly missed the wedding—not that we knew you were getting married till we reached the house and Kemp told us. I swear, Gifford could not even spend a month in Bath without having some kind of adventure.' Anthony smiled at Honor as he finished speaking and she liked him immediately. In the midst of all the drama and excitement he was so calm and reassuring.

'Indeed I could.' Gifford rose to the challenge immediately. 'A month in Bath. I will be bored out of my mind—but I will not have an adventure.' He frowned. 'Perhaps we won't set off just yet,' he decided. 'I want some of the wedding feast—is there any more?' He looked around hopefully. 'And I want to hear all your adventures, brother. Mine can wait,' he forestalled Cole's response. 'It's not my wedding day. I will get to dance with the bride, won't I?' he added.

'I like your brother,' said Honor, a long time later.

'I like him too,' said Cole, grinning. 'I'd forgotten what a damn showman he can be sometimes, though. What an entrance!'

'And I like Anthony.'

'Yes.' Cole was sitting on the edge of the bed. He pulled Honor between his knees and began to unbutton her dress.

'Did you find out yet why they're still alive?' she said over her shoulder. Gifford had been resolute in not turning the evening into a recitation of his and Anthony's adventures.

'Briefly,' said Cole. 'Apparently Giff and half the crew were taken prisoner by one of the privateers that attacked him, while Anthony and the rest of the men were taken on board the other privateer. Gifford managed to escape and gain control of the privateer he was a prisoner on. Then he went off in pursuit of Anthony and the rest of his men. He didn't tell me any more than that. I do know that both he and Anthony were afraid Anthony was going to be sold into slavery. That may be why they're not talking much about it.'

'Oh my God!' said Honor, appalled at the implications of Cole's words.

'There's a shadow in Anthony's eyes that wasn't there when I last saw him,' said Cole, momentarily entirely serious. 'I didn't press for details.'

'Of course not.' Honor shivered. 'But he's safe in England now.'

'Yes.' Cole slipped the dress off her shoulders and turned her to face him.

'Wait a minute.' Honor pushed his hands away before he could finish undressing her. 'You're distracting me. I want to tell you something.'

'Sweetheart, I hope I am distracting you,' he retorted. 'This is our wedding night.'

'I know,' she said breathlessly. 'This isn't normally the kind of thing the bride tells the groom on their wedding night, but—'

She broke off, looking down at him as he sat on the side of the bed. She slipped her fingers through his tawny hair as he gazed up at her, a half-smile on his lips, but his blue eyes narrowed questioningly.

'I was thinking,' she said, 'about what we were talking about before. And—and…I talked to Mama—because, of course, Susannah hasn't ever actually *had* any children—even though she's very well informed…'

'Honor?' Cole's hands tightened on her waist.

'And I've been thinking,' Honor continued even more breathlessly. 'About—about…well, I've been so *distracted* over the past few months, I wasn't paying proper attention. I mean, I just didn't *think* but maybe, I mean…I think it must have been the night I stayed with you in Spain—after you found out Gifford was dead—only he wasn't really, of course,' she finished in a rush.

Cole stared at her for several long, agonising seconds while he tried to disentangle what she'd just told him.

'*I think I might be pregnant already!*' she whispered, her eyes round with amazement and excitement. She'd held the news inside her for two days, eager to tell Cole, yet terrified that somehow she'd made a mistake.

Honor had taken Lady Durrington's sadness so deeply to heart, and made the unfortunate woman's fears so much her own, that it was hard for her to believe she might be capable of bearing a child. It was even more unbelievable to think that she might already be pregnant.

Cole took a deep breath. Much as he loved Honor, he still wasn't entirely sure she knew exactly what she was talking about. He made her explain to him in embarrassing detail why she thought she was pregnant.

By the time she'd finished she was bright pink all over and Cole was grinning with delight.

'Oh, sweetheart! I think you're right!' he exclaimed exuberantly.

He pulled her on to the bed with him and kissed her until she couldn't think straight.

'What will we do now?' she asked much later, her head resting on his shoulder as he idly stroked her back. 'Everything has changed again now Gifford has come back.'

'*Sir* Gifford,' Cole murmured lazily. 'I never did feel comfortable with that title. I was due the Oxfordshire estate if I married Bridget, but I can't say I really want to live a few miles from her father. I haven't had a chance to talk about it with Giff yet, but I thought I'd ask him for the Hampshire estate. We could rebuild the house that was burned in the fire. What do you think?'

Honor raised herself on her elbow, looking down at Cole in the dim light.

'That's where we camped on our way to London?' she said. 'Where you…' she blushed in the darkness '…covered me in apple blossom?'

'You look beautiful in apple blossom,' Cole assured her tenderly. 'We could make a good home there, Honor.'

'Yes, we could,' she agreed. 'I liked it. What are you going to do now that you won't have so many responsibilities?' she asked after a moment.

She was a little worried about Cole. Not *very* worried, just a little concerned. She didn't think managing one country estate was going to be enough for him.

'I'm not sure,' said Cole. He didn't sound perturbed. 'But if your mother can found a coaching empire out of nothing, I'm damned sure I can find something worth doing.'

'Oh, no!' Honor groaned. 'You really are just like her.'

'No, I'm not,' said Cole firmly, rolling Honor on to her back and positioning himself above her. 'In many ways I am nothing at all like your mother. But you must admit she has an admirable head for business.'

'Are we going to talk about Mama now?' Honor asked breathlessly.

'No.' Cole kissed her. 'I wasn't planning on talking at all,' he murmured against the warm skin of her cheek. 'Unless you really want to?'

'No.' Honor put her arms around him, pulling his strong body to hers. 'I don't want to talk either,' she whispered. 'Not right now. I want…' She hesitated, blushing in the darkness, and decided this was as good a time as any to overcome her shyness on certain matters. 'I want you to make love to me,' she said boldly.

Cole laughed softly. 'Yes, Mrs Raven,' he said huskily. 'Your word is my command.'

*   *   *   *   *

Modern Romance™
...seduction and
passion guaranteed

Tender Romance™
...love affairs that
last a lifetime

Sensual Romance™
...sassy, sexy and
seductive

Blaze.
...sultry days and
steamy nights

Medical Romance™
...medical drama on
the pulse

Historical Romance™
...rich, vivid and
passionate

MILLS & BOON®

Winner at

2001 IDEA INTERNATIONAL
DESIGN
EFFECTIVENESS
AWARDS

MAT5

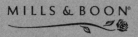

MILLS & BOON®

Historical Romance™

LORD CALTHORPE'S PROMISE
by Sylvia Andrew

Lord Adam Calthorpe had been rash when he promised to look out for a fellow soldier's sister after the battle of Waterloo. Katharine Payne flouted his authority at every turn! Such a headstrong chit would surely never find herself a husband. Only when an unscrupulous man started pursuing her did Adam realise that fulfilling his promise might involve marrying this golden-eyed virago himself!

Regency

THE DUTIFUL RAKE by Elizabeth Rolls

Marcus, Earl of Rutherford, is used to flirting with scandal. But when he places Miss Marguerite Fellowes's reputation in jeopardy, he's challenged to do the honourable thing. Marcus makes it clear it will be a marriage based on duty, not love, but as he watches proud Meg blossom in London society, the dutiful husband finds himself with far from innocent desires…

Regency

On sale 7th June 2002

Available at most branches of WH Smith, Tesco, Martins, Borders, Eason, Sainsbury's and most good paperback bookshops.

0502/04

0702/73/MB38

Coming in July

~·~

The Ultimate
Betty Neels
Collection

~·~

* A stunning 12 book collection beautifully packaged for you to collect each month from bestselling author Betty Neels.

* Loved by millions of women around the world, this collection of heartwarming stories will be a joy to treasure forever.

Available at most branches of WH Smith, Tesco, Martins, Borders, Eason, Sainsbury's and most good paperback bookshops.

FREE!

2 Books
and a surprise gift!

We would like to take this opportunity to thank you for reading this Mills & Boon® book by offering you the chance to take TWO more specially selected titles from the Historical Romance™ series absolutely FREE! We're also making this offer to introduce you to the benefits of the Reader Service™—

- ★ FREE home delivery
- ★ FREE gifts and competitions
- ★ FREE monthly Newsletter
- ★ Books available before they're in the shops
- ★ Exclusive Reader Service discount

Accepting these FREE books and gift places you under no obligation to buy; you may cancel at any time, even after receiving your free shipment. Simply complete your details below and return the entire page to the address below. *You don't even need a stamp!*

YES! Please send me 2 free Historical Romance books and a surprise gift. I understand that unless you hear from me, I will receive 4 superb new titles every month for just £3.49 each, postage and packing free. I am under no obligation to purchase any books and may cancel my subscription at any time. The free books and gift will be mine to keep in any case.

H2ZEB

Ms/Mrs/Miss/Mr ....Initials................................
BLOCK CAPITALS PLEASE

Surname...

Address..

....

....Postcode ....

Send this whole page to:
UK: The Reader Service, FREEPOST CN81, Croydon, CR9 3WZ
EIRE: The Reader Service, PO Box 4546, Kilcock, County Kildare (stamp required)

Offer not valid to current Reader Service subscribers to this series. We reserve the right to refuse an application and applicants must be aged 18 years or over. Only one application per household. Terms and prices subject to change without notice. Offer expires 30th August 2002. As a result of this application, you may receive offers from other carefully selected companies. If you would prefer not to share in this opportunity please write to The Data Manager at the address above.

Mills & Boon® is a registered trademark owned by Harlequin Mills & Boon Limited.
Historical Romance™ is being used as a trademark.